CU00588127

Netta Muskett was born in Sevenoaks
Kent College, Folkstone. She had a var
first teaching mathematics before work
owner of the 'News of the World', as well as serving as a volunteer
during both world wars – firstly driving an ambulance and then
teaching handicrafts in British and American hospitals.

It is, however, for the exciting and imaginative nature of her writing
that she is most remembered. She wrote of the times she experienced,
along with the changing attitudes towards sex, women and romance,
and sold millions of copies worldwide. Her last novel 'Cloudbreak'
was first published posthumously after her death in 1963.

Many of her works were regarded by some librarians at the time of
publication as risqué, but nonetheless proved to be hugely popular
with the public, especially followers of the romance genre.

Netta co-founded the Romantic Novelists' Association and served
as Vice-President. The 'Netta Muskett' award, now renamed the
'RNA New Writers Scheme', was created in her honour to recognise
outstanding new writers.

BY THE SAME AUTHOR
HOUSE OF STRATUS

SAFARI FOR SEVEN

Netta Muskett

HOUSE OF
STRATUS

Copyright © 1967 Estate of Netta Muskett
Typography: 2014 House of Stratus

All rights reserved. No part of this publication may be reproduced, stored in a retrieval system, or transmitted, in any form, or by any means (electronic, mechanical, photocopying, recording, or otherwise), without the prior permission of the publisher. Any person who does any unauthorised act in relation to this publication may be liable to criminal prosecution and civil claims for damages.

The right of Netta Muskett to be identified as the author of this work has been asserted.

This edition published in 2014 by House of Stratus, an imprint of
Stratus Books Ltd, Lisandra House, Fore St., Looe,
Cornwall, PL13 1AD, UK.

www.houseofstratus.com

Typeset by House of Stratus.

A catalogue record for this book is available from the British Library and the Library of Congress.

ISBN 07551 4306 X
EAN 978 07551 4306 1

This book is sold subject to the condition that it shall not be lent, resold, hired out, or otherwise circulated without the publisher's express prior consent in any form of binding, or cover, other than the original as herein published and without a similar condition being imposed on any subsequent purchaser, or bona fide possessor.

This is a fictional work and all characters are drawn from the author's imagination. Any resemblances or similarities to persons either living or dead are entirely coincidental.

Chapter One

David Parley

As he zipped up the front of his thin khaki wind-jacket, David wondered casually whether it would be warm enough for the chill of Johannesburg's July in the South African winter.

Six thousand feet above sea-level, the City of Gold sets a swift pace for living and the crisp, sunny cold of the winter does nothing to slacken its speed – speed to live dangerously, to get on with the business of living, to make money, to make more and yet more money for the expensive cars, expensive furs, expensive women, glittering with jewels; to take with both hands all the gifts which bountiful nature has showered upon South Africa, from the blue and gold of her skies to the white and gold for which men toil unceasingly beneath the soil.

But David Parley was thinking less of South Africa and of Johannesburg at that moment than of himself – twenty-seven, single, with no definite aim because after the wild, minute-to-minute life of a fighter pilot, nothing else seemed to be worthwhile. As far as he personally was concerned, wars should go on for ever. He lacked the type of imagination which had made the lives of some war pilots sheer hell. He had loved the life as much as he despised and hated the present one.

"*You!*" he apostrophised himself scornfully, with an unusual second glance at his reflection in the mirror of his small, bare bedroom in a cheap boarding-house. "You're nothing but a bloomin' shuvver, man! Drive me here. Drive me there. Take these ladies to see this or that.

And what else will there ever be to it? Don't even get a chance of one of the long trips. Nothing but trundling old ladies about Jo'burg!"

It was a good-looking face, even though at the moment it glowered, tanned by wind and sun, blue eyes like bright points of light, short; crisp fair hair; his mouth compressed for the moment out of its generous, good-tempered natural curve.

He shrugged his shoulders and turned away. What the heck?

His eyes caught sight of the one photograph in the room, and he paused and looked back into the pretty face. He had had to let Elissa go because he had nothing to offer her, and she was the sort of girl who asked a lot of life and of any man who would be brave enough to marry her. They had had fun whilst he was in the Air Force, even talked a little, not very seriously, about marriage, though probably neither had believed it would happen.

The end of the war had found him miraculously undamaged, but without his uniform and easy money he had lost most of the attraction he had held for Elissa.

They had talked things over with the frank sanity of the modern young people.

"I want things, David. I can't bear to be poor and I'm quite the wrong sort to help anybody to make good from the start. I'm not likely to find anyone like you with money, so I'll probably have to marry someone old and bald and fat, and I shan't mind so long as he has enough money to give me all the things that matter to me."

"Don't you want happiness, Lissa?" he had asked, trying to keep about her the delicate veils in which he had wanted to shroud her real self, wishing she would not so ruthlessly tear them away.

"My pet, I shall get it that way. Oh, I won't deny that I'll miss something – you, for instance, and the fun we could have had if you only had some money. Look, David, my sweet. Let's have fun before we end it. Take me away somewhere for a month – or a week-end if you think that would be enough to get us out of each other's systems. Make terrific love to me so that when I'm old I can remember it and tell myself that that was my finest hour!"

She had laughed as she said it, laughed with her lovely, seductive eyes, with her mouth which always left lipstick on his, laughed with a twist of her beautiful body and a gesture of the hands which would be exactly right for their diamonds and emeralds and rubies.

Why on earth had he not taken her at her word? She had told him airily that he would not be the first, nor the last, and he had looked at her and turned away and left her there, in the foyer of the hotel where they had arranged to meet after he had been demobbed. He had not even looked back, so that the last thing he had seen of her had been her laughing face and provocative eyes.

He had believed he was taking it badly, that he was suffering the pains of hell, but after the first few days he realised that she had killed at one blow whatever there had been or might have been between them. He smiled inwardly at the discovery, for he was no puritan, no stern ascetic, but lived the normal life of a healthy, virile young man. He realised that he had built Elissa up into something she never had been, never could be, and when she had ruthlessly demolished his façade, there was nothing there to love.

But he kept her picture there. It served to remind him that girls needed things he could not give them, and that therefore he must not get serious thoughts about any of them.

He ran down the stairs and into the street, hopped on a bus, got off in Eloff Street and went with his long strides down Commissioner Street, and into the street where the offices of his employers were situated.

He glanced at the clock. Just in time, but only just.

Mr. Van Essen, who gave him his daily orders, was also looking at the clock.

"Oh, there you are, Parley," he said. "I've just had a call from Court. He's ill. Most annoying. Most. You'll have to take on the Kruger Park. Know anything about it?"

He was a little, middle-aged, querulous man who suffered from arthritis and a nagging wife, and he spoke in jerks and in reporting style and had never been seen to smile or to regard any happening as other than a tragedy and a personal affront.

David felt his spirits rise. He knew very little about the great Game Reserve, though he had been into it once or twice in his boyhood, but not for the world would he have admitted ignorance

3

when the chance came to do something rather more interesting than what were termed 'taxi trips' about the city.

"Of course," he said blithely. "When do I start?"

"Now," said Mr. Van Essen pettishly. "You ought to have started half an hour ago, of course, but it can't be helped. Here's the list. Six people to pick up, and you'd better apologise to them for being late. Here are your papers for the Reserve and the rest camps."

"Everything booked?" asked David, surmising that at this time of year accommodation at the rest camps must he secured well in advance.

"Of course," snapped Mr. Van Essen. "You had better get off now. Take the big car, of course, and see that there is enough petrol. You can fill up at most of the rest camps."

David took the handful of papers, glanced at them as if they were familiar to him, though he had no idea what they were, and strode off to the side street where the cars would be parked.

He was still going to do chauffeuring, of course, but this would be a change, and he would be gone for five or six days, and during that time he would at any rate feel he was his own boss, and would have responsibility. If he wanted to do anything in particular with his life, it was in some way to make himself his own boss, to keep the money he earned, to know that the harder he worked, the more he would have.

Suppose he could have his own fleet of cars, for instance? Or even one good, roomy one? He was a good driver, and he knew cars down to the last screw. With his own car, he felt he could work up a connection, take small, select parties for long trips, attend personally to every item for their comfort and enjoyment. It might not be much of an ambition, but at least he would be on his own, working for himself, at nobody's beck and call.

He thought of Elissa and grinned. Elissa and a taxi-driver!

He wondered if she had found her fat, bald, rich old man yet, and if it was fun having mink and diamonds. It probably was – for her.

The car was big and roomy, and it could accommodate six as well as the driver, one in the front seat, three behind it, and two (less fortunate) at the back – less fortunate because the seat was hard and uncushioned. David remembered with a somewhat wry grin the discussions he had heard between the other drivers, the subject being the bitterness which was apt to crop up between passengers on account of that hard, uncomfortable back seat, where none of them wanted to sit, and the seat beside the driver, where all of them wanted to sit.

Well, his six must work it out amongst themselves.

He glanced down the list of names and addresses and began to sort them out in his mind. It would mean covering a good many miles of the Johannesburg suburbs to pick all six passengers up, and the office had supplied him with no specific information at all about some of the addresses, which were obscure even to his knowledge of his home town.

He began to check his levels methodically, oil, water, petrol, satisfied himself personally that the car had been properly serviced for the five-day journey, and set off.

Mr. and Mrs. Craye.

He had better pick them up first.

He memorised their address and turned the big car.

Chapter Two

The Crayes

Rowena Craye banged down the lid of the suitcase. It would not close, and she pushed it with her foot towards where her husband sat idly reading the newspaper.

"You shut the beastly thing," she said irritably.

She had been very pretty. At twenty-eight she should still have been pretty, but the last eight years of life had drawn the wrong lines on her face, had hardened her mouth under its orange-scarlet lipstick, had given a shrewish bad-tempered note to the voice which ought still to be filled with laughter.

Francis looked at her, raised his eyebrows and remained sprawled in the chair. His lantern-jawed face wore its habitual look of cynical amusement.

"How can you expect it to shut with the sleeve of that thingummy stuck out at the side?" he asked. "You should pack it properly."

"*I* should pack it! What about you having a go at it? The whole rotten thing was your idea, not mine. Why should I want to go to the beastly Game Reserve? What do I want with more wild animals? Haven't I got enough living with you?"

Once, possibly not even so many years ago, she would have laughed as she said that, and he would have joined in the fun. Now it wasn't fun, and they both knew it.

"How about me?" he drawled, returning to his newspaper. "I thought it would make a change for both of us to see how animals manage life in the raw instead of the civilised state," his bitter mouth curving on the adjective.

Rowena glared at him.

"I wonder if you have any idea how I hate you?" she asked, and longed passionately to be able to look at him and speak to him with the devastating coldness which seemed so easy for him to achieve. She always lost her temper.

"Some faint conception," he said. "I've often wondered why you don't leave me. Why don't you?"

"Just funk," she said. "Would you divorce me if I did?"

"No."

"Why not?"

"Because, my sweet, I have had enough of marriage myself, and therefore should not want a second wife," he told her calmly.

"What about me? Don't you think I might want a different sort of husband, so help me?"

"Possibly, but since you pursued me until you got me, and you make my life hell, why should I make it possible for you to do the same for some other poor bloke? But if you want to leave me and try life on your own, don't let me stop you," and he returned to his newspaper, crossing one leg over the other knee, his slipper dangling from his toe.

Enraged, she bent down and snatched off the slipper and threw it at him. He fended it off with the newspaper, after which she tore the paper from him and screwed it into a ball and flung it on the floor and trampled on it.

He smiled, rose from the chair and, walking past her, bent down to attend to the suitcase.

"I don't think I'll go with you," she said jerkily.

He shrugged his shoulders.

"All right, my dear," he said and opened the case again and began to take things from it, her things, putting them down on the floor.

"I shall need the case," she said sharply.

"What for? You can't go back home. The Mayhews are there, remember? Besides, you'd hate the scandal. And what would you do alone there? The car's in dock, too. You'd better stay here," and he went on turning her belongings out of the one case which, in Umveli, they had decided would be more convenient for them than two pieces of luggage.

Rowena glared at him, hating him. He was right, of course. The impossible thing was that he was always right. She could not go back to their Rhodesian home, since they had let the Mayhews and their teeming family have it for the week, and even if she could have gone back there, she would have loathed the gossip, the avidity with which women with too little to do would seize on her reappearance without Francis and interpret it with hideous exactitude.

"And what do I use for money if I stay here?" she asked.

"I wouldn't know," he said coolly.

"You mean you won't give me enough to live on if I'm not with you?"

"How well you know me, my sweet. I mean exactly that," he said. "Now I think that's everything. If I've overlooked some little thing, nylons or face-cream or anything, no doubt you've got enough on you to replace them."

She was silent, frustrated, helpless. He knew he had her trapped. Had he had any idea of this when he booked them in at this particular hotel, which catered for the wandering traveller rather than the resident guest? One paid for a comfortable room, morning coffee and bath, but meals had to be paid for in the dining-room as and when served. Arriving in Johannesburg early the previous day, Rowena had indulged in an orgy of shopping, and Francis knew that she had no more than a few shillings left in her purse. How could she stay here or anywhere? And especially without even a suitcase, and with only the few clothes she had brought with her for the week in the Game Reserve?

She crossed the room, pushed him out of the way, went down on the floor on her knees and began to replace her belongings in the suitcase, moving with the frenzied haste of anger.

He smiled and turned to go out of the room.

"Where are you going?" she asked sharply.

"To the one place in the hotel, my love, where it isn't usual for even wives to follow husbands," he said and left her.

She crammed the rest of the things into the case, shut and fastened it, and sat down on the edge of the bed and looked drearily and unseeingly out of the window.

People always said Johannesburg did things for them – Johannesburg with its height and its thin air and its hurry and zest for life. Well, the only thing it seemed to be doing for her and Francis was to set them even farther apart. The prospect of this week, with its enforced intimacy, with its unavoidable association with strangers before whom they must keep up some sort of appearance, was appalling.

Her thoughts ranged back through the years, back to the girl who, incredible as it now seemed, had been passionately in love with Francis Craye. She had been twenty, and he twenty-four. Her parents had lived for many years in South Africa and she could scarcely remember what England was like, but something inherent and inescapable had come rushing back to her at first sight of Francis, in his naval uniform, and intensely, typically British.

Like all South Africans, her parents had kept open house for the Service men who, during the war, had put in for various reasons at the ports, making them welcome, showering on them the open-hearted and open-handed hospitality which will live in the memory of the recipients with warm friendliness all their lives.

Rowena, delicately pretty in her dark, slender, wild-bird style, her Red Cross uniform enhancing the effect with its trim, starched severity, was an eyeful for most of them, but Francis Craye was different. His steely grey eyes and his rather grim mouth, the way he had of looking at her, his deep voice and unexpected chuckle, the tall spareness of his form in what must surely be the most becoming uniform in the world, that of the British naval officer – these things set him apart from all the others so that in the course of the few days in which his ship lay in Cape Town Dock for some minor repairs, Rowena was head over heels in love with him.

On his third evening as the guest of the Lovells, he went out on the *stoep* with her and pulled her into his arms and stood looking down into her eyes, searching her face and at last looking at her lips so that, flushed and suddenly shy, she had tried to draw away from him.

"No," she whispered. "No. Don't."

He laughed and held her there.

"Don't what?"

"Don't—look at me like that."

"How do I look?"

"As if—as if—"

She could not go on. She felt breathless, frightened and yet exultant. What did he want of her? Only what so many other men had wanted, but had never had? It had been so easy to refuse them; it would not be easy to refuse Francis Craye.

"Well?" he asked in his deep, quiet voice, a voice subtly exciting. "As if I wanted you? I do, you know. How do you feel about it?"

The bottom dropped out of her cloudy world. He was only like other men, then.

He felt the sudden cold of her and let her free herself.

"You mean you don't feel like it? You don't want me?" he asked, and there was still that uncannily exciting, low laughter in his voice.

"No," she said thickly, turning away. "No."

He shrugged his shoulders and lit a cigarette. She could see his strong, lean face lit up by the match in his cupped hands. Her heart seemed to turn over. Was she a fool to have said no? Did he know that it wasn't true? That she wanted him wildly?

"Let's go in, shall we?" he asked, and she turned blindly and went back into the living-room, where her mother looked up speculatively at them. Her father was away doing war work.

Mrs. Lovell was not a maternal woman. She had never really wanted to be a mother, but she had been a good one, and Rowena had not lacked for anything – except the one thing she had needed, her mother's love.

Francis talked for a few minutes in his charming way, and then took his leave.

"Come again when you like," Mrs. Lovell said in her friendly voice, and he had nodded and said he would.

"I expect we shall be here a matter of another six or seven days," he said. "I will, if I may. Goodbye. So many thanks. 'Bye, Rowena," and he had gone, leaving her with a feeling of empty desolation.

"Has he asked you to marry him, or anything?" asked Mrs. Lovell briskly.

"Not to marry me, but possibly – anything," replied the girl, pouring herself out a drink.

"Well, if you play your hand properly, you can get him, but don't sleep with him or you'll lose him. Give me one, please, Scotch – and not much soda."

"Mother, why do men always think that way, and only that way, about me?" asked Rowena suddenly.

"My dear child, all men always think that way about all women who are not absolute hags," said Mrs. Lovell, adding another squirt of soda to her glass. "Used properly, it gives a woman an advantage – unless, of course, she's idiot enough to fall for the man herself. Have you fallen for Francis Craye?"

"I think I have."

"Then go all out and get him. He's presentable, good family, a bit of money, and if he survives the war, he could keep you. Better, get him now, though. Every sailor has a roving eye." And she proceeded to give her daughter the advice of a practical, worldly-minded and unsentimental woman on the art of getting your man. Rowena, still a little starry-eyed and breathless, listened.

Between them, they set out to get Francis Craye, Rowena because she was in love with him and the few moments in his arms had been enough to set the bonfire ablaze within her, and her mother because she was tired of having Rowena always about.

Francis himself had not meant to do anything more than amuse himself with a light affair with this pretty, eager child. He had not intended the affair to go further than a mild flirtation. But almost before he was aware of it, he had fallen so much in love with her, with her gaiety, her happiness, her zest for living, that he wanted her as he bad never wanted any other woman, and it was made quite plain to him by her and by her mother that there was only one way to her – through the church door.

He left Cape Town intending to forget her, but he could not. It amused and intrigued him to realise that he was in love with her, really in love for the first time in his life. He thought of her at the most inconvenient moments, and when his ship was driven into harbour again, this time at Port Elizabeth, he contrived to get enough leave to go to Cape Town and find Rowena and marry her.

Rowena had a few days of wild, entrancing honeymoon and the world seemed to end for her when he had to rejoin his ship.

"Give me a baby, Francis," she pleaded with him that last night. "Leave me something that will always be yours."

He shook his head and kissed her with the kisses which seemed to draw her very life-blood through her lips to his.

"No," he said decidedly. "That will have to be enough until I come back for keeps."

"You may not. Oh darling, you may not!" she told him wildly.

"I shall," he said with his blithe confidence.

And he had come within a few months, slightly wounded and contriving in his uncanny fashion to be sent not only back to the Cape, but to the very hospital where Rowena worked as a V.A.D.

His wound, though not serious, kept him idle for three months, and at the end of that time he was offered, and accepted, a chance of doing a shore job, first in Kenya and then in Rhodesia.

Rowena had gone with him, and when the war ended, he decided to remain in Rhodesia, working and playing, but playing harder than he worked because in the meantime his father had died and had left him so comfortably off that it did not matter whether his farm paid or not.

They built a new house to replace the little one-storey place on the farm. They entertained lavishly, and their 'sun downers' became famous and increasingly extravagant in conception. Every evening the lines of cars stood outside their hospitable doors and many of them were still there in the early morning.

Life became for them a mad rush from party to party, and Rowena, who had been happy on one gin and tonic or a small sherry, became able to drink most of their friends 'under the table'. Gradually the atmosphere changed as their home life receded into no more than a few hours of sleep and many hours of entertaining and being entertained. They raced hundreds of miles over the long, dusty Rhodesian roads with their narrow, tarred strips, to and from wild parties. They had more than one accident and several narrow escapes from death, and by degrees the more serious-minded and hard-working of the Rhodesian settlers and farmers eased themselves out of the circle which revolved about the young Crayes.

"We can't live at your pace," they said as they dropped away from them. "Besides, we don't all have your luck, Francis. We have to *work* for our living!" half in envy, but also with the healthy contempt of their kind for the non-workers.

So whilst Francis lost the friendship of the best kind of settler, the men who had welcomed him and been eager and able to help him in his early difficulties, Rowena also lost their women-folk, the steady, clear-eyed, quiet-living wives and sisters who had come out to this young country and were helping it by their own work and vision to grow in healthy prosperity, a fitting land for themselves and their families, a good life.

And in losing all this, Rowena knew they had also lost each other, though she was never able to understand what it was that had come between her and the husband she had adored, and could still have adored had it not been for his baffling fending-off of her eager loving. They lived as husband and wife, but there was something in his love-making which seemed in some subtle fashion to insult her. It was as if he took her in spite of himself, and mocked them both in so doing.

Sitting in the conventional hotel bedroom, she wondered for the many hundredth time when and how it had started, this bitterness between them that was almost hatred, her total inability to understand him, the resentment against him which had drawn her into all sorts of attempts to escape from herself. Had there indeed ever been between them the love she had imagined at first there was? Had she ever agonised over the possibility, when he was late, that something had happened to him? That his car might have skidded on the tarred strips of the Rhodesian roads and he be lying somewhere, hurt and untended? Or that he had been bitten by a snake? Or trampled to death by a rogue elephant?

Then she would hear his car and rush down to open the gate, to hurl herself at him, to try not to think that his laughing kiss had been casual and mocking.

"What do you imagine might have happened to me?" he would ask, and laugh when she told him – laugh in that way which once had so much intrigued and fascinated her, but of which gradually she had become afraid.

So long ago – so long!

It seemed that it had come so gradually, and yet, looking back, had they ever been really happy? Happy with the quiet, sober, accepted happiness of the friends they had wantonly lost?

She wandered about the hotel bedroom restlessly.

It was an idiotic idea, this trip into the Game Reserve.

Somebody had once told them what a thrill it could be, that all sorts of things might happen, that a herd of elephants might trap a car and batter it to bits, or their car might not get into a rest camp before it closed so that the passengers would have to spend the night in the jungle. These were the most improbable happenings, but at the time they had sounded feasible, and Francis had suggested it as a relief from the boredom which both the Crayes felt with their uneventful life. It would make a change, he had said, to be devoured by lions, or hippo, or something.

The room telephone bell rang, and she got up listlessly to answer it just as Francis opened the door.

"All right. I'll take it," he said, picking up the receiver.

"It's the car here for us," he said to her when he had taken the call. "Are you ready? I take it you're going?"

"Oh, I suppose so," she said irritably, picking up her handbag.

He paused for a moment, looking at her uncertainly.

She was not the only one who now and then reviewed their lives and thought back into the past and wondered how they had reached their present position and where it would, or could, lead them.

She caught his glance and tilted up her head so that her eyes could look at him coldly beneath half-shut lids.

"Well?" she asked. "Are we going?"

He stooped to pick up the suitcase.

Downstairs in the foyer, a young man in a zippered jacket stood waiting.

He looked at Francis, hesitated, and then came forward with a smile on his frank, pleasing face.

"Mr. Craye?" he asked.

"Yes. Are you taking us on this wild-beast hunt?" asked Francis with a friendly smile. "My wife will be down in a moment."

"Is this the extent of your luggage?" asked David. "What a model passenger. I'll stow it away in the boot whilst we wait for Mrs. Craye."

Rowena appeared, newly powdered, calm, aloof.

"Where do we sit?" she asked, looking at the big *safari* car with its seven seats.

"You can pick, as you're the first," said David with his nice smile. "We usually change around a bit so as to give everybody a turn in the front seat – and also on the back seats," with a somewhat wry grin.

"I'll sit in front with you to start with," said Rowena calmly, ignoring the door which Francis held out for her to give her access to the wide middle seat.

He opened the front door for her instead.

"Just as you like," he said as indifferently, and David glanced at them briefly and went on stowing the luggage away.

"What goes on there, I wonder?" was his thought, but his face betrayed nothing as he got into the car beside Rowena. Francis was behind him on the middle seat.

He glanced at his list to see which was his next pick-up.

"Mr. M. Teckler at the Langham," he decided and let in the clutch.

Chapter Three

Mark Teckler had done what he had always intended to do and what, believing supremely in himself, he had been quite sure he would do.

He had made his pile and retired at fifty.

That is to say, he had left off doing the things out of which he had made his original pile, and was now concerned only with making that pile grow by careful, skilful dealings on the stock market. That was one of the things that had brought him out from Lancashire to Johannesburg; another of the things was the need to satisfy at long last his longing to travel, to see what the rest of the world was really like and how its people lived; also he was going to see for himself just what was the matter with England, if indeed anything at all were the matter. Nothing he had seen abroad so far had confirmed in him the vague uneasiness that there was anything the matter.

At fifty he was still as vigorous in mind and in body as he had been at forty, and at forty he had been more vigorous at least in body than he had been at twenty, because at that age he had worked almost to death a physique impaired by lack of good food and fresh air. His frame, of middle height, was spare and hard and he watched with relentless eyes for any sign of thickening girth. His thick, grizzled hair topped a face which was a square of forehead and jaw and lank cheeks. His mouth was usually shut like a trap, but it could relax into almost womanish softness, though the occasions for such relaxation were very few.

He had practically been born in a cotton mill, his mother having dragged herself away from the loom only just in time, and a week later, she was there again, the baby in a box on the floor beside her. Because she was one of the fastest workers and the most careful and the most silent, a blind eye had been turned to the box by manager and overseers alike, and as soon as Mark could work, he was put to the sort of jobs given to boys of tender age in the earliest years of the century.

The next thing he learned to do was to fight with his fists, to kick with his feet, to bite and scratch like the untamed young animal he was, and the first need to fight arose from the taunts of his fellows that he had no name because he had no father. He had no particular affection for his mother, but she was his, and the only thing in the world that he could claim; therefore he defended her without understanding the thing against which she had to be defended.

He was fourteen when she died, and he did not grieve over her death. He was already self-supporting, and there was no longer any need for him to help her with the irritating little tasks connected with their shared life in their one poor room.

He was a silent, friendless boy, watchful, distrustful, careful of every penny. Nobody liked him, but everybody was aware of him, and though they resented his promotions which took him amongst men and women twice his age, his ability could not be denied.

All his workmates would have been amazed and incredulous had they had any inkling of the real truth about Mark Teckler, which was that he was conscious of himself and his loneliness in a way which bit into his very soul. He longed for friendship, but could not give any, and the more he was attracted to another person, the more harsh and bitter was his attitude out of his fear of being rebuffed.

He was twenty when he met Lizzie Hart.

It was a wet night, the rain streaming down pitilessly, and his only suit was soaked through before he had gone more than a hundred yards from the mill. A lighted lamp swung over an open doorway, and some of the mill hands brushed past him and ran, laughing and pushing, into the lobby beyond the doorway.

"Let's get in outa rain. Chapel's bettem' a soakin', any road," laughed one of them, and Mark found himself carried along with the rest, up the step, into the lobby and into the place itself, the small hall which served as chapel, Sunday school and recreation room for one of the many Nonconformist sects of the city.

There was a function of some sort going on, part religious meeting, part social, and when somebody had finished singing 'The Holy City' others began to bustle about handing round plates of sandwiches and buns, and cups of tea. Mark said a curt "No" to the girl who offered him a cup of tea with one hand and a plate of sandwiches with the other.

She was not a pretty girl. She was small and thin, and her dun-coloured hair was scragged back untidily and her eyes, if not actually crossed, were not quite straight. She wore a black shawl tied crosswise over her flat breast, and though even in those days very few of the mill-girls still wore clogs, her feet were encased in them below the uneven hem of her grey dress.

"No," said Mark again as she pushed the plate nearer. "I don't want any."

"Why not? They're free," she said, giving him a frown of surprise.

"I didn't come in here for that. I came to get my coat dry. I don't belong here," he said curtly.

Her surprise deepened.

"You speak different," she said. "Don't you belong Lancashire?"

"Yes," said Mark and closed his lips again.

"Oh. Oh well – if you don't want it," she said and as everyone else in the vicinity seemed to have been served, she set the cup and saucer and the plate down on a window-ledge and wandered away.

He knew that he spoke differently. It was part of his scheme for his life. It was not that he despised his county or its particular quality of speech, and on the rare occasions on which he was stirred out of his monosyllabic taciturnity he would relapse into the broad accents of his fellows and his own childhood; but he had realised that it might be a disadvantage to him when he went out into the world, as he meant to do, a rich and powerful man, if he were always to be associated with his beginnings by the mere fact of his speech, and therefore he had set out to change it and to listen to and acquire the vowel and consonant sounds which would not betray him.

He was, as ever, hungry; and seeing that nobody appeared to want the food he had refused, he turned his back on the company and quickly wolfed the whole plateful of sandwiches and washed them down with the tea.

"Changed yer mind, then?" asked a voice beside him, and there was the girl who had brought him the food.

He felt himself flush a little, and he nodded.

"Wanted that, didn't you?" she asked, and he nodded again.

"I didn't take time for my dinner," he mumbled in self-justification.

"That's bad. You should always take yer vittles," she said. "I'll find you some more," and she turned away before he could prevent her, to return a few minutes later empty-handed.

"Not a blessed thing left," she said disgustedly.

"I don't want any more," said Mark. "Have you had anything?" thinking of her belatedly.

She shook her head.

"Don't specially want it," she said. "I live just down street and I left t'soup on hob. It's stopped raining, so I'll go before it starts again."

"I'd better do that as well," said Mark, and so it came about that a minute or two later he found himself walking down the street with a girl for the first time in his life.

She stopped before one of the doors set flush on to the mean, shabby street.

"This is my place," she said. "Why not come in and take a drop of t'soup? It'll be good," and she turned the handle of the door and went in, leaving him to follow, so that it was difficult for him to take any other course.

"I live at top," she said, and they went up the stairs and into a room even smaller and pokier and more drab than his own, and this, too, gave him that unprecedented sense of protection towards her.

Over their basins of soup, which was hot and appetising, the two talked awkwardly, a guttering candle their only light in addition to the dying embers in the tiny, rusty kitchen grate.

"My name's Lizzie," she volunteered. "Lizzie Hart,"

"Mine's Teckler. Mark Teckler," he told her gruffly. "I'm at Coller's."

"You don't sound like a mill hand," she told him, and he found himself telling her something of his life, his ambitions, the small

19

successes he had already had with simple inventions, and of what he not only hoped to achieve, but intended to achieve.

In the flickering, dim light of the candle, her eyes looked soft and he forgot that they were not straight. She had taken off her shawl, and the small V of her grey bodice showed a triangle of white neck. Her little, work-roughened hands lay looking singularly defenceless in her lap. Something quite unexpected and unknown welled up in him, whilst at the same time his inherent wariness made him draw back.

"I don't know why I'm telling you all this," he said roughly, pushing aside his emptied soup bowl. "I'd better go now," and he stood up.

She rose as well.

"I've never 'ad a lad before," she said, her eyes and voice filled with wistful regret.

"Why haven't you had one then?" he asked, his lip curling.

From the conversations he listened to daily in the mill, girls had as many lads as they liked, and when and how they liked.

She gave a little, bitter laugh.

"Didn't you take a good look at me in 'all?" she asked. "Lads don't fancy kissing lassies like me."

"Why, what's wrong with you?" asked Mark, feeling that strange drawing towards her again, that knowledge that she was small and helpless and, like him, lonely.

"If you don't know, why should I tell you?" she asked with that bitterness which hurt and yet drew him because it had its echo in his own mind.

He hesitated.

"Hasn't any lad ever kissed you?" he asked stumblingly.

She shook her head.

"And I've never kissed a lass," he said, "Dost want me to kiss thee, lass?" not even knowing that he had dropped into the old form of speech.

She nodded and looked down.

"Happen I do," she said.

He had to bend to touch her cheek with his lips and after he had done it, he straightened himself again and looked down at her.

"Seems a lot o' fuss for almost nowt," he said doubtfully.

"Were it nowt to thee, Mark?" she asked in a small voice.

Nobody had called him by his Christian name since his mother died six years ago. It shook him badly.

Timidly at first and then with more courage as the first knowledge of his manhood became urgent, he touched her, put his arms about her shoulders, drew her against him. The candle-light made a whiteness of her neck as her face lay against his breast. He turned her small, submissive body in his arms until the whiteness was the triangle of her throat where it slipped down into the buttoned bodice. His hand pulled at the worn grey stuff and the buttons slipped from the loose, shabby button-holes. His fingers touched the flatness of her small breast, fumbled with a sort of desperate, half-afraid eagerness.

Instinctively she tried to evade his touch, putting her own hand to pull his away.

"No," she said, frightened. "No, Mark," but with the use of his name again she spurred him on.

His fingers found the soft immaturity of her breast and held it cupped in a grip that hurt her whilst his lips came down on hers. She was still afraid, desperately afraid, and yet within her was the thought that, just as this was the first time a man had ever wanted her, so also it might be the last time. If she refused him now, he would go, and he would never come back, or if he did, it would be to see her in the light, as she was, plain and unattractive and with eyes that squinted.

"Soft, cool skin tha has, lass," he whispered. "Happen 'tis all soft and cool, all of thee," and with hands that were big and none too gentle, he pulled the dress back over her shoulders with the cheap, poor underclothes she wore, and when in an agony of half-shame, half-surrender, she hid her naked breasts against him, he put out a hand to quench the light of the guttering candle and held her to him in the darkness.

In the tiny room, all they had had for seats had been her narrow truckle bed. He pulled her down beside him. Her only coherent thought was that now she need not be afraid he would see her eyes.

Dawn was struggling through the skylight when he woke.

She was asleep beside him, pressed against the flimsy wooden wall of the room. In the faint light he could see that his clothes were hung over the edge of the table where the last warmth of the fire could complete their drying. She must have done that. He dimly remembered flinging them on the floor.

He rose quietly and dressed without waking her and crept out of the room and down the stairs and out into the street. The earliest workers were on their way to the mills, but there was no need for him to go to his work yet.

He was experiencing a strange mingling of well-being and disgust. His body still tingled with the emotions of the night whilst his mind accepted the prosaic business of the day.

Well, be thought, so that was it, was it? Never again could he feel that somewhat disdainful detachment from the other men when they boasted of their prowess of the night before, or of some other night, or some future night. He was one of them now. He had slept with a girl.

He began to think of the girl, Lizzie Hart. He had gone wrong there. He ought to have given her some money, but in his haste to leave her before she woke, he had not thought of it, nor had he the least idea what sum he ought to have left. How could he find out? Could he ask her? That would mean seeing her again, though, and he was not sure that he wanted to.

He went back to his room, washed himself all over in ice-cold water, towelled himself into a glow, had a cup of strong tea and a hunk of bread and jam, and strode out into the street again, clear-eyed, exultant, glad to be alive.

That evening when he left the mill, Lizzie was waiting for him. She was in the same grey dress and black shawl, still in her clogs, but she was neater than she had been the day before, and when he looked at her in a panic of uncertainty, he saw that she was smiling.

When he reached her, she turned to walk beside him. Neither of them spoke until, at the end of the street in which she lived, he stopped and looked down at her.

"I—I wanted to see you," he said awkwardly.

She nodded and kept her eyes downcast. She was agonisingly conscious of their distortion.

"There's stew for thee in pot," she said.

"You mean—you mean—in your room?" he asked.

She nodded again. It saved her having to look up at him.

"Art coming, lad?" she asked, and took his answer for granted by clattering along again in her wooden clogs.

They ate, sitting side by side on the truckle bed in almost complete silence. Tonight she had lit the gas, a fish-tail of flaring light which showed up the tawdry poverty of the room, its makeshift oddments of furnishing, the broken, rusty stove, the barest necessities of life.

They looked at each other furtively when they had finished eating, and then Mark put his hand into his pocket and pulled out some coins and fingered them in his palm uneasily.

"I—I don't know—I left you—" he stammered, not daring to look at her and suddenly she threw herself face downwards on the pillow and burst into tears.

He sat looking at her, bewildered, frowning. Then he put the money back in his pocket and stretched out a hand to pull her up until her head rested against him.

"What is it, lass?" he asked with surprising gentleness.

"Mark, Mark," she wept. "'Tisn't thy brass I'm needin'. It's thee for my lad, Mark."

"Well, and isn't that what I am?" he asked her gently.

"I 'aven't never 'ad a lad before, Mark," she whispered.

"Nor me a lass, Lizzie," he said.

She struggled to her feet and turned off the hissing jet of gas so that they were in darkness.

She crept back into his arms, no longer afraid but triumphant because he was with her again, her lad, a lad of her own, who called her his lass.

It went on for six weeks or so, until his workmates began to nudge one another and smile and whisper, began to chaff him until he whirled round on them with murder in his heart and in his eyes. Then came the day, a Saturday afternoon, when Lizzie met him in their accustomed spot with an anxious look in her eyes and fear tugging at her again.

They walked by the banks of the canal, as they usually did on a Saturday afternoon, winding up the day with a cup of tea at a stall, cheap seats at the cinema, and then back to her room to share a parcel of fish and chips.

But today she did not want to go to the cinema, seemed nervous and could not suggest anything she wanted to do.

At last she led him to one of the seats set at intervals along the canal bank, and poked the dust about with the toe of her shoe, no longer a clog but a real leather shoe.

"What's wrong today, Lizzie?" he asked her, frowning.

She did not look at him but continued to stir the dust with her foot.

"Mark," she said at last, "if I had to ask it of thee, would tha wed me?"

He drew a deep breath, understanding. How had he been such a fool as not to think of that? He did not want to marry her, or anyone – not yet, anyway. It was not a part of his scheme. He travels fastest who travels alone, and he had meant to travel very fast. He wanted every penny of money he could save and scrape together to complete the working model of an addition to the old looms which Edwin Coller still used in preference to the newer models. With the addition he had in mind, all the advantages of the new style of loom would be gained without the expense of scrapping the old ones and buying new. He had not yet dared to talk of it to Mr. Coller in case it did not work out as he hoped in actual practice, but he knew that the old man was scrupulously honest, and if the thing worked, Mark would get a fair deal at the hands of his employer. It was a big thing to him, the biggest he had so far attained even in thought, and he had planned and dreamed and exulted over it whilst he scraped together the wherewithal to complete his model. It was no part of his plan to go to Mr. Coller beforehand and enlist his interest and help. The invention was to be his, Mark Teckler's, and it would be known as the Teckler Shaft.

But now, if what Lizzie was suggesting was true, the whole scheme would fall to pieces.

"Mark?"

Her voice, tearful and afraid, interrupted his gloomy forebodings.

"I heard," he said, not looking at her. "Are you sure? How can you be? Isn't, it too soon?"

She shook her head.

"No, lad," she said.

"We'll try to get something," he suggested wretchedly.

"I've tried.'"

They sat in silence again, pushing their feet about and trying to see into the future. Lizzie was petrified with fear. What if he would not marry her? Mark saw his whole plan for life in danger if he did.

But of course he must, if it were true and they couldn't find anything they could do about it.

They waited another month, and then Mark married her.

Three days after their marriage, she found that it had been a false alarm. He need not have married her.

He had taken her to live in his room, since it was better than hers, and he had had to buy things which had not been necessary to his bachelor state. He had bought a larger bed, blankets to replace the collection of old coats which had served him so far, some cooking pans which he would never have used but for which she asked him. Those in her room had belonged to her landlady.

When she told him about herself, watching him anxiously, he sat on the edge of the bed, his hands hanging loosely between his knees, his head bent. There was a well of bitterness within him because of the futility of the thing he had done, and yet he was fair enough to know that it was no more her fault than his – except that he had asked her to wait another month and she had been afraid her condition might show too soon after their marriage.

"I'm sorry, Mark," she whispered.

His conscience pricked him. He did not look up, but he stretched out one hand to her and she slipped hers into it, and sat down on the floor beside him and leaned against him.

He reflected that there was some consolation to be had in the fact that there was to be no child, since now she would not have to leave the mill, but could just go on working as she had done so far, and out of their combined wages he could save the money he needed and reimburse himself for what he had had to expend on their home, such as it was.

The bitter part was that in all the subsequent years of their marriage, no other child had been conceived. It was as if their resentment and hostility towards that first embryo had made Nature turn her back on them and refuse them for ever the gift they had once spurned.

But to compensate for it, Mark Teckler prospered in everything he undertook – everything except that marriage to Lizzie, his wife.

The Teckler Shaft was followed by other modifications and improvements until finally the Teckler Power Loom itself was in action and on the market. Edwin Coller had not failed him, and by the time he was thirty-five, Mark had a stake in the business, and when Coller died five years later, a childless widower, it was found that he had left to Mark Teckler his entire interest in the great mill.

He seemed indeed to have the golden touch, for he rarely, if ever, made a mistake. He worked with an iron determination which excused neither himself nor anyone else for failure. He was just, but without mercy. His employees, who had once been his fellow workers, feared and hated him, but respected him as a man of unswerving honesty who never broke a promise nor forgave a wrong. Friends he had none, for he had never learned that friendship must be given to be received, but he told himself that he felt no lack. Acquaintances he had, business associates, men who hoped to get something from him, men who feared his enmity and therefore made a parade of friendship.

Apart from his wife, there were no women in his life, and it was very quickly established in their married life that that marriage had been a mistake for them both. Beginning on the shallow basis of a young man's physical need, and the urgency of her fear of pregnancy, marriage was an unreal bond which held only their bodies together, and when after the first few years it seemed obvious that there would be no children, he was glad that circumstances made it easy for them to live their separate lives.

They moved from their one room into their own small house on the strength of the Teckler Shaft, and it was Lizzie who suggested two beds then instead of one.

"You're restless, Mark," she said. "We shall sleep better in beds of our own."

He had disguised his satisfaction over the arrangement so skilfully that when a year or two later, he suggested a larger house and separate rooms, she raised her eyebrows in astonishment,

"Mark, art tha sure that's how tha wants it?" she asked.

"Don't you?" he asked roughly. "You've never wanted it, and I don't need it any more."

His manners had not improved with the years, though he could, when occasion and his own advancement demanded it, be what he termed derisively 'the perfect gent'. With his wife he seldom if ever troubled to be even polite, and it never occurred to her to resent it.

So by the time he was thirty-eight or so, and she a few months younger, they had ceased to share anything but their meals, and with increasing frequency as the years went by not even those. Lizzie, with too much money to spend and nothing on which she really wanted to spend it, began to have fancies about herself.

She went to a fashionable psychoanalyst in London, and he gave her the idea that she was in a state of acute neurosis through the lack of any sex life. She returned home, dressed herself in the new, extravagant and unsuitable clothes she had bought in Bond Street, rouged her cheeks and painted her mouth and had her hair dressed in baby curls, and displayed herself to Mark, to his stupefaction and disgust.

"What's the idea of getting yourself up like a toy poodle?" he asked.

She touched her hair in a gesture she had seen used by one of her film heroines.

"Don't you like me like this?" she asked in mincing tones, out of which she unsuccessfully tried to push her honest Lancashire accent. "I did it to attract you."

He stared at her.

"Have you gone mad?" he asked.

27

"No, but I might do. That man I've been to see, the man they all rave about, the psycho-something, he says I am suffering from mal—mal—mal—something of my love life, and that that's what I need."

She squirmed against him and he pushed her away.

"You make me sick," he told her brutally. "Your love life! You don't know the meaning of it. You haven't any sex in you. You never have had, right from the first, when you got me in the dark and caught me, pushing yourself at me, showing me your neck, knowing I was young and silly and ignorant and going all limp and coy and pretending to be frightened when I pulled your dress open and felt your bosom. You never had an honest sex feeling in your life, and if you fancy you might get a thrill out of it now, it's too late. You don't attract me. In fact, you're repulsive to me, with your frizzed hair and your lips all stuck up with paint and your squint. You're revolting," and he pushed past her and stalked out of the room and locked himself in his workroom and forgot her.

Lizzie stood for a long minute where he had left her, her face working oddly, her mouth pulling into all shapes, her eyes with their squint hideously exaggerated. Then she fell like a log to the floor.

One of the maids discovered her some time later, and Mark and a doctor were hastily summoned, and the inert form was undressed and laid in the bed from which she never rose again.

Mark suffered horribly. He had never known love for her, nor love for any human being, but he stood arraigned before the most ruthless and merciless of judges, his own conscience, for what he had said to Lizzie, who had not deserved it of him. And now, because of him, she lay there, like this, horrible to look at with her twisted limbs and distorted features and those dreadful, in-turning eyes. She was completely helpless to move even a finger, or to nod or shake her head. Only by her eyes could it be seen that she heard and understood.

When she died, eighteen months later, the relief was almost unbearable, and during those eighteen months, his thick brown hair had gone grey and there were lines graven on his face, and deeper lines graven on his memory.

For two years after her death he worked on with tremendous energy which spared neither himself nor anybody else, and at the end of those two years he completed his plan for living.

He was fifty, and he turned the Coller-Teckler Mills into a company which could be operated without his active ownership and told himself and his acquaintances that he had retired.

"I'm going to travel," he said. "Where? Oh, everywhere. I'm going to South Africa first, to make a bit of money for a change. What's all this about Johannesburg, the City of Gold?" with his laughter which never held any mirth in it nor called any forth.

Somebody told him that whilst he was in that part of the continent, he should take an opportunity of going through the great Game Reserve.

That was how it was that, on that July morning, he was ready in his comfortable suite at the Luthjes Langham Hotel in Johannesburg, waiting for young David Parley to pick him up.

Chapter Four

Yvonne Dubois; Miss Koetse

"Any sign of the car yet, Yvonne?"

"No. I think it's that they have lost the road," said the girl who, perched on the brick rail of the *stoep*, had for the past half-hour been craning her neck to catch a glimpse between the trees of the quiet side road, in the Johannesburg suburb where she was staying for a visit with her friend Marie, now Mrs. Hofmeyr.

"I described on the phone just how to find the house," said Marie, coming out to join her. "If he does not come, I shall support it because it will mean having another week with you before you must return to France."

Talking, they slipped into the luxury of their native French. It was a nostalgic delight to Marie, who since her marriage to her South African husband had not been able to speak in her native tongue. She and Yvonne had been friends in their home town, and they were renewing their association after three years apart.

Yvonne sighed and slid a hand under her friend's arm. She was a little thing, dark-haired, dark-eyed, the vivacity natural to her race making it unimportant that she had no real claim to beauty. "Quite passably attractive," one might think carelessly at first meeting, but after that no one ever thought of her as other than enchanting company, gay with unexpected touches of gravity, responsive, charming in her many moods.

The sigh was because she did not want to go back to France, to her home and the man who would be awaiting her, to whom so very soon after her return she would be married and, as she had said privately to Marie, live bored ever after. Jean Lafitte was fifty, going bald, very fat and jolly, loving food and wine and (this was what mattered most to Yvonne's parents) had enough money from his silk factory to satisfy all his own and his wife's needs and whims.

The marriage had been arranged according to the usual French custom, and though Yvonne had been frightened and had begged her parents to refuse Jean's offer for her, she had been told not to be foolish, as of course these things work themselves out, and after marriage there would be plenty of time for love and romance. The important thing was to secure a rich husband who was fond of her, but not so fond as to prove an embarrassment or too tight a bondage.

Yvonne had meekly acquiesced, and because of her submissive obedience, her parents (with Jean's somewhat reluctant consent) had allowed her to accept her dear Marie's invitation to come to stay with her in South Africa for a three months' holiday. Now, after one of these months had already fled like smoke in the winds Yvonne was doing something which Marie's husband, Jan, had urged her to do – namely taking the *safari* through the Game Reserve. Marie would have loved to go with her, but this Jan would not allow, since she was pregnant with her first child.

The Hofmeyrs lived as far out of town as they could, consistent with the needs of Jan's business, and since she knew it was difficult to find, Marie had given explicit directions to the travel agency over the telephone, and she had been told that the instructions were clearly understood and that the car would call at her address for Miss Dubois at half-past eight in the morning.

David Farley was getting hot and anxious at his inability to find the house, since Court, who should have been driving the *safari* car, had neglected to pass on to him the directions he had been given, and though he knew the city and its nearer outskirts well, the whereabouts of the Hofmeyrs' house eluded him. Up and down various roads he went, knowing that he must be in the near vicinity of Riss Road, but unable to find it.

He consulted his list again.

There were two more people to pick up, Miss Koetse and Mrs. Ellman.

Miss Koetse lived not far from the district which he was combing in his vain pursuit of Riss Road, so perhaps he had better call for her now, and see if by any chance she could tell him where to find the address of this Miss Dubois.

Miss Henrietta Koetse had been sitting bolt upright in one of the high-backed stinkwood chairs of her elegantly furnished sitting-room, tapping the floor impatiently with the toe of her substantial, expensive shoe.

She glanced for the twentieth time at the clock and tinkled a little brass bell which stood on the low table on whose top were scattered ornaments of fine Indian workmanship. It was a beautiful room of wide proportions, with a series of long windows opening, South African fashion, on a broad, tiled *stoep*. The furniture was of stinkwood, dark, beautifully and simply carved, substantial, made to wear and to be lovely for many more generations. The polished floor of parquet blocks had a few priceless Persian rugs here and there, enough for comfort but not enough to spoil the somewhat severe elegance of the large room. The curtains and fabrics were of a sober blue, without pattern, and there were neither flowers nor ornaments, except for the Indian brasses on the one small table.

Miss Koetse was completely right for her home and it for her.

Tall, spare, with grey hair drawn firmly back beneath her expensive, uncompromising hat of grey felt, her features grimly classic and unrelieved by art, her suit of grey, herring-bone tweed as classic as her face, she might have been made to fit into the plain, sober, elegant and expensive house to which she always referred, correctly, as 'my house' and never 'home'.

She had recently had (not celebrated) her seventieth birthday, but she looked exactly as she had done ten, fifteen, even twenty years ago. She was old but ageless, because she had never been young. People might have regarded her as one of life's tragedies, too often repeated all over the world, since she had sacrificed her youth and her own chances of personal happiness to her family, first to her widowed mother, and then to an invalid brother whose death a few months ago had left her, for the first time in her memory, with no one to study but herself and no one to whom she need offer any more sacrifices.

Not that she had ever looked on these sacrifices nor her life as a tragedy of self-immolation. She assured herself and her few friends and her large circle of acquaintances that she was and always had been perfectly happy.

"You see, I have never had the least interest in marriage for myself," she had said on the few occasions when the subject had been raised. "I am not well disposed towards men in general and never when I was young met one in whom I took any interest, nor have men displayed any interest in me. I never had any beauty, nor was I gifted in any way. I was perfectly happy in the Cape as a child, and after my father died and my mother and my brother and I came to this beautiful house, my happiness continued, except for the natural grief of my dear father's death."

Her voice, cool and calm and remote, did not suggest that the grief was any more deeply emotional than the happiness. In fact, Henrietta Koetse had never known, in her seventy years, one intense emotion of any sort. She had never wanted for anything, never known any extremes of poverty or of sickness or excitement or grief. Quietly and peacefully she had loved and waited on her parents and her one invalid brother until each in turn died, leaving her their accumulated fortunes – not great wealth, but enough to provide her with every comfort and luxury even had she wished to live on a far more extravagant scale.

Her car was a vintage Rolls-Bentley, and she had the distinction of employing one of the very few white chauffeurs in the country who are in private service, an elderly Londoner who had come out in his youth to make his fortune in the gold-fields, but who was perfectly contentedly ending his days as Miss Koetse's chauffeur.

It was whilst he had gone on his annual visit to his one relation, his married sister in Kenya, that Miss Koetse had had the oddly inconsistent impulse to go on one of the organised trips to the Kruger National Park. Some of her friends had recently been, and she felt that she might be interested and informed by seeing her national wild animals at large. The idea of going alone in her own car, with Pain to drive her and make all the necessary arrangements for the rest camps, had not attracted her, so that she had booked a seat for herself in the *safari* car and told Pain he could take his annual holiday to see his sister.

She was not at all sure she was going to enjoy being herded together with strangers in a hired car, but she had stipulated to the travel agency that of course she must be properly accommodated in the rest camps, where she understood there was an ample supply of hot water and baths.

"Wherever possible, I shall expect to have a suite with a private bathroom," she had said in her letter, and the clerks in the travel office had passed the letter round and grinned.

"She'll be surprised!" said one of them.

"And how!" and her letter was answered with skilful evasion of the question of the private bathroom in the rest camps.

But, whatever discomfort she might be expected to survive, Miss Henrietta Koetse certainly did not expect to sit in her house, ready and with her expensive suitcase standing packed and locked in the hall, waiting long past the hour at which she had been told the car would call for her.

She went out on the *stoep*, her face severe, her eyes frosty with disapproval, her back straight as a ramrod.

Perhaps it was because the scene was too familiar to her that her eyes did not soften and glow at the sight of the colours in her South African garden, the trees of flaming poinsettias which flanked the stone gateway, the scarlet of their great blossoms intensified by the absence, at flowering time, of their leaves; the beds of multi-coloured larkspur and stocks; the zinnias like a carpet of yellow and orange against the green of the short turf, which was kept green only because the hose was kept constantly playing on it; the hibiscus still in flower, cups of red and pink and rose; over the pillars which ran from *stoep* to the balcony above, great trails of bougainvillæa, not only the natural purple but also the pinks and reds and mauves of the hybrids in glorious, riotous banks of colour. By the side of the house was the broad pathway leading to the garage where the Rolls-Bentley sat in silent state. The way to the garage had been roofed with latticed woodwork so that over it could be trained the exuberant golden shower, with its great racemes of orange and gold, sweeping in a bower of lavish magnificence beneath the African sunshine.

But the eyes of Miss Henrietta Koetse, the owner of all this delight, were fixed on the approaching car and waiting for the hot-faced and worried young driver to explain why she had been kept waiting.

"You are nearly an hour late," she said pontifically when he had brought the car to a standstill and jumped out.

"Miss Koetse? I am terrible sorry," said David, "but I have been wandering about everywhere to find one of the addresses at which I have to call."

"Why did you not make yourself familiar with the addresses before you started out?" she asked icily. "That is surely part of your duty?"

"I had not very much time, Miss Koetse, and I thought I knew every road and street within many miles of the city," he said apologetically.

"What an old so-and-so!" he thought, his heart sinking, but he felt it wiser not to attempt to justify himself any further. After all, it would not be good policy to tell his passengers that this was his first important commission, and the first time he had conducted a party through the Kruger Park. He was remembering that a special point was made on the advertising brochures that every party was accompanied by 'an experienced and courteous European driver'. It would hardly behove him at the outset to say what he was thinking – namely, "It's the first time I've done this, you old bag!"

When they came back from one of the long trips, the drivers usually foregathered to exchange comments on their recent passengers, so David knew he must expect a considerable mixture in his party, but at the moment he was secretly chagrined at what he had collected up to this point.

There were the Crayes, who were not on speaking terms, apparently, one of them sitting in the front seat beside him and the other on the middle seat. Beside Mr. Craye sat the only other male member of the party, Mr. Teckler, who had already half-scared David by insisting, before he got into the car, on being shown the written arrangements for the tour in order to assure himself that full accommodation had been reserved in advance.

"I'm not going to do any sleeping in tents," said Mark Teckler in the best Teckler manner, which was to become more familiar to young David Parley in the days to come.

David himself had no intimate knowledge of the arrangements, but he had been assured that all accommodation had been booked, so that his party would not reach any of the rest camps to find there was nowhere to sleep.

He thumbed through the various lists and vouchers which had been pushed into his hand at the last minute by Mr. Van Essen, looking frantically for anything which said what type of accommodation had been arranged.

Mr. Teckler grew impatient. He was not used to being kept waiting when he asked for information. Efficiency had been his password. He gave it and demanded it, and it made no difference to him that he was no longer in his mill in Lancashire, but in South Africa, about to set out for the Game Reserve with only a sixth share of the attention of David Parley.

"Come along," he said impatiently. "Are there or are there not proper reservations?"

"Yes, sir, there are," said David, taking a chance and hoping desperately that Van Essen and Court between them had not let him down. This old buffer was likely to paint the Reserve red if everything did not go as he wanted and expected it to go!

So Mark Teckler had climbed into the car beside Francis Craye, and the two men eyed each other warily, Francis spick and span and slim in his well-cut, immaculate grey whipcord slacks and blue Harris tweed jacket, Mark in a town suit with a disreputable hat of floppy brown linen covering his grey head to provide shade against the African sunshine.

They were an ill-assorted trio, at any rate, David was thinking, and now he had to add to the trio this old war-horse, Miss Henrietta Koetse. How on earth was she going to fit into the party?

"Where would you like to sit, Miss Koetse?" he asked courteously, eyeing the only available seats, the two at the back and the third one with the two men.

Miss Koetse gave a cursory glance into the car.

"I presume you are not expecting me to sit on those seats?" she asked, indicating the hard, uncushioned bench behind the middle seat.

"We change round, so as to give everybody the same chance of seeing the game," said David cheerfully, groaning inwardly and wishing he had picked up this lady first.

Miss Koetse glanced at the remaining middle seat and then at the one beside the driver, occupied by Mrs. Craye.

"That is the one I should have preferred," said Miss Koetse haughtily.

Rowena sat in serene indifference, looking straight ahead of her. Did the woman think she was going to get up and give her the best seat in the car, and seat herself either on the back seat or next to Francis? Not *Pygmalion* likely!

David threw her an appealing glance, but she would not intercept it, and he stood with the door of the car open, awaiting the new passenger's choice. That door gave access to the remaining middle seat or to the back seats.

"Very well. I will sit here," said Miss Koetse, and stepped into the car like a French aristocrat getting into the tumbril *en route* for the guillotine, and seated herself beside Francis Craye, who had perforce been obliged to shift from his window seat into the middle, between Mr. Teckler and Miss Koetse.

Each of them was thinking the same thought: "We're in for a pretty dreadful trip with companions like these!"

David got back into the driving seat.

Somehow he had to find Riss Road and pick up Miss Dubois, but he dared not ask Miss Koetse now!

However, with only the two back seats left, there could not now be any argument about where they were to sit. Until they stopped for lunch, there would be no opportunity of changing seats.

And, as luck would have it, taking by sheer chance the turn to the right instead of to the left a few minutes later, he saw Riss Road right in front of him.

His spirits rose and then fell at the sight of the two girls standing beside Yvonne's small, neat case and evidently expecting him. His first reaction was, "Well, anyway, here's someone young and human at last!" and his next, "How on earth will either of those two fit in with the job lot I've already got?"

"Miss Dubois?" he asked, bringing the car to a standstill beside them.

Yvonne came forward with a smile. It was a heart-warming affair after the grim silence of the Craves, the fussy questioning of Mark Teckler, and the haughty disapproval of Miss Henrietta Koetse.

"You've come for me," said Yvonne. "This is all the luggage I've got," and she turned to embrace her friend again.

"Goodbye, Marie darling," she said in English with the most delicious touch of a French accent.

"*Au revoir, chérie,*" said Marie, and, turning to David as he picked up the suitcase. "Look after her, won't you? And don't let the lions or anything eat her. She's wanted back!"

He laughed, glad to feel young again, and to be adding the gay youth of Yvonne to his sober party.

"I'll bring her back personally, and safe and whole," he said.

He and Yvonne chanced to be looking at each other at the same time, and through Marie's mind there flashed the sudden thought: "Now that is the sort of man for my Yvonne, not fat, bald old Jean Lafitte! Pity. That's life," and she stood waving to Yvonne, who had the back seat to herself, until the car had passed out of sight.

"And now only Mrs. Ellman," thought David, "and she's on the way out."

"I hope there are no more or the car will be uncomfortably crowded," said Miss Koetse, who had bestowed one swift, critical glance at Yvonne in her pleated, heather-brown skirt and yellow knitted jersey, the jaunty little brown felt cap.

Yvonne rightly felt the glance to be one of condemnation, but she asked herself why she should care. They were a dull-looking crowd, anyway, even the smartly dressed woman on the front seat who had scarcely troubled to look at her. The only bright spot, as far as she could see, was the young driver, and he was about as far from her as he could well be.

"There is one more passenger," said David with bravely assumed cheerfulness.

"Four would be quite enough in this car," said Mark Teckler curtly, "and there are five already, six including you."

"Oh, these cars are planned to take six and the driver," said David. "If we change around a bit, we shall all be quite comfortable and happy."

"I don't think!" he added mentally.

"I hope you know exactly where you are to pick up this other person and will not have to waste our time driving round and round Johannesburg," snapped Miss Koetse, who did not at all like the prospect of at some time or other being required to sit in the back seat, and who was privately planning how to avoid it.

"Yes, this will be quite easy," David assured her. "Actually, we have to go almost to Pretoria before we pick her up, and her house is just off the main road. We can't miss it."

"Another woman! What an unbalanced party," commented Rowena from the front seat.

"You can hardly strike a more balanced party with seven than a three and a four," said Francis unpleasantly.

"Quite," agreed his wife, matching his tone.

"I realise you would have preferred an extra man, however," said Francis.

"How well you know me, darling," said Rowena acidly, and relapsed into silence.

"I agree," said Mark Teckler. "I'm not so fond of being in a party of mostly women myself."

Rowena turned her head just sufficiently to give him an annihilating look – if Mark Teckler could possibly have been annihilated by any look.

"How very fortunate for women," she said sweetly.

He glared at her and was silent.

David Parley set his lips and drove on.

The sooner this particular trip was over, the better as far as all of them were concerned, he thought!

Chapter Five

Domini Ellman

The Barlows had always been Somebodies with a capital, even before Sir Elwin Barlow was knighted for work in India about which nobody knew very much, probably Sir Elwin least of all. He had been plain Elwin Barlow when he married the Honourable Maud Delarayney, but even then she had seen in him a suitable future for herself. She was one of the prettiest of the season's debutantes, with half a dozen possible husbands hovering about her when she had selected and married, at St. George's, in ivory satin and diamonds and with a train of bridesmaids themselves like a bouquet, young Elwin Barlow.

The results justified her choice. After a successful number of years, first in Lisbon, then in Vienna, finally in India, she found herself Lady Barlow, her husband knighted and notified that, his term of office triumphantly concluded, he could now retire to England to enjoy the remainder of his life. He had not even had to wait until the evening of life. It was still no more than late afternoon when Lady Barlow was able to inform her friends, and her young son and daughter, Jervis and Domini, of the imminence of their return.

It was early in 1938, when Domini was eighteen and Jervis two years older, and during most of their lives the two had been what Domini termed 'farmed out', which is to say they had spent most of their lives at school, being sent for the inevitable holidays to various (usually unwilling) relations. Both parents were fortunate in having a multiplicity of married brothers and sisters who consciously did their duty towards the fluid nephew and niece.

On the night before their ship was due at Tilbury, the aunt of the moment had reluctantly allowed Jervis and Domini to go to London alone and, of necessity, to stay the night in a quiet, carefully chosen hotel. Aunt Jane had been more than dubious of the propriety of the procedure.

Domini had challenged her doubts gaily.

"What on earth is likely to happen to us in one night?" she asked. "It's not as if we were children, either. I'm eighteen and Jervis is twenty, and the same thing is bound to happen to us as happened to the girl who wore woollen stockings – nothing!" and she laughed at the slightly scandalised look on her aunt's face.

Domini's laughter had a lovely sound, young and gay and lively and vibrant with the sheer joy of living. She was a brown-haired, brown-eyed thing, slender as a reed and swaying, it seemed, with every breeze that blew on her pliant, eager mind. What she did, she did with passionate intensity. If she liked, she loved; if she disliked, she hated. There were no half-measures, no lukewarm emotions about Domini.

Aunt Jane eyed her with disapproval; but then she always had disapproved of her brother's only daughter, though Jervis was of different material, more tangible and reliable.

"Well, I must leave you to look after the pair of you, Jervis," she said, "since it seems impossible for you to go up from here in the morning in time to meet the boat, and my rheumatism simply will not allow me to take the journey."

"You can rely on me, of course, Aunt Jane," said Jervis in the somewhat prim way he had, and Domini made a grimace at him and ran off to complete her packing. Lady Barlow had written that they had better pack for a week or two as she would probably want to stay in Town before going to Bath to meet the family.

Once in the train, and in an otherwise empty first-class compartment, Jervis saw that his sister was provided with what Aunt Jane considered suitable reading matter, and himself retired behind the columns of a financial newspaper.

When they still had another three-quarters of an hour's journey to London, the train stopped at a country station, waited there a brief few minutes and then started again. With the train actually on the move, the door was suddenly wrenched open and a young man precipitated himself into the compartment.

A porter on the platform, voicing imprecations, slammed the door again and the brother and sister instinctively put out their hands just in time to save the intruder from measuring his length on the floor. The young man thanked them with considerable embarrassment, dusted himself down and was just taking his seat when he realised that it was a first-class compartment.

"I say, I've got into the wrong bus," he said. "I didn't notice this was a first. I'll charge down the corridor," and he was preparing to do so when they all heard the voice of the inspector at the next compartment.

"That's rather torn it," said the intruder. "Will you bear me out that I've only just got in?"

Quick as thought, Domini took her own ticket out of her bag, pushed it into his hand and got up.

"Here. Show him this," she said. "I'll go along to the lav., and if he sees me when I come back, I'll say Jervis has got it."

She was gone before either of the two men could say anything, though Jervis flushed with annoyance and the other young man looked embarrassed.

"Idiotic of her," said Jervis. "That's so like her."

"What had I better do now?" asked the other, but at that moment the inspector arrived, glanced at the two tickets, smiled politely and went on to the next compartment.

"I feel in a very awkward position, but of course I'll clear out into my own part of the train. May I give you your—the—this ticket?" said the stranger.

Jervis accepted it and slipped it into his pocket with his own.

"Not much point in that now," he said carelessly. "I believe the train is pretty full and you may not get a seat. Better sit down. I don't suppose he'll come through again."

"It's a rather embarrassing position," said the other. "By the way, my name is Ellman, Keith Ellman, and I'm haring back to my job. I'm in a solicitor's office and I've had to go and get some signatures on a document."

Jervis Barlow accepted the unsought information with a barely perceptible nod and returned to the periodical he was reading without offering any return of the introduction. His whole expression and bearing was of arrogant indifference, and Keith Ellman flushed, decided he would clear out to the other end of the train even if he did not get a seat, but was frustrated by the reappearance of Domini.

She was smiling, her candid friendliness very different from her brother's attitude.

"He's gone," she said. "I met him in the corridor and told him my brother had my ticket."

Jervis gave her a suppressive look, but she pulled a face at him and settled down to make the most of the chance encounter with such a very personable young man.

At twenty-one, Keith Ellman was the answer to many a maiden's prayer, though there was certainly little about him which would measure up to the standard Domini had so far set herself in Jervis, for he was a good four inches off Jervis's six feet, and he was fair-haired, slenderly built and lacked the look of the open air and of strenuous athleticism which belonged to the young man still at the University and not taking life too seriously.

Domini could not have said what it was about Keith which first attracted her interest; in fact, at no time in the future could she ever discover what that nebulous something had been, but by the time they reached London the two had run the gamut of possible subjects for conversation, both of them aware of the silent disapproval of Jervis from the other side of the compartment.

And at the last moment, Domini did an entirely reprehensible thing.

She scribbled on the margin of one of the pages of *The Reader's Digest*, closed the book and put it into his hand.

"Why not take this with you?" she said. "We've finished with it, anyway, and there are some quite good things in it. Shall I call out to a porter, Jervis?" turning away from him to her brother.

43

"Of course not," said Jervis. "Can't you keep still and quiet for once? I'll see to things," beginning leisurely to put together the various pieces of their luggage.

"I'll say goodbye then – and thanks again for being so decent about the ticket," said Keith, opening the door.

"I expect I shall end up in prison," said Domini blithely, "but this time I seem to be saved again. Goodbye," and her brown eyes, that were both soft and gay, held his blue ones for a moment before she turned away to help Jervis.

In the bus on his way to his City office, Keith hunted through the magazine and found what he wanted.

"Clegg's Hotel. Ring 7. Barlow," Domini had scribbled.

He read it several times, and chuckled, and put the book carefully away. There might be some fun in this, and life for a very junior clerk in a City office was not often productive of fun.

What name had her brother called her? Sounded something like Domen or Domino, but whoever heard of a girl called that? It was probably a nickname of some sort.

Anyway, even if he had had something better to do (which he had not), he would have taken a chance and rung Clegg's Hotel that evening at seven.

Domini had stayed there before and knew that there was a telephone in each room and that therefore by merely being in her room at seven o'clock, she would get that call if he had found the scribbled message.

In the decorous, conventional environment of the hotel itself, she began to wish she had not yielded to such a mad impulse, and she was hunting about in her mind for some way of getting out of the situation when the telephone bell rang.

She hesitated and then went swiftly across the room to the instrument.

"Miss Barlow? A call for you, madam," said the voice of the hotel operator, and then Keith himself spoke.

"Is it you?" he asked.

"Yes—Domini Barlow," she said, speaking softly.

"I'm thrilled to be doing this."

She laughed.

"And I ought to be thoroughly ashamed of it," she said.

"Are you?"

"No."

She heard his answering laughter.

"I don't know what the next move is," he said then.

"Of course there ought not to be one."

"The things one ought not to do are always nicer than the other sort. How long are you staying there?"

"I don't know. We're meeting the parents tomorrow, unless their ship is delayed. They're coming back from India."

"So if it isn't delayed, you've only tonight?"

"I expect so."

"Then how about it?"

"You mean—tonight?" she asked fearfully, wondering how she was going to accomplish anything without, Jervis's knowledge.

"Can you?" Keith was asking. "Will you meet me? Where? What time?"

"I'm just going to have dinner and I don't know what my brother will want to do after that, so I don't think I can make any arrangement," she said. "Just let's say goodbye, shall we? I went a little mad."

"I went more than a little mad—about, you," he said. "Look. I don't know where this hotel of yours is, but there's sure to be a corner near it. I'll find out where it is and I'll get there round about eight and I'll wait at the first corner from the hotel, on the right of it and on the same side of the pavement and—well, I'll just hope that you'll be able to come."

"Oh no—no, please don't!" cried Domini in alarm. "I mean, I may not be able to—"

"I'll be there and I'll wait just the same."

"But if I don't come?" she asked.

"I think you will," he said and laughed, and she heard the click that finished the connection and slowly replaced her own receiver.

Of course she would not dream of going, she told herself. People like the Barlows simply did not do such things. But unconsciously

45

Jervis played right into her hands by developing at dinner an excruciating headache.

"I'm sorry, old girl, but I'll simply have to go to bed," he told her apologetically when, desperately, she had suggested their going to a cinema after the meal. "Do you mind frightfully?"

"Of course not. It would just happen, though, wouldn't it?" said Domini, and she did not mean what he thought she meant.

It was half-past eight before she decided to go – no farther than the corner, of course, and then only to tell him how impossible it was for her to stay, or to go out with him.

She had not changed into an evening frock, so all she had to do was to slip a loose coat over her plain, tailored frock.

"He may not be there," she thought, half hoping that he would not, but she saw him at once, his fair head touched into gold by the light of the street lamp, his face watchful and eager.

He came to meet her, began to offer his hand and then drew it back. Her shyness fled at the realisation that he was much more shy.

"I've been willing you to come. Did you feel it?" he asked her.

She looked, laughing, into his eyes and looked away again.

"I've really come to say I can't come," she told him, but she found herself turning with him and walking back to the comer and round it.

"Shall we hop on a bus?" he asked, and the next moment she found herself clambering to the top of the first bus that came along.

"Where are we going?" she asked in a somewhat delirious mixture of excitement, pleasure and trepidation. Domini Barlow simply did not do things like this.

"No idea," he said. "Do you mind?" and she shook her head and found that, for some undiscoverable reason, she could not let his eyes hold her own. They were such blue eyes, she thought confusedly.

The bus went along Park Lane, and they got off it and wandered in Hyde Park, aimlessly, talking of themselves and their dreams.

What had they talked about? she sometimes asked herself afterwards, and could remember scarcely anything that had been said. Their clinging hands, the sense of each other's nearness, had been enough without a spate of words, though she remembered that he had told her of his life in a City office, and she had told him of her parents due to arrive at Tilbury the next day.

"It's odd to think that we shall never meet again, or know what's happened to each other's lives," said Domini whilst they waited for their return bus.

He gave her a quick glance.

"You don't think that's what will actually happen to us, do you?" he asked. "Just hullo and goodbye."

She gave him one of her quick, shy glances and he registered again the softness of her eyes and the sweep of her lashes against her smooth young skin.

"It will have to be—won't it?" she asked. "I mean, we're not likely to meet again."

"You say that as if you were sorry, Domini. Are you?"

She nodded.

"Yes. Yes, of course I am. I—"

She broke off in confusion and he wondered desperately what it was she had started to say.

"It need not end, Domini," he said softly, and just then their bus drew up beside them, and they climbed to the top again and sat very close to each other and for some time in silence.

"How can I find you again?" he asked at last.

She shook her head.

"We can't," she said.

"Why not? You mean because you're not going to live in London?"

"Yes," she said, but that was not what she had meant. She had had a vision of the reactions of her family to Keith. She knew just how they would regard him, as out of their world, just one of the people who of course had to exist for the proper maintenance of life's machinery, but who could have no possible contact with their own world. If she presented Keith to them, they would be too well-bred to say what was in their minds, but they would look, and the looks would speak volumes and would hurt Keith intolerably.

But he understood what was in her mind and spoke with the flavour of bitterness in his voice. They were off the bus now and making their way slowly back to her hotel, their fingers no longer entwined.

"What you really mean is that they wouldn't let you know me," he said. "After all, why should they? Sir Elwin Barlow and a solicitor's clerk who has no hope of being anything more."

She slipped her hand into his and gave it a little squeeze.

"You're hurt," she said; "but it's you who are doing the hurting. You know it wouldn't be like that."

"Of course it would be," he said, and she could still hear the pride and the resentment in his voice.

The quiet street was almost empty. There was no one at all on their side of the road. The hotel loomed very near. In a few seconds he would be gone, and she could not see how or where they could ever meet again.

She stopped, holding his fingers tightly.

"Please, Keith, kiss me," she said, and offered him her lips.

He hesitated and then put his own on them, lightly and quickly.

Unfortunately for Domini's future, it was that very moment which Jervis caught, coming out of the hotel and looking along the pavement to where the two stood kissing.

"Good Lord!" he said to himself, and moved to the pavement from the hotel steps.

It was this that Domini heard, and when she had glanced round she gave Keith a little push.

"Better go. That's my brother," she said quickly, and turned and left him, hurrying to meet Jervis. Keith lost no time in going in the other direction, though inwardly he longed to be the sort of man who would have stood his ground and not been intimidated by anyone's brother.

"What on earth is all this about?" asked Jervis angrily, taking her elbow in a vice-like grip and hurrying her back to the hotel. "Wasn't that the man you got so friendly with in the train?"

"Yes," said Domini meekly, though meekness was a thing she neither possessed nor cultivated. On this occasion, however, until Keith was safely out of her brother's reach, she thought it better to be meek.

"Pretty disgusting," said Jervis, and that was all until they had gone upstairs and he followed her into her room.

"What on earth possessed you?" he demanded angrily, making sure the door was shut.

Domini raised her eyebrows at him. "Do I have to account for my doings to you?" she asked with resentment.

"Yes, you do, in the circumstances," said Jervis. "You know quite well that Aunt Jane was against our coming to London alone, and we gave our promise to her—"

"You did. I didn't."

"Tacitly, you did. At any rate, do you for a moment imagine that Aunt Jane would not make any objection to your going off on some assignation in the dark with a man you picked up casually in the train? Some pettifogging clerk?"

In the midst of her anger, Domini began to giggle.

"Oh, Jervis, what an amusing word for you to have found! Pettifogging! I thought it went out with Victoria."

"It isn't funny, and don't try to confuse the issue," said Jervis. "Haven't you any sense of decency? Heaven knows you've had enough spent on you."

"I don't see that it is any of your business what I do," said Domini hotly, the more hotly because she knew he was right.

"It's my business because I am older than you and because Aunt Jane, acting for Mother and Father, thought I could be trusted with you. Where have you been with this man?"

"Into Hyde Park," said Domini, chin in air, deciding to give Jervis a real fright for his interference in her life.

"Good heavens, haven't you *any* sense?" he asked furiously. "Only prostitutes and girls looking for that sort of thing would go into Hyde Park at this time of night."

"Oh well. I suppose you know, Jervis," said Domini with the little devil of mischief in her eyes and her soft, sugary voice. "I take it you've seen for yourself what goes on? If so, there's not much need for me to enlarge on why Keith and I went there."

He stated at her, the colour rising in his pale face.

"Well!" he breathed at last. "Well! Now we *have* learned something. Of course I shall tell the parents."

"How sweet and considerate of you to spoil their homecoming," said Domini. "I may as well tell you that what you so disgustingly assume to have happened did certainly not happen."

"I've only got your word for it," said Jervis, and the hot colour ran up to her cheeks as brother and sister stared at each other in bitter hostility, each seeing the other as if for the first time.

His headache had been excruciatingly painful and he had at last in desperation gone to Domini's room to see if she had any aspirins, he having emptied his own bottle. A chambermaid who saw him go into the room told him that she had seen Miss Barlow go out.

After waiting in frantic dismay and apprehension for her to return, he had dressed and gone downstairs and, still having no idea where she had gone nor how he was to set about finding her, he had gone out at the door of the hotel just in time to see Domini and Keith kiss and part.

Jervis was no more immaculate in his own private life than most of his contemporaries, but that did not prevent him from being disgusted that his sister should have any such little affair as this; in fact, it was probably because he could have indulged in such a thing himself that he felt so affronted, and in his own mind imagined far worse a thing than had actually happened.

Domini, alone in her room when he had left her there, put her hands to her hot cheeks and looked at herself in the mirror, into her eyes which were miserable and ashamed and angry.

"Why should I feel like this? What is there to be all het-up about, after all?" she asked herself, and though in her heart she knew she had done nothing of which she need feel ashamed, nothing which had degraded her, she could not rid herself of the feeling,

Jervis greeted her with hostile disapproval the next day; nor did his manner improve during the long, dreary wait at Tilbury whilst the liner lay too far off for anyone without binoculars to distinguish individual members of the crowd hanging over the deck-rails.

At last Domini spoke nervously, in a voice too low to reach those about them.

"Jervis, you don't mean you actually intend to tell them about— about last night, do you?" she asked.

"Certainly I do," he said.

"Why?" she asked bitterly. "Because you want to spoil their homecoming by getting me in wrong with them? Do you think it will improve your own position with them?"

"I'm not thinking of myself," he said loftily.

"You're certainly not thinking of them," said Domini, who looked pale and tired after an almost sleepless night. She had hoped so much from this reunion with their parents, looked forward so happily to a real home, to a settled life with a garden and dogs and cats, things that belonged to her and not just other people's belongings which she was allowed temporarily to share.

"I was entrusted with the responsibility for you and I failed in that trust," he said. "Since you are the sort of girl who can do what you did last night, sneaking out of the hotel when you knew I could not see you, meeting a casual man picked up in the train, and a man caught travelling first with a third-class ticket at that, it would not be fair for my mother at least not to know."

"She's my mother as well," said Domini, blinking away the tears of misery and apprehension, and at that moment there was a movement in the crowd and a surge forward as the rumour went through that they were to be allowed to go on board the ship by launch.

Domini hung back.

"I'd rather wait here," she said.

"Don't be a little idiot. I'm not going to tell them the first minute I see them," said Jervis, but the rumour turned out to be a false one, so that the waiting went on until eventually the passengers themselves were brought ashore by launch, and after the preliminaries in the Customs sheds, the four Barlows were together again.

Lady Barlow was like a delicate watercolour, fragile and transparent, with pale china-blue eyes and fluffy grey hair, and a grey travelling suit that exactly matched it. Beside her, her husband was large and robust, red-faced, loud-voiced, energetic.

"Hullo, you two," he boomed, pumped Jervis's hand and kissed with a tickling, bristly moustached mouth the daughter who surprised him delightfully. She had been a brown, long-legged, coltish thing when he had seen her last.

"My two darlings!" breathed Lady Barlow in a small, light voice like a breath of summer breeze. Jervis kissed her, but Domini lost the opportunity by struggling out of her father's embrace, by which time mother and son were going on ahead to the waiting taxi.

Both parents were a little amused at the hotel to which their children conducted them, and within a few hours had removed them to a suite, with two extra bedrooms, at the Ritz.

"I must be in the centre of things," said Lady Barlow in that faint, slightly deprecating and apologetic voice which suggested to those who did not know her that as a rule she gave way with sweet unselfishness to the wishes of others, whereas the actual truth was vastly different.

Sir Elwin grinned. Since he was in England again, and since for the moment it had to be London, he was content, and his eyes were affectionate as he watched her walk with her graceful, swaying movements to the window, to stand looking entranced down into Piccadilly.

"What do you think of the brats?" he asked her, giving his waistcoat a tug and wondering whether his old cutter was still at his favourite tailor's in Conduit Street, and whether he could disguise the unfortunate bulge of the years.

"Nice," said his wife casually. "Jervis seems a bit prim, but he will grow out of that, and if Domini learns how to stand and walk, she'll be quite lovely. She ought to marry well."

"Oh, not yet surely? I shall enjoy having her about."

"Elwin, you know quite well how things are, and that a good marriage is the best thing for her, for both of them, in fact," said Lady Barlow with a touch of asperity in her voice, and Sir Elwin coloured slightly more deeply than his tan. He knew what she meant. He was an inveterate gambler, and Maud herself was extravagant, and between them they had practically exhausted what had once been a good inheritance so that they would be obliged to live henceforth on very little more than his pension and a small private income of her own which neither had been able to convert into expendable capital.

He sighed and fidgeted with his waistcoat. Maud was right. Dammit, she usually was. The brats would have to marry well, and by well, of course, she meant to well-to-do partners.

Chapter Six

Domini Ellman (Continued)

If Domini had hoped that Jervis would change his mind about telling the tale of her escapade with Keith Ellman, she was soon disillusioned, for on the second morning at the Ritz, Lady Barlow sent the maid to summon her to her bedroom.

There was no possibility of ignorance that she was in disgrace.

Her ladyship was sitting up in bed, her breakfast tray taken away, her laces and chiffons completely at variance with the look on her carefully preserved and made-up face.

"Lock the door, Domini; and *walk*, don't slouch. You may sit in the chair. No, not on the side of the bed. Now, what is all this that Jervis has told me about you? That you actually slipped out of the hotel, without his knowledge, and met some common young man whom you had picked up in the train? Did you?"

"I did, but not in the way you make it sound, the way Jervis-probably made it sound," said the girl, gulping.

"Never mind that. What did you do?"

"Just walked and—and talked."

"Where?"

"In—in Hyde Park, I think it was."

"H'm. A fine thing. So that's the way you have been brought up, is it? I hope by this time you're ashamed of yourself."

"No," said Domini, getting up from the chair to help her courage, her brown eyes looking mutinously into the blue of her mother's eyes, as blue as china and as hard.

Lady Barlow's voice had the same unyielding, inflexible quality as, very quietly, very evenly, very fluently, she told her daughter just what she thought of her and how, in the future, she would conduct herself so that this regrettable, disgusting episode might not be allowed to mar that future.

Domini listened, at first bewildered and not understanding, but gradually having understanding forced on her startled, horrified mind by the plain words her mother used.

Her mother thought *that* of her! And that, too, was what Jervis had thought, that disgusting, impossible, hateful thing!

She had nothing to say. There were no words in which she could have expressed her horror and shame and disgust, and in the end her pale face and staring, appalled eyes began to spell their meaning so that Lady Barlow's voice faltered a little, hesitated for words and finally ceased.

"Am I mistaken?" she asked at last. "Did things not go that far?"

Domini continued to stare at her. She was still standing. She had not moved during the whole of the tirade. Now she swallowed painfully and the few words she was able to force from her aching throat were harsh and quite unlike her.

"You can believe what you like," she said, and turned away, walked quite steadily towards the door, unlocked it and went to her own room.

Her mother's treatment of the affair had served to impress Keith Ellman indelibly on her mind, whereas, left alone, she would have forgotten him, or at most thought of him only in the half-tender, half-contemptuous way in which one remembers the emotions of childhood. Now she could not forget him. He was there in her life. As the days went by she found herself thinking more and more of him, wishing she could see him again, remembering with increasing insistence that he had told her where he worked, that he had said he was usually alone in the office between one and two o'clock, when everybody of more importance was out at lunch.

And the day before they were due to leave London for Bath, she found an opportunity to slip down to a telephone in the hall. She was afraid to use the one in her bedroom in case the number were recorded, to appear on the bill.

She recognised his voice, but her own went unexpectedly thin and high.

"Keith, is it—do you know—who it is?" she stammered.

"It isn't you, Domini, is it?" he asked doubtfully, and she nodded and managed to say "Yes. Yes, it is."

"It's lovely of you to ring me up," he said.

"I—I just thought I would. We're going away tomorrow."

"Away from London? Where to?" he asked.

"Bath first, to stay with the aunts, and then they're going to look for a place to rent, but it won't be in London, though Mother says it must not be too far away. Perhaps—perhaps—we should be able to meet. If you'd like to, that is," she added.

"Of course I would. I've thought about you such a lot, Domini. I suppose I couldn't see you today somewhere? Where are you? At that hotel? I haven't liked to ring up."

"No; we're at the Ritz. I don't know how I could meet you, unless—unless you could be somewhere near here so that I could slip out whilst Mother's dressing."

"What time? I leave the office at five and it wouldn't take any time to get there on a bus."

"I could be ready by about quarter past six."

"All right. You know the park next to the hotel? The Green Park? I'll be walking up and down the path there, waiting for you. I'll be there before six in case you can be earlier. Domini!"

"Yes?" she asked. She had been about to ring off.

"Thank you for calling me," he said.

"That's all right. I—I wanted to," she said, feeling suddenly very young and shy, and rang off and slipped up to her room.

Coming upon him as he paced the path waiting for her, she felt that something exciting and dangerous had been added to the situation, as indeed it had, for her. Keith was in some way different, she thought. For one thing, he was in his office suit, slightly worn and shabby, and he wore a grey felt hat that needed cleaning and re-blocking. He was shy, too, and tongue-tied, and in his whole attitude there was that indescribable thing which appealed to Domini's quick sympathy, which made her less shy herself so that she did most of the talking, told him what she had been doing, of the theatres, the cinemas, an exhibition of French pictures which had bored her beyond words, the endless shopping expeditions in which her mother took such an exhausting interest.

"Of course I like clothes myself. Who doesn't?" she asked, "but I can't get passionate about them, or want to spend hours discussing the shape of a sleeve or a particular colour. I know what I like and whether I think it suits me, and that's the end of it. But Mother! And there's another awful thing, Keith. She wants me to have a London season, a real one, all dressing up and going out to things and meeting people, and I shall hate it."

"But you'll be in London, at any rate," he said.

"Yes, but—"

She broke off. How could she tell him that, of all people in London, he would be the most difficult for her to see? The one person she would he least able to present to her mother or invite to her home?

He understood, at least in part, though he thought it was only a matter of social grading.

"I know," he said in a low voice. "Do you think I don't understand that I'm not your sort, Domini? That—that your people wouldn't let you know me, if they knew?"

They had wandered as far away from the Piccadilly side of the park as its limits would allow. It was getting dusk, and involuntarily she paused, turning to face him. She felt that he was hurt, and she hated anybody or anything to be hurt.

"Keith, don't speak like that. Don't think of me like that, ever. You know that's not the way I think, don't you?"

They were in the shade of a tree. He pulled her into his arms and held her there, loosely, without compelling her.

"You're sweet, Domini," he said unsteadily, and she swayed forward so that their lips met and for a few moments clung together.

"I shall have to go now," she told him, and he nodded.

"I know," he said. "Shall I ever see you again?"

"I don't know. Shall I telephone you when we come to London again?"

He nodded, not ready believing that she would.

The next day the Barlows went to Bath, and a few weeks later Sir Elwin told them he had decided to take on lease Cranby Hall, old and not very convenient in itself, but far enough into Sussex to give him the country life he loved without being too far to allow Lady Barlow quick and easy access to the London life she herself adored.

That was in 1938, and almost as soon as they were established there, the vague rumours of war began to grow less vague, to grow menacing and almost certain of fulfilment, and everybody began frantically to make preparations according to his or her conception of the need. Lady Barlow bought enormous stores of food and candles and organised First Aid classes in the huge, otherwise unusable drawing-room of Cranby Hall. Domini, who was nineteen, wanted to join one of the women's services already being talked about, but this her family flatly refused to allow, and she had to content herself with joining First Aid classes, taking instruction in air raid precautions and passing them on to men, women and girls recruited from the village, dealing out gas masks, studying the horrifying and alarming pamphlets describing the various types of gas warfare which must now be anticipated.

Sir Elwin rushed back to the War Office and got himself the best job open to him, though he grumbled continually of its inadequacy. Jervis, up at Oxford, was easily persuaded that his first duty was to complete his science course, which would, if necessary, provide him with the necessary exemption from at least immediate military service. His father had nothing to do with that decision. The arguments which it occasioned between him and his wife were the nearest approach to outright quarrels they had ever had.

Though the projected London season, in a modified form, had been discussed for Domini, it was obvious that it would have to be abandoned, for which she was devoutly thankful. She was full of vitality and loved fun and amusement as much as any girl, but her mother's plans for her had offered her little choice and no freedom, and it had been impressed on her that her first duty was to secure for herself a suitable husband, the suitability being chiefly a matter of bank balance. Domini saw herself up for sale, and resented the picture so formed.

The prospect of war gave her sudden release both from the formal London season, and, for the moment it seemed, from the need to find the suitable husband.

Domini found herself with unprecedented freedom of movement, since Lady Barlow was too busy now to keep constant watch on her daughter, as she had done for so long after the thing which she called, in her own mind, 'that regrettable affair'. Domini had given her no further cause for anxiety, had proved amenable and docile, and her mother had had not the remotest idea that a regular correspondence had been going on under her very nose. Keith's letters being addressed to Domini at the Post Office at Wengate, the small market town five miles from Cranby where the weekly shopping was done. As Domini drove the car, it was the simplest possible matter for her to call and collect her letters when she went to park in a side road conveniently near the Post Office, leaving her mother in the High Street.

With her new freedom, she was able to meet Keith in London now and then, to have lunch with him, even (on an occasion when he played truant from the office, pleading an appointment at the dentist's) taking her one afternoon to a cinema, where they sat hand in hand, eating sweets from a paper bag.

A few days before the actual outbreak of war, Sir Elwin died, ending his days ignominiously under the wheels of a lorry whose brakes failed.

Domini and Jervis were stunned rather than grief-stricken. They seemed to have known their father so short a time, to have been little more than acquainted with him. Lady Barlow was appalled at her loss, realising almost for the first time what good friends they had been, she and Elwin, how much she had relied on him and owed to his good-natured generosity of mind as well as of pocket.

Since his pension died with him and he had made no provision for her, she was in considerable financial difficulties and, hauling down the flag of her pride, she applied to Elwin's estranged family for help in the settling of his debts. They helped her grudgingly, even offering her a small annuity, but this she disdainfully refused, was glad to accept the offer of a Government department to relieve her of the rest of the lease of Cranby Hall, and took a small service flat in Holland Park for herself and Domini. Jervis, realising that in the end he would not be able to escape military service, used his new University degree to get into the Intelligence Department, and settled himself in considerable comfort in the Somerset town where his section was securely housed, far from the battle front.

Domini begged again to be allowed to join one of the women's services, but her mother could now plead her widowed state, and also that in her straitened circumstances, it was the girl's plain duty to add what she could to the family exchequer.

"I can't type or anything, but I suppose I can learn," said Domini doubtfully. "Can you afford to pay for lessons for me?"

"I can, if necessary, but I should have thought your common sense would suggest an easier and pleasanter way of helping both yourself and me," said her mother in the sharpened tone which was becoming habitual to her since her husband's death.

"What do you mean?" asked Domini, frowning,

"My dear girl, why pretend to be so dense? You know quite well why Aubrey Bessingway comes here."

The brown eyes widened in sheer surprise.

"Mr. Bessingway?" she repeated almost stupidly as her mother's meaning dawned on her.

Aubrey Bessingway was in his forties, far nearer Maud's age than her own, a widower living in considerable comfort on his late wife's fortune, childless and to Domini's mind intolerably boring and self-opinionated.

"Oh, Domini, for heaven's sake, when are you going to grow up?" asked Lady Barlow, at the girl's incredulous expression and repetition of the name. "You surely don't imagine he comes to see *me*?"

Actually, Maud was sorry that he did not, though she realised that it was much too soon after Elwin's death for her to be able to consider a second marriage; nor did she actually want to marry again. It would suit her much better to get Domini married to a man wealthy enough, and grateful enough for his connection by marriage with Lady Barlow to provide handsomely for his wife and reasonably for his mother-in-law. Aubrey Bessingway did not, perhaps, match up to the standard she had once set for her daughter, but then things had changed, and Aubrey, if not actually a gentleman, had acquired a sufficiency of good manners to be presentable. Domini need not be ashamed of him, and he was kind and would probably be generous.

"You can't imagine that I'd ever think of *marrying* Mr. Bessingway, Mother!" said Domini, still wide-eyed.

"Why not? Or have you an inflated idea of your charms?" snapped Lady Barlow.

Domini flushed. She was not very fond of her mother, and there were times when she actually hated her. This was one.

It was soon after this that the air raids on London started, and Domini's life was further complicated and yet in some ways made simpler, since so little was demanded of her by way of explanation of where she was going, where she had been and when she would be back.

Her life and her mother's had almost ceased to converge after the abrupt sundering of their sympathies in the matter of Aubrey Bessingway. Domini came and went, did her job in a City office creditably, spent a proportion of her nights fire-watching on the roof of the office building, and in other respects lived the normal life of a business girl in wartime London. She spoke very little of her home life or background at her office, and nobody had any idea that her mother was a titled woman until one night, fire-watching with two girls from the adjoining set of offices, one of them suddenly said to her, "Isn't your mother a lady?"

Domini laughed.

"I expect she'd say so," she said.

"No. I mean, isn't she *Lady* Barlow?"

Domini hesitated. She enjoyed the position she had found and made for herself, Domini Barlow, without the help or aegis of her parentage. She had no wish at all to be set in a place apart from these other girls, friendly, courageous, unpretentious working girls who had accepted her as one of themselves.

"Well—yes," she had to admit. "Why?"

"Well, it's such a scream, you working here like one of us and never saying a word," said the girl.

"Who told you?" asked Domini crossly.

"A man I know. He's on the A.A. post on the Common with my brother, and Alf brought him home to supper the other night. I was telling him all about the office and us fire-watching and all that, and I mentioned your name and he caught me up like anything. 'Domini?' he asked. 'Not Domini Barlow?' and when I said yes, whoever else in the world had such a funny name as Domini, he said he knew you, if you were the same girl that had Sir Somebody Barlow for a father, only he was dead. Ellman, his name is. Do you know him?"

"I—did once," said Domini and then the red warning replaced the amber in the shaded row of lights and the girls sprang to their places in readiness for watching and reporting on the fall of the first of the incendiary bombs for the night.

Domini, automatically watching her roof area, thought of Keith, whom she had not seen since her father's death, and from whom she had had no letter after the difficult, stilted one offering her his sympathy. She had written hurriedly in reply, merely telling him that they would be leaving Cranby, so he had better not send any more letters there. After that, she had not written for so long that in the end she felt it better to let things stay as they were. Her life was so much changed, her future so uncertain, and Keith would inevitably be caught up in the relentless maw of the war. Better to let it end there.

But it gave her a feeling of warmth and sweetness to know that he had remembered her. She thought of him gratefully. Keith. It had been a very young, a very tender, an almost passionless romance. He had been so sweet with her, gentle, undemanding, unpossessive, grateful for so little.

And a few days later she had a letter from him, addressed to her at the office.

"Dear Domini," he wrote, "Do you remember me? Keith Ellman? I have thought about you so much, and about the good times we had together, and how sweet you were to me. Have you thought of me at all? Or have I been forgotten amongst all the other boys you must have had by now? Fancy it is more than a year ago now, and you are in London. I wasn't able to join up because I have a duodenal, but I am on an A.A. station now. If you remember me and would like us to meet, I would like it very much. I could never forget you.

"Keith."

She carried the letter about with her in her bag for several days before she answered it, and then she suddenly decided that she would meet him again, and they made an arrangement to meet on his free evening and go to the pictures together.

He looked very different in uniform, bigger and more manly and important, and he had acquired with the uniform a new appearance of responsibility, it was he who was making the plans for them now, not Domini, and she liked it. He was a man rather than the boy he had been.

They began to meet regularly. She did not tell her mother anything about it, though she felt that now she must be allowed to choose her own friends and her life. She was tempted at times to tell, because Lady Barlow was still trying to thrust Aubrey Bessingway down her throat, but what, after all, was there to tell? It was not as if she were engaged to Keith, or had any thought of being engaged to him. They kissed when they met, briefly and without passion, and they kissed again at parting; they held each other's arms when they walked in the black-out as otherwise they might quite well have lost each other in the inky darkness; they held hands in the pictures because, having done it once, it seemed the expected thing, each of the other.

But there was nothing else until one night things happened, as they had a way of happening during the war on Loudon. It was towards the end of 1942, when the raids were at their height.

It was not Domini's night for fire-watching, and when Keith had managed to make his free evening coincide with hers, they usually went out into the country, as far as they could get from the bombing, trusting to good luck to get them back even if, as sometimes happened, the buses had stopped running.

On this occasion, their luck did not hold, however, for there were very few cars other than official ones on the road, there were no buses, and such cars as might have stopped to pick them up were disinclined to do so.

Then it began to rain.

"Well, that's rather that," said Domini.

"I must find you somewhere to shelter," said Keith anxiously. "Is that a barn or a shed or something over there? Shall we have a shot at it? We can't stand out here."

They trudged, slipping and sliding, across a ploughed field to where the building stood, derelict and only half-roofed, but at least providing partial shelter. A pile of sacks thrown over some trusses of straw had kept them dry, and the pair of them, laughing, managed to scramble up the slippery straw and find a comfortable, dry perch on the top. Keith pulled some of the sacks over them. They felt snug and warm.

His arm had stayed about her shoulders when he had pulled the sacks about them, and she leaned back against it and closed her eyes.

"Lovely," she said drowsily, and the next moment she felt him kissing her.

"*You're* lovely," he said, and she opened her eyes and laughed up at him.

"Keith! That's almost the first compliment you've ever paid me," she said. "And I'm not lovely, you know. I'm just very ordinary, and at the present moment my hair is all straggly and there's rain running down my nose and I've eaten all my lipstick long ago. Keith!" breaking off perforce as his kisses took from her lips whatever of lipstick might be left.

"I'm in love with you, Domini. Domini darling. Will you let me love you?"

His voice was unfamiliar, but then everything had suddenly become strange. He did not seem to be Keith any more; she did not feel she was the Domini Barlow she had known.

Her eyes looked back into his, so near to them. Her lips were wet with the rain and with his kisses. Dimly outside the small refuge the guns thundered and the rain beat on the battered, corrugated-iron roof in a mad orchestration. The noise beat into Domini's brain.

Nothing any longer had any meaning, made any sense, nothing but the cacophony of sound and Keith's kisses on her mouth, his whispers which she barely distinguished, the close hold of his arms making a world within chaos.

"Let me love you, Domini. Domini darling," he whispered.

"I want you to love me. I love you so much," she said, and he looked into her clear eyes, deep, trustful, unaware, and sprang away from her and went slithering down the bales of straw to stand at the doorless opening, to watch, unseeing, the blazing of the distant sky.

He could not take her, not like that, ignorant and trusting and so unaware.

Soon she came to him, slid a hand beneath his arm and rested her head against his shoulder. She was strangely happy and at peace. This, then, was the meaning of things, of her restlessness, her sense of unfulfilment and longing. She and Keith were in love, truly in love, and they would marry. Whatever her mother or Jervis said about it, she was going to marry Keith. She was twenty-two; she was earning her own living. They could do nothing to stop her now.

She lifted her face to his.

"Kiss me again," she said, and he kissed her, briefly, lightly.

"We ought to go," he said. "It's terribly late. It's not raining now, though the raid's still on, of course."

"Well, we can't wait for *that*," said Domini, who, like the rest of her generation, had accepted air raids as just part of life. It was beginning to be difficult to remember what it had been like without them.

She looked at her watch.

"Heavens, is it really eleven? And we're miles away from home. Mother'll be having a fit. She knows it's not my fire-watching night, and by the time we get home, the cinemas will have closed hours ago. Come on, darling. I'll make the very first car stop for us somehow. You watch me!" and in the glow of love and happiness, she felt that nothing could defeat her.

Nor in this instance did it. An enormous chauffeur-driven limousine drew silkily up at their appealing signal, and the next moment she and Keith were scrambling in, Domini laughing and quite at her ease with the elderly, important-looking man, Keith feeling awkward and out of his element as he tried to mumble the thanks which she expressed so easily and gaily.

The owner of the car explained regretfully that the shortage of petrol prevented him from taking them all the way to Holland Park, but he put them down at an Underground station.

The raid was over when they emerged and began to walk towards her home, and tonight for the first time Domini did not ask him to leave her at the corner.

"It doesn't matter now, does it?" she asked him softly, and did not release his arm, but held it lovingly right up to her doorstep.

And then, without warning, the door opened and in the wavering light of an electric torch, Lady Barlow appeared with Jervis, unexpectedly on leave, behind her.

Keith would have obeyed the impulse to clear off as quickly as possible, but Domini's hand slid from his arm and gripped his fingers tightly.

"Might as well be now as any other time," she told him, and with determination in every feature and movement, she pulled him forward and gave him no option but to climb the three steps and stand at the top of them, facing her mother and brother.

"Mother, this is Keith," said Domini, though now that she was in the actual presence of the two who had so far dominated her life and ordered its comings and goings, she felt her heart quail a little. "We are engaged," she added quickly, and then stopped, swallowing hard.

Well, it was out now, anyway. The words could not be unsaid. It made her feel better actually to have them spoken.

Lady Barlow looked from her to Keith and back again. When she spoke, her voice was inflexibly cold.

"You had better come inside," she said. "No, Jervis. Leave me to deal with this," as her son made a movement towards Keith which caused him instinctively to draw back.

They went upstairs, the four of them, Keith acutely uncomfortable and wondering if there were any way in which he could get out of this totally unexpected position. It was perfectly true that he loved Domini. He supposed he had loved her from the beginning. It was quite on the cards that he would love her for the rest of his life. But engaged? Married? How could they be? She being who she was, and he who he was? And no security? And the war still on and likely to go on?

His mind was confused. Clear thought was impossible. All he could do was trail up the stairs with Domini and her mother and brother and let life take charge of itself for him.

in the sitting-room, a room poor enough in Lady Barlow's estimation, in spite of all she had tried to do for it with her own furniture and her few good pictures, but the extreme height of elegance to Keith, the four of them automatically separated into two pairs, opposing camps, Domini straight and determined beside Keith, a little in front of him, her mother that little ahead of her son.

"Now what is this nonsense?" she asked, addressing Domini.

"It's not nonsense. It's just plain common sense, Mother." said the girl, gathering all her courage about her. "Keith and I are in love with each other and we're going to get married."

"Indeed? Am I to suppose you are in a position to keep my daughter? I take it that you know who she is?" demanded Lady Barlow of Keith, icily.

Domini took the lead again. She had suddenly lost her fear of her mother.

"Mother, don't be so absurd," she said. "As if anyone were anyone nowadays! All that's been washed out for ever, and a good thing too. As for Keith keeping me, why should he? I can keep myself until the war's over. Everybody does. How can anyone in the Forces keep a wife? Not unless they're colonels or things, and Keith, poor lamb, isn't even a lance-corp."

"You've got a lot to say, Domini. Suppose Ellman speaks for himself," put in Jervis in a superior voice.

Keith cleared his throat. He was in it now, and he was not at all sure that he wanted to be anything but in it. Domini was splendid, bearding them like that, and after all, as she herself said, what were these Barlows that he was not, nowadays?

"I haven't much to add to what Domini has said. We want to marry each other," he said.

Lady Barlow's blue eyes were turquoise pin-points of anger and frustration. Only that afternoon Aubrey Bessingway had been to see her, had offered her in unmistakably plain terms, even if they were not in actual words, the free use of his comfortable little flat in Bournemouth and his elderly housekeeper, who would suit her admirably, if and when by marrying Domini he would find the flat too small and therefore superfluous. She had, also in innuendos plainer than words, assured him that Domini had indicated that she had changed her mind about her repeated refusals of him and would very shortly be ready to leave this undignified job in the City for the comfort and dignity of being Mrs. Aubrey Bessingway.

And now this ridiculous, impossible position had been revealed to her! She recalled something of the silly flirtation Jervis had told her about, all that time ago, when she and Elwin had come home from India. Wasn't this the same young man? The name had a familiar ring. If so, then the affair must have been going on all this time behind her back.

She must now take a very firm hand. Whatever Domini said about the new freedom and social levels, she hoped she could still control her own daughter.

"It is quite clear that you, at any rate, do not know how to manage *your* own life, Domini," she said icily. "Any thought of your marrying this young man is, of course, out of the question."

She turned to Keith.

"You must realise that the only thing you can do is to go, and in future to leave my daughter alone. I presume that you know who I am, though possibly you may have quite a wrong idea of my financial position—"

Keith, stung, found the courage to retort.

"I do know who you are, Lady Barlow, but as for any thought of money—"

Jervis suddenly stepped forward. He was several inches taller and twenty pounds heavier than Keith, and he seemed to tower over him.

"You heard what my mother said, Ellman. Are you going to get out, or am I going to have to throw you out? You're not welcome here, nor will you ever be."

Domini, white-faced, her brown eyes almost black in her excitement and her anger, laid a hand on Keith's arm.

"There's not the slightest need for violence, Jervis," she said. "Come along, Keith. We'll go, shall we?"

"If you go now, and with this man, you need not expect me to have you back," said Lady Barlow.

Domini held her head high and tightened her grip on Keith's arm.

"If that is the way you feel about it, Mother, I shall not want to come back," she said quietly. "Ready, Keith?" and he found himself turning and walking out of the room with her, out of the room and the flat and the house, out of the life she had known and into something she could not even vaguely begin to visualise.

In the street, they turned to look at each other, both of them still startled, only half aware of what had happened.

Then Domini laughed. It was a natural, familiar sound and it started to restore them to normality. It was not that she felt amused or happy. It was the obvious reaction to all the drama and the comitragedy of the past half-hour.

"Well, that's rather that, isn't it?" she said. "You've got me for life, Keith, whether you want me or not. Do you, by the way?'

There was only one possible answer.

"Of course I do, darling," he said, and kissed her. "What do we do now? I can't take you back to the camp with me. Do you really suppose your mother meant you were not to come back?"

"Whether she meant it or not, I'm not going," said Domini. "I can go back to the office for what remains of the night. There are all the fire-watchers' beds there, and I bet some of them have gone home now that the all-clear's gone. Tomorrow we can decide what to do and find out how soon we can get married."

Chapter Seven

Standing at the window, waiting for the car to pick her up and take her to the Game Reserve, Domini Ellman looked back along the ten years of her marriage to the man who lounged, disgruntled, peevish, in the room behind her.

She had not seen him come in, had not heard the protest of the springs of the shabby couch as he flung himself against them, but she did not need to turn her head to know exactly what she would see – the figure no longer slender, but even at thirty-seven thickening with soft, flabby flesh, the fair hair raggedly in need of a barber, the blue eyes set amongst too-early folds and lines, the mouth sagging petulantly. It was not easy for her to remember him as he had been when she had married him.

When she had married him!

Her mouth grew tight as her mind caught and repeated the phrase and thought how well it expressed what had always been the wrong thing about their marriage. She, Domini, had married Keith; she had been from the first the motive force, the deciding factor.

From the first. From that night when, her arm firmly holding Keith's, she had turned with him and walked out of her home, away from the incredulous mother who would have called her back, forced her to remain, but for the stern, unyielding Jervis at her side.

Domini had not realised in the least how scared Keith had been, how unwilling to accept the situation suddenly thrust upon him. In her young pride, in her passionate love for him brought to a head by that tender hour of love-making so swiftly followed by her mother's condemnation of her lover, it had never occurred to her that Keith might not be as ready as she was to accept the consequences of her defiance of her family.

It had been almost daylight when they reached her office building. After seeing her to the door, he had had to rush away, back to his A.A. station to meet trouble there for his absence.

"When can we see each other?" Domini asked, clinging to him for a last brief embrace. "I must find a room or somewhere to go until we can make arrangements."

"Arrangements?" he echoed nervously.

"To be married, silly," she told him with a little laugh and another kiss. "Oh, Keith, I'm happy—happy! Aren't you?"

"Well, don't forget that I may get in jug for this," he said moodily. She laughed again.

"Isn't it worth it? Can I come and bail you out? Make eyes at the C.O. or whoever might jug you?"

"It's all very well to laugh," he complained, but he was not proof against her gaiety of spirit, her tenderness, her open, unhesitating surrender to her love.

They had been married by special licence a few days later. Few obstacles were put in the way of marriages in wartime, and theirs occasioned no great upheaval to their respective way of life except that now Domini lived in a room near her office instead of with her mother, and Keith came to her whenever he could for brief, ecstatic hours, sometimes a night together, sometimes a snatched week-end as far from London as they could get.

Those were the happiest times. She realised it now, though at the time she had longed passionately for the end of the war, the end of the perpetual, terrifying fear lest Keith should be hurt, possibly even killed.

How, she thought now, was it that she had never realised that what she had loved had been love rather than Keith – Keith, who even then had been unable to respond to her or to satisfy the hungry craving which she herself had not understood?

Poor Keith. She had thrust herself upon him, had hustled him off from her mother's doorstep and married him out of hand, and only by slow degrees, painfully, unbelievingly, had it begun to dawn on her that he did not really love her. It was not that he cared for anyone else or wanted anyone else; it was merely that he was incapable of feeling any wild tumult of emotion. All he wanted was for life to flow along in peaceful monotony, taking him with it without any volition of his own.

The war ended and he went back to his office and to the inadequate salary which had been his before. Domini found herself pregnant, and was torn between a deep joy at the prospect of motherhood and anxiety as to how they were going to manage without her earnings.

"Darling, you must go to Mr. Gain, remind him that you are still on the same salary as you were four years ago, tell him that you can't manage, that it isn't reasonable," she urged him.

"He won't give any increases. He's refused everybody else," said Keith uncomfortably.

She kept returning again and again to the subject until he had burst out, "Don't nag! You're turning into nothing but a nagger. I do all I can for you, don't I? What more can I do?"

"You can go to Mr. Gain," she said, but the thrust had found its mark.

Perhaps it was true. Perhaps she was turning into a nagging wife, a shrew. And yet how were they going to manage unless he got more money, and how was he to get more unless he asked for it?

Finally, he told her he had been to Mr. Gain and had been refused. She looked at him, held his eyes with her own until his gaze shifted and she knew that he was lying to her. He had not been to his employer at all.

Frantic, knowing that within a few weeks she would have to leave her office, she went boldly to Mr. Gain herself without Keith's knowledge.

"But, my dear Mrs. Ellman, surely it is your husband's job to apply to me for an increase in salary, not yours," he said with deceptive mildness. She recognised the flinty hardness of his eyes and knew she had done Keith no good, but it was too late now.

"Yes, I suppose it is," she said frankly, "but he feels that—that—well, he is quiet and retiring and is nervous—"

She was not making even the best of a bad job, and she knew it.

"Possibly that is the real trouble, Mrs. Ellman. Your husband is too quiet and retiring and nervous, so much so, in fact, that he does not feel capable of taking on the added responsibilities which alone would justify an increase in salary."

"How can you possibly know that unless you offer him these added responsibilities?" she asked.

"You are evidently not fully in your husband's confidence, Mrs. Ellman. He has been offered such responsibility, but he declined it, saying that he did not feel able to carry it."

Domini flushed hotly and looked down at the carpet. What was there to say to that? Keith had lied to her then, and not for the first time. He had told her that he had asked for a better job and had been refused. Her pride would not let her question Mr. Gain, and she knew instinctively that he, at any rate, was telling her the truth.

She rose to go.

"I apologise for taking up your time, Mr. Gain," she said evenly, her head high.

"I'm sorry, Mrs. Ellman," he said. "I appreciate the difficulty of your position, and the only thing I can suggest is that perhaps your husband might be happier and—er—get on better with a different job."

"Thank you for your patience," said Domini very quietly and turned to go. "You won't, of course, tell my husband about my visit?"

"Certainly not," he agreed and she left him.

There was a cold anger in her mind mixed with a sense of frustration. What was she to do now? Where was she to turn? Somehow they had to have more money in the near future, and it seemed hopeless to look to Keith for it.

Gould she get work to do in her own home? They had what passed in post-war London for a flat – that is to say, they had a bedroom and a sitting-room, with a gas cooker and a sink on the landing and a share of the communal bathroom, which she hated, but about which she had been able to do nothing. They paid about as much in rent as the whole house was worth, and if they complained about anything, however justifiably, they were told that there were plenty of people who would be only too glad to take the rooms if they vacated them, and at an increased rental.

She hired a typewriter and managed to get a little private work which she did in the evening, but in a very few days the landlady informed her that there were complaints from the other occupants of the house about the noise of the machine and she had to choose between giving up the work of giving up the rooms.

And then, in the fifth month of her pregnancy, she caught her heel in a frayed strip of carpet on the stairs and lay there, in intense pain, until someone found her and she was taken to a hospital in a hastily-summoned ambulance.

It was many hours later before Keith was allowed to see her, and he was shocked out of his usual complacency by the change in her, not merely a physical change from the agony she had endured, but a mental change. She seemed a stranger lying there, looking up at him with something at once fierce and defeated in her eyes.

"Have they told you?" she asked him harshly.

"About the baby, yes. I—I'm so sorry, Domini."

She laughed. It was a dreadful sound. He felt himself flinch from it as from a physical blow.

"About this one and all the others," she said. "There won't be another, ever."

"Domini, I—I—I don't know what to say," he told her miserably.

"Well, if you did know, it would be that you're glad, wouldn't it?" she asked in that new, bitter voice which seemed not to belong to her at all. "I can always be relied upon to do the right thing, can't I? You couldn't have supported a family, so the fates have been kind to you and relieved you of the problem," and she turned her head on the pillow, shutting him away from her sight.

Part of her bitterness lay in the fact that she had repeatedly asked him to see what could be done about the worn-out strip of carpet, for which, since it was on their own flight of stairs, he was responsible.

"Yes, I'll do it, dear," he had said comfortably, and though she could have done it herself, it was one of the things she had been determined he should do.

Well, he had not done it, and neither had she, and she was the one to pay the penalty. She felt it to be hideously unfair.

But gradually, lying there in the hospital ward, waiting until they said she was now able to get up and go home, she realised bitterly that this was, after all, the best way out. She could no longer blind herself to the fact that Keith was not and never would be a 'provider'. He would always be content to sit back and let others pass him. He had never raised any objection to the fact that she was earning her own living, nor ever hinted that there might come a time when he would do it for her.

From that moment she recognised the definite cleavage between them, and when she returned home, taking up her office work again, she found herself watching and criticising Keith with a clear perception of his weakness, his dependence on her for any choice that had to be made, his inability to make up his own mind.

And yet, seeing his weakness, knowing him to be very few of the things she had believed him to be, he could still hold her love, not the passionate, demanding love in which she had married him, but with her defeated and frustrated maternal sense. She made excuses for him even to herself, constantly spread over him a protective mantle so that others should not recognise his weakness, despised herself because, despising him, she could still love him.

She had had no contact of any sort with her own family since her marriage, and though it did not hurt her to be cast off by her brother, there were times when she ached for reconciliation with her mother, especially after the loss of her unborn child. She wrote to Lady Barlow whilst she was still in the hospital, but received no reply. The salt was rubbed into her wound.

It was some two years later that she had the communication from her mother's solicitors which opened the wound afresh and yet began the healing. The letter told her of Lady Barlow's death, adding that in a will made a few weeks before death, her mother had bequeathed to her everything of which she died possessed.

Whilst she sat, tearless, but with a sword piercing her, Keith came home, surprised to find her sitting by the dying fire instead of being, as usual in the kitchen preparing the evening meal.

"Hullo? Anything wrong?" he asked.

She handed him the letter in silence, wondering what he would make of it. She could never anticipate Keith's reactions to things which concerned herself.

He read the letter through and whistled softly.

"Well," he said then, "who would have thought of the old lady turning up trumps after all? They don't say how much it is, do they?"

She lifted her head to look at him.

"It's my mother, Keith," she said quietly.

"Oh. Oh yes, of course. Of course, my dear," he said. "It's a long time since you've seen her though, isn't it? I mean—"

"Yes, I know what you mean, Keith," said Domini in the same quiet voice. "I'll let you know as soon as I am told how much better off we are going to be by my mother's death," and she went into the kitchen and began mechanically to prepare the meal.

She had not known that her mother had anything of her own, but it now appeared that there would be some eight hundred pounds plus whatever the furniture and personal possessions might bring in. Keith suggested that they should look over these personal belongings first.

"I mean, there may be some valuable stuff amongst it, and we may as well get the benefit of whatever there is rather than let some rascally auctioneer knock the best bits down to himself for a song."

Domini's eyes were cold.

"You can go if you like," she said.

"But I mean—what I mean to say—" he began blusteringly.

"I am not interested in what you mean to say," said Domini curtly. "I think you understand what it is I mean to say, which is that I do not intend to go poking and prying into my mother's things. She will have left everything in good order and the solicitors will see to everything and have everything sold – everything."

Keith had not gone. She knew he would not, unless she motivated him. Jervis must have known where she was, since he was named as the executor of the will, but he did not contact her. When the small estate was settled, there was something rather less than a thousand pounds paid into a bank in Domini's name.

It was then that she decided that they should leave England and make a fresh home and a fresh start in South Africa, and for once Keith was enthusiastic.

"It will be one in the eye for old Gain," he said, "when I give notice and tell him I am going fruit-farming in Africa. He's never thought I had it in me," and for a few days he actually swaggered, giving to the uninitiated the impression that this migration to South Africa and the prospective purchase of the fruit farm was due entirely to his energy, courage and resource.

Domini watched him with a queer tugging at her heart. He was at such a moment once again the man she had married, boy who would never be really man. Was it that immaturity which had at first attracted her? Had he roused in her only the mother, never the mate? Although at first she refused to recognise it, she herself had always been the real force, the leader, desiring more of the marriage both physically and mentally than Keith had been able to supply. She knew now that she was consciously unsatisfied, but that there was nothing she could do about it. All their lives she would have to do the thinking, the planning, make their life for them and continually spur her husband on to make the needed efforts to effect the plan.

At first he had been wildly enthusiastic over the South African project, rushing here and there, buying books, writing for pamphlets, consulting this and that supposed authority, coming home with all sorts of fantastic propositions, some of which would overthrow in a moment everything that had so far been decided.

Domini kept her head and went on steadily with her planning, listened to him, perhaps nodded amiably as to an excited child before a holiday – and went quietly ahead.

Finally, she secured an option on a piece of land in the Transvaal, and she and Keith sold up everything they had in England, bought before sailing such simple machinery and implements as expert authorities had thought advisable, and said goodbye to her native land, possibly for ever.

Even at the last moment she had hoped to see Jervis. She had written to tell him of her plans, and what she proposed to do with the money left her. She had had a brief acknowledgment of her letter, written and signed by his typist, but that was all. Leaning on the deck rail as the ship made ready to sail, she scanned the crowd of people on the dock, but he was not there. Keith was running about the ship, peeping into this and that lounge or smoke-room, trying to talk to the young officers who had their jobs to do and no time at such a moment for the passengers.

It was a sore point with him that Domini had insisted on taking cabin class accommodation rather than first class, and they had had a quarrel over the matter which had threatened to wreck the whole scheme and also their marriage.

"Damn it, Domini, why should we be herded with a lot of emigrants and cheap tourists? It's not as if we were their sort."

"I don't know quite what you mean by *their* sort, Keith. They are the workers, the people, who, like us, are going out to a new country to try to make a new life and earn a living. We definitely are their sort, and I'd far rather be with them than with rich pleasure-seekers, or people going out on other people's money. We're workers, aren't we? And the difference in the fares for two people will be a valuable saving once we get to the Transvaal."

"But, Domini, don't you see? We might meet people who can help us."

"We've got to stand on our own feet."

"I know all about that, but in a place like South Africa it matters enormously the sort of people you know, the houses you visit."

"Keith, for heaven's sake! We've got to and our own level, and the sort of people we shall know, or want to know, will be workers like ourselves. They are the people who can and will help us, not wealthy mine-owners and suchlike. Besides, how do you know, any more than I do, what kind of people we shall be amongst? What kind of people will be willing to know *us*?"

"Well, after all, we *are* somebody, Domini. Your father was Sir Elwin Barlow and—"

"That's enough," she said sharply. "There is not to be one word of that sort of thing, Keith. We are nothings and nobodies and it is from that point that we start, and if there is any bandying about of my father's name, or any suggestion that it is an asset, I shall pack up and leave you."

It had taken him some days of moody silence to get over that episode, but in the end he had apparently accepted it, though she knew it was useless to expect that he would not at some time or other insinuate into his new contacts the information that his wife came from a titled family.

By the time the ship reached Cape Town, Keith knew most of their fellow passengers, but Domini only a very few of them. It was Keith who threw himself with unprecedented energy into the business of organising the ship's games, himself a prominent member of the committee, going about the decks and public rooms with lists and pencil, urging this and that reluctant passenger to enter for deck quoits, for shuffle-board, for the tote on the day's run. Yet, like most things he attempted, most of the actual work was done by others, and by the end of the voyage Domini would have been genuinely surprised if she had known that it was she and not he who had been the more popular of the two, that it was she who had incurred quite a lot of interest and sympathy.

"She'll have to carry him all the time," was the general view, though when the moment came for disembarking, it was Keith who was rushing here and there, determined to say goodbye to people and to collect a few last addresses, whilst Domini stood at the deck rail, her eyes fixed on the skyline of the new country, on Table Mountain with its sentinel peaks, on Cape Town itself packed at the foot of the mountain and already beginning to spread out into the great tract of land reclaimed from the sea and planned with the long vision for generations yet unborn.

What message had it for her? What would it mean to her, to them, this land of sunshine and of opportunity, this strange land where her own tongue was spoken and yet in its heart and in the daily life of so many families another and (to her) alien tongue marked a cleavage of race, of habit, of thought? Would this country welcome her? Take her to its heart so that in the end it might become her country too, its fortunes her fortunes, its dangers and strife her own?

It was a long business getting through the Customs, since they had brought with them articles which were dutiable and which had to be declared as such. But at long last all formalities had been complied with and they were free to go. By arrangement, they were to meet Mrs. Joubert, the wife of the man who was selling them the property in the Transvaal, and spend a few days with her at her hotel before proceeding north, where her husband remained in temporary possession until their arrival.

She had sent a car to meet them at the dock. It was a distance of some seven miles to Camp's Bay, and the road lay along the coast. Domini leaned forward to watch, with a tugging at her heart, the lovely rock-bound bays, their almost white sands lapped by the sparkling blue and white of the sea. At either side of the little bays, great rocky arms stretched into the sea and against them the spray of the breaking waves was flung high into the blue, translucent sky.

"It's like Cornwall," she said, home-sickness in her voice already.

Mrs. Joubert, tall, gaunt, with the heritage of her proud old Dutch forbears in every line of her calm face, in her dark, deep-set eyes was at the entrance to the hotel to meet them. Domini liked her on sight. Here was someone to be trusted, to be liked and revered perhaps rather than to be loved, someone as stable as the stalwart pioneers who had fought and persisted and taken hold for ever of the land in which they had sought freedom.

"I am glad you have come, Mrs. Ellman," she said in the unfamiliar, clipped English of the born Afrikander. "Come in. The boys will see to your luggage."

But Keith must fuss about with it first, it seemed, dictating to the coloured servants about which trunk to take and how to handle it, announcing in loud tones which carried along the length of the *stoep* that there were valuable articles in the cases.

Domini flushed a little as she caught the slightly scornful look in the old lady's eyes, and followed her into the hotel, one of the older ones of the Cape, long and low, with the old Dutch gables harmonising with its setting amongst blue gums, palms and hibiscus. Managing the hotel was a charming young Scottish couple who made them feel welcome, though Keith glanced round the bedroom disparagingly and could scarcely wait until their hosts and Mrs. Joubert had left them to start complaining about the amenities of the room.

They were to stay in Camps Bay as Mrs. Joubert's guests for three days before taking the long train journey to Johannesburg. Keith was popular in the hotel, frequently to be found in the bar, drinking with anyone who would drink with him, paying for his round when he could not escape it, always ready with an amusing story or a compliment to a woman.

It was a relief to Domini when the train left Cape Town Station and they were alone and on their way to their new life.

"Rotten, poky little hole this to spend a couple of days and nights in," observed Keith disparagingly of the coupé which Mrs. Joubert had, with some trouble, managed to secure for them. In their ignorance of the needs of the long-distance train travelling in the vast continent, they had not known that such reservations were essential.

The coupé was admittedly very small, consisting only of the one full-length seat which at night would form a bed, and another above it which would be let down like a ship's bunk for the second passenger, but at least they had it to themselves. Without Mrs. Joubert's help and trouble, they would have had to share a four-berth compartment with two strangers.

"Oh, Keith, for heaven's sake stop finding fault with everything and try to be pleased with at least something," snapped Domini, and he stared at her, astounded.

"Oh well—sorry, old thing," he said. "I only just said it was poky."

"I know what you said."

He decided it would be wise to change the subject. Pity Dom was getting so snappy. Feeling the heat, perhaps. Poor old Dom.

"You know," he began conversationally, "I can't help feeling sorry we're leaving Camps Bay. They were a nice crowd, and we've got to start all over again now. Pity we couldn't have stayed in the Cape."

"We were on holiday," said Domini uncompromisingly. "What lies ahead of us is work."

"Well, all right. I know. I hope you're not going to keep up this way of snapping at me whatever I say," he told her with an injured air. "I don't know what's happened to you lately. You never used to be like this."

She turned to him, a retort on her lips, but at sight of his face, the disconsolate face of a slightly bewildered little boy, her anger evaporated. Instead, she put her hands on his arms and stood there, facing him, holding him lightly.

"I'm sorry, dear," she said. "I haven't meant to be snappy. It's only that—well, it's natural for us both to be a bit worried and anxious about this new life, wondering what we shall make of it, what new things there will be to go wrong, how many mistakes we shall have to make before we get things light and going our way."

"Oh, we shall get on all right," he assured her with that jaunty cheerfulness which once had been, so appealing, but which by now had become something to be afraid of because it left her so much alone, so responsible for them both.

Inevitably on the long, dull journey across the Karoo, hundreds and hundreds of miles of nothing but flat, dry, empty land where not even sheep could find meagre pasture, Domini sent her thoughts forward into the unknown future whilst Keith made his facile friendships with people on the train, chatting and smoking in the corridor, greeting as old friends people met for a second time in the dining-car, telling his endless tales, so many of them redounding to his credit. Domini blushed for him, catching the little meaning, amused glances of his listeners as he boasted of this and that, of what he had done in England, of what he proposed to do in this new country of which he would admit no lack of knowledge.

"Well, look us up any time you happen to be our way," he told all and sundry of these chance acquaintances when the long journey ended in the bustle of Johannesburg, the City of Gold, with its streets too narrow for the tremendous surge of traffic they had to carry, confusion and danger inevitable in spite of the many sets of traffic signals which sought to control the teeming thousands of huge, gleaming cars. Their drivers seemed never to have enough time to reach their destination. The slightest delay brought a protest from a dozen hooters, whilst the unfortunate who missed his gears, or whose car for any other reason refused to rush forward again at the first sign of the amber light after the red, rapidly became the centre of an angry maelstrom of cars and people going in every direction.

They had only a night and a day in the city, and then on towards Pretoria, where Mr. Joubert was to meet them and drive them the twelve miles or so to the farm which was to be their home and their livelihood henceforward.

It was dark, with the swift darkness which follows the day without a twilight, when the taciturn, elderly Afrikaan stopped the car and announced that this was as far as the road went.

They peered out. It seemed to them that they had come to the end of civilisation. All around them was the tract of dry, rough earth, with the dark bulk of trees blocking their way, protective or menacing. Which?

Domini climbed out of the high-slung, old-fashioned car which went with the property and was now theirs. She wondered how Keith was going to like that! He had been silent for once during the drive from Pretoria and she could only guess his thoughts.

There was no sign of any habitation and from amongst the trees dark forms came on bare, silent feet, and a black hand closed on the case she was holding. Instinctively she clutched it to her.

"I take, Missus," said a high, soft voice, and again the black hand touched the case.

"That's right, Sixpence," said Mr. Joubert. "Take that one and the boss's. Is Pony there?"

"Yaa, Baas," said another of the strange soft, high-pitched voices, and Domini felt they were surrounded by the faceless voices, the silently treading feet, the black hands.

She caught their names vaguely, strange, incredible names: Sixpence, Pony, Table, Green Beans, Zombie, and surprisingly, Macallister.

Their eyes grew accustomed to the darkness so that they could follow their host and the servants between the trees and to the house itself, low-built under its ancient thatch, smaller than Domini had imagined it would be, lit by oil lamps and furnished sparsely in the old Dutch style with the minimum of bare necessities, but each piece finely made by unhurrying hands, some in the beautiful native stinkwood, some in *imbuia*, but all beautifully kept by careful hands which had loved their task.

Mr. Joubert was leaving at once. Every detail had been settled already between the lawyers, so that when he had handed over the keys and some final papers, explained which were the outdoor and which the indoor servants, and introduced to them Inkuzi, the huge Zulu foreman, there was nothing to keep him. Pony, who was the general handyman employed about the house and farmyard, was to drive him back to Pretoria and bring the car home again.

When he had gone, the Ellmans stood at either side of the table in the general living-room and looked at each other, Domini flushed and starry-eyed, Keith unusually silent.

"Well, we're here and it's started," said Domini, and her voice shook a little.

She came to the other side of the table and slid an arm round her husband's neck and laid her face against his shoulder.

"I want you to be happy here," she said softly.

His arm came to enfold her almost shyly. There had been little love-making between them of late, none at all since they had left England. He wondered if she had minded about that, wondered a little at himself for not wanting to make love to her. She was Domini, his wife, and beautiful in her own way, and surely desirable. And yet for so long he had not desired her.

"Are you going to be happy, my—my dear?" he asked mumbling the endearments a little.

"If you are. Kiss me, Keith. This is a new beginning for us both, my darling. Let's put everything that's not been happy behind us for ever. Kiss me."

She turned her face to him and gave him her lips. They were warm and seeking. They held his own with a new, or perhaps an old forgotten, tenderness.

"They've all gone to their quarters. We're alone," she said. "Lock the door. Our own door, our first home in a new country," and whilst he turned the key and shot the heavy bolt in the thick, impregnable door, she turned out the lamps, all except one which she carried into the inner room, their bedroom with its great double bed, the linen on it hand-woven many years ago, the soft blankets spun from the fleece of sheep which their own land had pastured.

Over everything brooded a deep, quiet peace. Beyond the open windows, heavily barred at a time when no white man had known safe sleep, the blue gums moved softly in the night wind, and the sharp, bitter tang of the wattle, not yet in flower, drifted into the room to mingle with the smell of beeswax on the bare floor, and the all-pervading and imperishable smell of kerosene.

Domini put down the lamp and turned to her husband as he came into the room, held out her arms to him and gathered him into the deep warmth of her embrace.

"A new life," she said again. "Can we make our love new again too? Get back the things we've somehow lost? We have only each other now, each other's strength and faith and love."

Yet that night, lying in the big bed beside her, he failed her. Knowing that she was ardent for his love, giving herself with a new passion, yet he failed her and could not give her the response she sought.

Though there had been no other man for her, no desire for any other man, she knew that he had not always been faithful, but in that hour she made herself forget that – forget it and utterly wipe it from her mind. He was her husband, her man, her young, lost love who surely now would come back to her as she to him?

Yet he failed her, and they lay at last in silence and apart, her mind and body unsatisfied and bewildered, his knowing such abasement and shame as they had never known before. What was he, then? No longer and no more a man?

He felt in the darkness for her hand. It closed on his and held it, but there was no clinging of her fingers now, no more than a half-reluctant tenderness,

"Domini, I'm sorry. Do you hate me?" he whispered in the darkness.

"No, of course not."

"Despise me then?"

"No, my dear."

He tried to interpret her mind through her voice, but could not. It was expressionless.

"The journey—and all that—the excitement," he said haltingly.

"Don't," she told him and turned from him a little.

It was unbearable that he should have to find reasons, make excuses for not being able to love her. She had been ready, eager, ardent for his loving. The bitterness sank deeply into her. Was she then no longer lovable? No more to be held and loved and cherished by the man she still desired? To whom she had offered herself in love?

She never asked for that loving again, nor did he try to offer it.

There was, she found, a second bedroom in the little house, crudely furnished and probably very seldom used by the Jouberts, but she made it into a room for herself, and Keith could find nothing to say.

And the years had gone by, years with their hard work, their mistakes, their many failures and their few successes, years which had brought with them some sort of companionship because they had been obliged to live them together, doing shared work, making plans, learning the hardest way which did not break their hearts only because, it seemed, they had no longer any hearts to break.

Chapter Eight

It had been Domini's own idea to go into the Kruger National Park, and without Keith. It was not that she had any particular desire to go there, nor that she thought she would feel more than a passing interest in wild animals; as to that, people had told her you could sit with craned neck and your eyes popping out of your head for days on end and never see more than a herd of impala or a few buck.

The attractive feature for her had been the fact that, once embarked on such a tour, she would be cut off from ordinary life, shut right away from the everyday affairs, unable to be reached by any outside contact, for the best part of a week. She knew that she and Keith were at the stage when they must make a decision, and she could not make it unless she could get away from his actual presence, away from the intolerable irritations, her own contempt for his weaknesses, the anger which it seemed she could no longer control.

What were they to do with their lives, she and this man whom once, incredible though it now seemed, she had adored and loved with all the force of her young, ardent spirit? For more than ten years she had fought and struggled, planned his life as well as her own because he seemed entirely incapable of any plan. She had held him to their purpose, kept him from the payment of his own folly, guarded his feet, and when he had slipped from her hold and fallen by the way, she had dragged him upright again. Afterwards, by almost superhuman control of her own very human reactions, she had forced herself, if not to forget his follies, at least not to hold them openly against him.

There had been the time when, gambling in a petty, niggling way, he had begun steadily to get into debt, had been afraid to tell her and had borrowed the firm's money. That had been only a few months before her mother's death and unexpected legacy had enabled her to get him away from these temptations. She had discovered his defalcations by chance, and because even in such matters he was too weak to be able to lie convincingly. She had given him the money, her own earnings, to straighten out the books before the visit of the auditors.

"I swear to you I'll never let it happen again, Domini," he had said humbly, and his very humility had been the more irksome to her. He could not even sin in a big way.

"You'd better not," was all she had said to him, then or later.

She had had to trust him when they had started the farm in the Transvaal. It had been impossible for her to do everything alone. Besides, in new surroundings, amongst a fresh set of people, neighbours, tradesmen, dealers of all sorts, her pride would not let him be seen for what he was, a mere dependent on her capability and resource and hard work. It had not taken her long to realise that he was cheating her, not out of big sums, but by petty pilferings, a few shillings here, a pound there, the price of purchases and of sales altered when she had to get him to make the twice-weekly journey into Pretoria with fruit and vegetables, eggs and table poultry and her home-made butter and cheese for the market.

She wondered contemptuously whether he knew that she was aware of the petty defalcations. When he had been altering the accounts, he always offered her elaborate explanations of the bills for the day's trading, so that she knew, when he did not offer them, this was one of the rare occasions when he had not cheated her.

Cheated *her?* That was part of the bitterness, for it never seemed to occur to him that he was cheating himself as well by making her work more difficult and less profitable, since she put back everything into the farm and their home.

Now, alter their second full year, she could look back at the difficulties and mistakes and feel that the worst of them lay behind them. With the loyal support of Inkusi and the majority of their "boys" (though inevitably there had been mistakes there too), they had come through a long drought and yet shown a small margin of profit. Part of their home was still the small, inconvenient one they had bought from the Jouberts, but she had contrived to add to it, putting on two extra rooms, another and more modern bathroom with a proper water supply, and better plumbing. In her mind was a series of further alterations and improvements, even the addition after another year or so of a small electric plant.

And then had come the discovery, sickening and disgusting her, that Keith was betraying her in a new way.

When they had come to Reit's Kloof, their nearest neighbours had been seven miles away, with Pretoria five miles beyond that, but during the two years other small farms with their homesteads had sprung up in the valley, shallow but comparatively fertile, which had been dignified by the name of *kloof* merely by comparison with the flat land around it. Their nearest neighbours now owned land which bordered on their own, a taciturn Scot and his wife, who, having no children of their own since their two sons had been killed in the Second World War, had adopted and brought out with them to this new country an orphaned niece, Flora Pearce, the daughter of Mary McBane's younger sister.

Domini had taken an immediate liking to the Scottish couple, though there was little coming and going between the two homesteads, the McBanes preferring to keep to themselves. Small neighbourly acts when they had first built their home and started to farm their land had been appreciated by the newcomers, but the acquaintance did not ripen into friendship and Keith complained that they were 'stuck-up and stand-offish'.

Flora, a girl of about twenty, pretty in a pert, over-coloured fashion, seemed quite out of place both with the quiet, middle-aged couple and on a Transvaal farm. It was she who drove the farm car, however, and she relieved the monotony of her life as much as possible by frequent visits to Pretoria, from which she seldom returned before midnight.

"I expect the McBanes worry about her when she's so late," remarked Domini one night when, sitting up unusually late herself to complete her accounts, she heard the rattle of the car as it turned into the joint road they had made for their mutual convenience.

"Well, it must be pretty dull for an attractive girl like Flora, stuck here in the back of beyond," said Keith, who had nothing to do, but had lounged in a chair watching Domini at the table, surrounded by books and papers.

"Attractive? Flora Pearce?" asked Domini, glancing up in some surprise before getting down to her work again. "Oh, yes, I suppose she is, if one admires that style," and she thought no more about her until one evening when, hearing their own car returning, she had gone down to open the gate and found to her surprise that Pony, the Basuto boy, had returned alone.

"Where's the *baas*, Pony?" she asked.

"*Baas* stay Pretoria, Missus," said Pony. "He say him come bime-by."

She frowned. Then, since it was undignified and unwise to question the boy, she accepted the position and went back into the house.

It was nearly eleven o'clock when Keith returned, strolling casually into the house.

"Thought it best to send Pony back with the car in case you were worried," he said. "Met old Cranby. Did a jolly good deal with him over the pawpaws. He's going to take all we can let him have for that new hotel he's opening. Sorry I'm so late, old girl, but had the devil of a job with him, haggling over the price and so on. Had to stand him one or two spots, of course, but clinched the deal in the end."

She looked at him levelly. He met her eyes for a second and then dropped his own.

"Did he bring you home?" she asked.

"Er—yes—yes, of course. Couldn't do less when he'd kept me haggling there all this time," he said with a laugh.

Her lip curled contemptuously.

"Keith, why not tell the truth?" she asked. "Do you think I don't recognise yet the sound of the McBanes' car and the way Flora skids round the corner?"

"Oh well—matter of fact, she passed us, so as it would take Cranby out of his way, I hailed her and got her to take me on board for the last mile or two."

"And apparently you thanked her suitably?" asked Domini.

He stared.

"What do you mean by that?" he asked.

"Only that even in this light I can see that you've got lipstick all over your mouth and chin," said Domini. "I didn't realise that you went in for that as well as everything else."

"What do you mean, everything else?" he demanded aggressively, the attitude of a weak man at bay.

"Oh, Keith, don't you realise that you don't hoodwink me at all?" she asked with weary impatience. "Do you think I don't know all your mean little tricks, the cheating and the lying you seem to think you have to do, when if you really needed more money than it was agreed each of us should take for ourselves, you should know you could have it?"

"Well, dammit, how can a man possibly manage on the miserable pound or two you dole out?" he demanded. "One has expenses to meet."

"Drinks, you mean?" she asked.

"Well, of course – and not just for my own pleasure, as you try to make out. I have to stand men drinks in the ordinary way of business."

"As this evening, you mean, getting Cranby to make a deal over the pawpaws?" she asked steadily – so steadily that if he had not been trying so hard to cover himself from another possible charge, he would have been warned.

"Well, of course," he said. "Cost me quite a bit too, best part of a couple of quid, but I suppose that's got to come out of my own money as usual?" with a sneer.

"Keith, you may as well know that this evening, just after five, Mr. Cranby called here to see me and I concluded the deal with him, not only for pawpaws, but for pines and sweet potatoes as well."

Her voice was as steady and expressionless as her face, and Keith stared at her, flushed, and then looked down at his feet as he shifted them about oil the floor and could think of nothing to say.

"I suppose the two pounds went on entertainment for Flora Pearce?" asked Domini inflexibly, and, as he did not answer, she went on bitterly: "I said just now that you had not been able to deceive me, but I was wrong. It never occurred to me that you were doing this sort of thing as well."

"I won't see her again, Domini. I swear it!" he said, breaking in at last. "She's a rotten little bitch, anyway, but she's been difficult to shake off."

He stopped, realising into what his tongue had betrayed him.

"So it has been going on some time?" she asked. "Long enough, in fact, for you to have got tired of her? Well, I've got to hand it to you for once, Keith. You've managed to keep me entirely in the dark about one of your little ways. You should be proud of it."

"Domini—"

"I think that's about all I can stand tonight," she said, cutting him short. "I'm going to bed. That will also give you time to think up a fresh set of excuses and explanations – only they must be good this time."

She would have passed him and gone into her bedroom, but he caught her arm and held it.

"Domini, I can explain."

Her anger and disgust and weary despair burst the bonds of her restraint and she lashed out at him with her tongue, scalding him and herself with the bitterness of her vituperation, spewing out all the pent-up gall of the years until, half sobbing, she flung herself from the room and bolted her door and threw herself face downwards on her bed, worn and spent and sick of herself and of him and of the hopeless futility of their life together.

Of what use to go on? And yet what else was there for her to do? This farm project had been her last throw, and into it had gone everything, material and immaterial. If she left Keith, she would walk out penniless because, foolishly she realised now, in her determination to make a man of him if she could, she bad put the farm in his name so that she could establish no legal right to it if he wanted to keep it.

And it took only a few days for her to realise that he would go to those lengths if she parted from him of her own accord. He told her so, doggedly and in so many words. She had not been sure that he knew the place stood in his name, but he had obviously discovered it.

"You haven't spoken to me for days, Domini," he said, opening the attack with a courage unusual to him, so that she suspected that some stronger will than his own was actuating him, Flora Pearce's possibly. "I want to know what you're thinking, what you're deciding to do.

"I'm not ready to tell you. I don't know myself yet," she said wearily.

"Only if you've got any idea of cutting adrift from me, wanting me to go and leave you or anything like that, you can't, you know," he said cautiously.

She turned to look at him. She was ironing his shirts. He had complained that the native girl did not do them well enough, and she had added this to her other tasks.

"I wonder what makes you think that?" she asked.

"Well, this place is mine, you know," he said.

She drew a sharp breath. She knew that it had been a completely silly thing for her to do. Actually she had known it at the time, but the quixotic gesture had fitted in with the then state of her mind. Keith had seemed so keen. She had actually believed in him!

"You could hardly run it by yourself if I were to leave," was all she said, going on with her careful ironing of the collar.

"Who says I'd try?" he asked, aggressively.

She put down the iron and with exaggerated care and fingers that were not quite steady, began to fold the shirt.

"You have a plan, then? You have thought it out?" she asked.

"Supposing I have?"

"I take it you mean—Flora Pearce?" she asked.

"Well, if you cleared out, I'd have to have someone, and she knows the work and is a good one at a bargain."

She gave him a long, scornful look.

"You think she'd consider you a bargain?" she asked. "Well, it is up to me to decide, after all, isn't it?" And she went out into the kitchen and hung the finished articles on the line.

What should she do? Stay and see this through? Do as she had done for years? Make the best of a job that was getting daily, yearly, worse? She could not blind her eyes to that fact.

If she could only get away from it for a little while, long enough and far enough to see it at a distance and get it into its right proportion, she might be able to decide what to do.

It was then that she remembered someone telling her of the five days' tour into the Game Reserve and of the curious detachment from life which it afforded. What if she did that? It was not too difficult a time to leave the farm, and Inkusi, she knew, was to be trusted to carry on in her absence. Of course, if she went, it was more than probable that she would be throwing Keith right into Flora Pearce's arms, but then, if that was where he actually wanted to be, why not?

He had been a little frightened when she told him what she had decided to do.

"You—you do mean that that's what you're going to do, Domini?" he asked anxiously. "You're not—not leaving me? For good, I mean?"

She looked at him with that expression which had become so familiar to him now, a look compounded of pity, of scorn, of regret, of a hopeless frustration.

"I wonder whether you think it would be for *good* if I did go?" she asked.

"You know I don't think that, Domini," he said in a low voice. "I don't want you to go. I want you to stay, not just for now, but always. I—I love you, Domini, though I don't expect you to believe it."

Her expression did not change. You poor fool, she thought to herself. Poor fools, both of you. Caught up in this endless tangle which nothing and nobody will ever be able to sort out, which can only be cut right through and thrown aside.

Aloud she said: "You say that, Keith, and I suppose I must believe it, but just how much is it worth, I wonder?"

"Come back to me, Domini, and I'll show you. I'll prove to you that it really is worth having. I—will you at least believe that whilst you're away, I won't even see—Flora?"

She gave a little shrug.

"I shouldn't make any promises if I were you," she said. "For one thing, you won't be able to prevent her from coming here once she knows I've gone. All I ask is that I shan't find her here, in my home, when I come back."

He stood with her at the open door whilst they waited on that Monday morning for the *safari* car to pick her up. There was a freshness in the air, a crisp buoyancy of the coming of spring. It was a day on which it should be glad to be alive, though neither of the two felt much gladness in life.

"I can hear the car coming now," said Domini and stooped to pick up the small case she was taking with her, just the barest necessities.

"I'll take it," said Keith. "Domini, will you—may I—may I kiss you?"

She turned her face for his kiss and received it without response.

From where Mark Teckler sat in the car as it turned in front of the house, he saw the action, the kiss, the averted face, the expressionless acceptance.

"Cold bitch," he said to himself, his lips curling. "Who do these women think they are?"

"Domini, you'll come back? You promise?" asked Keith with sudden, frightened insistence.

She smiled for a brief second. The smile had no warmth.

"My dear Keith, one doesn't get eaten by lions nowadays, and not in the Game Reserve," she said, and walked to the car and got into the only empty seat, at the back next to Yvonne.

"Well, that's our full load at last," said David Parley cheerfully. "Everybody all right? Comfortable?"

There was a faint, confused murmur of sound from the six passengers.

"Right away, then," he said, and the *safari* had started.

Chapter Nine

It was a beautiful day, fresh with the crisp chill of a July morning in the Transvaal, the sunshine filtering through the dark leafage of the stately blue gums, and the bare branches of the trees still waiting for their spring glory, though here and there already they were misted with the first faint gossamer touch of green. Against the pale blue of the sky, palms threw up their feathery fronds, stalwart against the long months of drought which had turned the veld into an arid waste, brown, dry, giving no hint of the palette of rich, glowing colour which the first rains would bring through the parched earth.

Very soon, crowding to the very edges of the city, came the great yellowish-white dumps from the gold mines. Side by side with the dumps were the surface erections of the mines themselves, their great steel stanchions above the shafts, and running from them the carrier belts, the enormous tubes conveying the hewn rock to the crushing mills from which, after innumerable and still primitive processes, the gold itself, in a thin stream, would emerge.

David Parley's six passengers reacted, according to their type and needs as the city gradually slipped into the area of the gold mines interspersed with small towns, mining villages and stretches of bare veld.

Rowena Craye, sitting beside the driver, looked straight ahead of her. Though the scenery was very different from that of Rhodesia, she could not yet detach herself sufficiently from her own personal life to be interested in it. She was still angry that she was even there, committed to what now seemed an utterly foolish and futile expedition. If she wanted to see wild animals, what about the Johannesburg Zoo? Or any other zoo for that matter? And as for going off into the wilds like this, with none of the ordinary comforts of her own way of life and only these deadly people for companions, why had she been so mad as to subject herself to it?

David gave her a sidelong glance every now and then and hoped it would not be long before his passengers rearranged themselves to give him someone more human than this Mrs. Craye looked – the little French girl, for instance.

In the seat behind, Miss Koetse sat as straight as a ramrod in her corner, conscientiously looking out of the window, but finding nothing at all remarkable or even interesting in a scene with which she had been familiar for seventy years.

In the middle, next to her, Francis Craye lounged as far as his position there permitted him, his long legs stretched out, his light grey eyes expressionless, though they automatically took note of anything unfamiliar in the scene. His mind, too, was occupied with his personal affairs, especially with the memory of the little scene which he had enacted with Rowena before they left the hotel. Why did they stay together when it seemed they had drained completely dry the cup which once had been filled with enchantment and delight for them, and which had seemed then inexhaustible? Why did he not let her go?

He could not find the answer to that question – unless it were that he still wanted her? Not *needed* her, since in this country life could be completely comfortable for an untrammelled man, but *wanted* her, a very different thing? They said such bitter things to each other and meant them and would say them again, but just how much of truth was there in these bitter words?

It was not the first time by any means that he had taunted her with chasing him until she got him, and it would probably not be the last time. To some extent, that was true. She and her mother between them *had* chased him, but had he run very far or very fast? Looking back (and his hard eyes unconsciously softened) he saw her as she had been, bright-eyed, dartingly swift in her mind, her movements, her speech, so that all the time one had felt a little breathless in her company, oddly excited. Where had that alluring quality of hers gone? She was still quick, but quick now to hurt, to gibe, to scorn. She was bad-tempered and unpleasant to live with, she did as little as she must for him, and that grudgingly, and he knew that there were other men intimately in her life. She was like that, and yet he did not want to let her go.

His mouth twisted into a cynical contemptuous smile, and it was at that precise moment that Rowena happened to turn her head, not so much to speak to him as to take another look at her fellow passengers. She caught the twisted, bitter smile, and turned back to stare again out of the windscreen. How she hated that smile of his! And it was galling to reflect that, even now that he was having his own way and had dragged her off on this expedition, he could not forbear giving her that look.

In the other corner of the middle seat, next to Francis Craye, Mark Teckler sat with his disreputable khaki linen hat pulled down over his grizzled hair to shade his eyes, and took a keen and perceptive interest in everything in the passing panorama.

He leaned forward to speak to David, to ask thoughtful questions about the mines, more questions than David could answer.

"You've got me there, Mr. Teckler," he admitted with a rueful smile. "I've never even visited a gold mine, though I believe this can easily be arranged."

"How do I arrange it?" asked Mark, pulling from his pocket a small notebook and his fountain-pen.

"I think if you write to the Transvaal Chamber of Mines in Johannesburg, they will arrange a visit for you," said David, and Mark wrote in his small, precise handwriting in the notebook "Gold Mines. To visit. Apply Tvl. Chamber of Mines, Jbg." and put the book back in his pocket.

Francis Craye gave him a lazy smile.

"Methodical man," he said, a touch of contempt in his voice.

"That's the only way to get on, young man," said Mark, his North Country accent more strongly apparent as if in defence. "I started life in the cotton mills – born in them, as you might say – and worked my way up to the top, where I am now, and I could not have done that if I hadn't had method."

Francis did not reply save by another of his lazy smiles, which had an infuriating quality in them.

"Cheeky young cub," thought Mark with an inward growl and turned his eyes and his mind back to the contemplation of the trail of natives, huge and powerful for the most part, dressed in dirty rags with the almost inevitable greasy felt hats to top their woolly heads, passing to and fro amongst the various mine buildings.

In the uncomfortable back seat, narrow and uncushioned, sat the two most cheerful members of the party, Domini Ellman, who was determinedly putting aside everything from her mind but her present enjoyment and her five days of freedom, and Yvonne Dubois, to whom everything in life, and especially in South Africa, was still fun.

"Do you think we shall be scared of the wild animals?" she asked Domini with a little shiver of pleasant affright.

Domini smiled. Having looked at the other passengers, she felt herself lucky to be sharing a seat with the little French girl, who at least looked cheerful.

"We shall be safe in the car," she said. "We're not allowed to get out, you know."

Her voice carried to the front seat and Rowena turned her head.

"That's nonsense," she said in her clear, decided voice. "If I want to get out, I shall."

David gave her a dubious glance.

"I certainly hope you won't want to, then, Mrs. Craye," he said. "I'm supposed to see that all the passengers remain in the car. Regulations, you know. Not mine."

She gave a shrug.

"The only compensation I can hope for for the discomfort I gather we shall have to suffer will be if I can take some really good photographs. I presume that at least you stop the car when game is sighted?"

"Oh yes, certainly," said David warily. He foresaw that he might have a spot of trouble over this determined young woman.

"That will be all right, then, if I do want to get out," she said.

"Don't be an idiot, Rowena," observed her husband idly. "If the driver says stay in the car, then you'll stay like the rest of us."

She flung him a look of amused scorn.

"I shall do as I always do, which is exactly what I like," she said and turned her head again.

"You sound a very objectionable young woman, and one who proposes to risk the safety or even the lives of the rest of us to satisfy a whim," said the stiff, frigid voice of Miss Koetse suddenly. "I hope that there will be at least someone who will have sufficient control over you to see that you are not able to do this," with a severe glance at Francis, who gave her his slow, lazy, enigmatical smile as his sole response to her challenge.

Privately he was thinking that it would take more than all of them to stop Rowena from any course on which she had set her mind and that opposition would only make her determination the greater.

David thought it time to try to bring back the conversation to something less personal. He began to fear that this bickering was to be the normal atmosphere of the trip.

"We shall not see anything more of the gold mines now," he said. "We came out of our direct course in order to pick up Mrs. Ellman, but now we shall rejoin the direct route to the Reserve."

"Shall I be able to get any more films?" asked Rowena. "By the way, what do we call you? What is your name?"

"David Parley," he said shortly, disliking her tone and beginning to feel more than sorry for her husband. "We shall be going through several small towns. I'll stop at the next one, though you will be able to buy films in the Reserve."

In the next town, he stopped at a chemist's shop.

"I want some money, Francis," said Rowena to her husband, and as Francis pulled out some notes from his pocket and handed her one, he caught her eyes and read in them her furious dislike of having to ask him for it.

She stalked into the shop, and David, standing by the door he had opened for her, looked in at the others.

"If anyone would like to have a turn in the front, please say so," he said hopefully, trying not to look in the direction of the back seat.

"I shall want to have my turn when we get into the Reserve," said Mark. "As for that back seat, I don't think anybody ought to be asked to sit there. It must be most uncomfortable, with no proper cushioning. I hope I shan't be expected to sit there."

Miss Koetse gave him a withering glance.

"You will take your turn there just as everyone else will," she said and pursed her lips and looked away again.

"I don't mind sitting here," said Yvonne.

"Oh, but you must have your turn in the front as well," said David quickly, and for a moment their eyes met and Yvonne unaccountably flushed and looked away.

"I'm all right where I am for the present," said Domini, "and if Mr.—did you say your name was Heckler?"

"Teckler," grunted Mark, whilst Francis Craye gave a little appreciative chuckle in Domini's direction.

"If Mr. *Teckler*," went on Domini serenely, "feels that he really cannot occupy this seat, I shall be quite willing to take his turn for him."

Her brown eyes, steady, calm, inscrutable, looked into his as she spoke. He wondered if he only imagined that there was scorn in them. Looking down at him, indeed? Who did she think she was, anyway, to look at him, Mark Teckler, like that?

"It's for the driver to tell us where to sit," he said sourly, and looked away from her.

Domini repressed a smile and then began to chide herself. Was she turning into a shrew? An actual man-hater because of Keith?

Then she told herself that one need not be a man-hater to dislike this uncouth North Countryman, who obviously was not used to the society of well-behaved people and had not acquired their habits and manners.

Mark was feeling slightly discomfited without knowing why. That look she had given him, and the cool, outward courtesy of her speech when she offered to take his turn for him – well, could you bcat it? Except for the little French girl, there was not one of them he would have chosen to share this trip with, but he made a mental note that on any and every occasion he would see to it that he avoided all possible contact with this Mrs. Ellman.

And calling him Heckler, too. She probably knew his name, but reckoned on getting a titter out of the rest of them – and had got one from that young Craye.

Rowena came back with her films, got into the front seat without offering to change with anyone, and they resumed their journey, stopping for lunch at an hotel in Machadodorp, where one large table had been reserved for the seven of them.

David adroitly managed to place Yvonne next to him, but his hopes of improving the acquaintance were dashed by Mark Teckler, who sat himself at the other side and spent the entire meal plying him with questions about the trip, writing down the answers with meticulous care in his notebook until David laughingly protested that he must not be held too closely to the information he could only give in good faith.

"I've not actually made this trip before," he explained.

"Oh?" asked Mark. "But I thought we were to have someone well-experienced with us?"

David coloured at his slip, but Domini, at the other side of the table, laughed.

"That caught you out, David," she said. "Is it all right if we call you that? I can see that by the end of these five days we are all going to get to know one another *very* well, so we might as well be friendly where and when we can!"

He gave her a grateful glance.

"I should be honoured," he said, and thereafter he was David to all of them, even to the unapproachable Miss Koetse, who contributed little or nothing to the conversation, but sat as stiff and formal as she had been in the car, and clearly held herself aloof from them all.

When they went to take their seats again, it was Francis Craye, with the lazy efficiency they were to recognise, who rearranged the seating.

"How about you having a turn in the front, Miss Koetse?" he asked. "I'll have a go at the back seat and perhaps someone else will volunteer for it as well?"

His light gaze flickered round the little party, mockingly as for a second it met Rowena's, and Yvonne spoke quickly.

"I don't mind sitting there a bit," she said. "It is for me quite comfortable."

"All right," said Francis. "That leaves Mrs. Ellman and Teckler and you, my dear Rowena, for the middle seat."

His wife gave him a direct look with lifted head.

"A very nice arrangement," she said lightly, inferring by look and tone that he had planned it previously with the French girl. He caught the look and smiled, almost as if in agreement, whilst Yvonne flushed uncomfortably.

Mark Teckler without a word climbed into the middle seat and took his former place by the window, making no offer to give it up to either of the two women. Rowena lifted her eyebrows with a meaning glance at Domini, who merely smiled.

"I don't mind sitting in the middle," she said, and got in next to Mark, who was occupying considerably more than his third of the wide seat and made no attempt to occupy less.

"One of the delights of this sort of expedition," said Rowena in her clear voice, "is that one meets such charming people, so considerate. I'm so much looking forward to the rest of the communal delights."

Domini gave her a slow, quiet look, a speculative look which asked a question Rowena would not like to answer.

Rowena had already sized up her fellow passengers and put them into her own classifications. "The Ellman woman," she had decided, was prim, stodgy, uninteresting, probably a prude, no doubt happily married, and there is no woman more sure of herself, less tolerant to her weaker sisters, than the happily married woman. Nothing there for her, Rowena had thought, consciously for the first time admitting to herself that she was putting out tentacles for help.

But that look which she caught in Domini's eyes gave her sudden pause. There was nothing condemnatory about it. It was an expression composed of interest and kindness and – could it be sympathy? Rowena would have shivered away instantly from any thought of pity. Insensibly her mind softened and she felt even a little ashamed of herself. It was not actually Mark Teckler who had betrayed her into what she knew had been a breach of good taste, but rather Francis, who she knew had deliberately provoked her. None the less, she felt ashamed that she had been guilty of bad taste.

Domini spoke quietly,

"The results of these trips into the Game Reserve are, I am told, a matter of the sheerest luck. One may see everything or nothing. I hope we're going to be amongst the lucky ones, in which case all sorts of discomforts will be worthwhile – if there are any. Actually I believe it is possible to be quite comfortable in the rest camps if one is anything of a traveller."

That opened the way to a stream of steady conversation between the two women, Rowena interested, even animated. Francis, watching her face when it was turned to her companion, listening to the almost forgotten animation in her voice, felt a little stab. There was still, then, in her the girl he had married, though for him that girl had been so long dead. What was this thing, marriage, that it could so change and stultify the lovely things brought to it?

He talked in his amusing light-hearted, half-bantering fashion to Yvonne, but his mind was with Rowena and this rather grave, quiet-voiced woman who, it seemed, had the magic key which in an instant had unlocked the close-shut door to Rowena.

Mark Teckler, looking out of his window and listening to the animated burble of conversation, thought disgustedly: "Couple of chattering females! Suppose we shall have to put up with that the whole time. Why must women always talk? Can't they ever let a man be quiet and think?"

David turned his head to them for a moment.

"I shall have to drive a little more quickly, though it is the best scenery here. We must get into the Reserve before the gates close or we shall have to stay in the car all night or else find an hotel."

"I should very strongly object to remaining in the car all night, young man," said Miss Koetse severely. It was almost the first remark she had made since occupying the seat next to the driver. It had left him free to concentrate on the road, which for the last few hours had been through beautiful country; it had also given him time to think about Yvonne Dubois, still as far away from him as the car would allow, but still, heaven be praised with her turn at sitting in the front seat to come.

"There is very little danger of that," he said with his friendly smile. "You must forgive me, though, if I drive rather faster."

In spite of that, however, they had still some miles to go to the Mtimba Gate when Mark Teckler announced that he wished to have the car stopped so that he could take a photograph. He had two cameras with him, a cine-Kodak and a complicated and expensive 'still'.

David hesitated, glancing at his watch and the sky.

"There's still plenty of time before dusk," said Mark in his domineering way. "I shan't be long," and David found himself, as most people did, giving way before the compelling strength of the older man's personality.

"There's no twilight in this country as there is in yours, Mr. Teckler," he reminded him, but pulled to the side of the quiet country road, quiet except for the cars which were now hurrying forward, obviously with the same object in view – namely to get into the Reserve before closing time.

Mark took his photographs with maddening precision whilst the others reacted according to their temperaments. Francis Craye lounged back as well as the narrow, high seat would allow, Rowena looked supremely indifferent, Domini a little anxious, Miss Koetse severely disapproving of the whole thing, David apprehensive and constantly consulting his watch, whilst Yvonne looked at them all in turn, not really minding what happened since this was her last fling before being caught and firmly held in the bonds of marriage to Jean Lafitte. If she had any particular feeling about the difficult moment, it was sympathy with the obvious anxiety of David Parley.

Mark took his photographs with maddening deliberation, and at last David got out of the car and went to him.

"I think, if you don't mind, we shall have to go on now, Mr. Teckler," he said with some diffidence. "The gates close at 5.40 and it is past five o'clock now and still some distance to go."

"Young man, I am paying quite a considerable sum for this expedition almost entirely so that I can take photographs for my records. You can drive as fast as you like afterwards, but I am not going to be hurried into making wrong exposures," said Mark firmly.

"I am obliged to remind you, Mr. Teckler, that you will not be the only one to suffer if we do not reach the Reserve in time to get our accommodation in the rest camp. There are five other passengers," said David, gathering courage when he saw that this particular passenger was going to make the whole trip burdensome and irritating if not taken in hand now.

Mark Teckler shrugged his shoulders and shut his camera with a disgusted snap. He clambered back into the car, his crop of thick, greying hair standing up defiantly now that he had removed the flapping sun-hat. Domini, looking at him as she edged farther along to make room for him and his impedimenta (though Rowena whispered, "Take a bit more room and squash him up for a change"), wondered what his background was, what things in the past had conspired to give him that look of defiance, of arrogant defence.

Mark, still angry at having been obliged to lose his photographs, gave her a casual, hostile glance as he elbowed for enough room without taking off the camera slung over his shoulder. Oddly, he felt the look arrested by something he surprised in her eyes, something compounded of compassion and even a faint amusement.

Compassion and amusement on his account! He drew a quick breath and turned his head away from her. What confounded cheek! Who gave her the right to pity or to laugh at him, Mark Teckler? And his mind enumerated defensively all the things he had achieved in life, the things he owned, the power he had.

David had to take the car at almost unwise speed to reach the Mtimba Gate just as the native guard was closing it. By hooting furiously, he was able to attract the man's attention so that he held the gate open to allow the car to pass inside the Reserve.

A fine thing if on this, his first *safari* to the Kruger Park, he should have his car shut outside for the night, with sleeping accommodation for his passengers reserved inside!

Chapter Ten

After the long drive, and particularly the inevitable jolting occasioned by the speed made necessary by the delay, the little party got out of the car and gratefully eased their limbs when they were safely within the boundary of the rest camp itself, Pretorius Kop.

A high wire fence and sturdy gates formed a necessary protection for the camp, since it was set well inside the Game Reserve, and outside it all kinds of wild life were free to range.

That part of the camp to which David had brought them consisted of permanent buildings, substantial, small bungalow-like rooms, brick-built and with thatched roofs and joined together in terraces, their doors opening from long, narrow verandas which served as connecting passages. The terraces of rooms were arranged in rectangles, each rectangle enclosing a plot which was paved or grass-covered, forming a pleasant contrast to the acres of woodland, scrub and forest beyond the camp.

In addition to the terraced rows of square rooms there were the *rondavels* – round, as their name suggests, with sturdy white walls and thatched roof, each with door and window, just a small, circular hut developed in design from the native huts of grass or wattle or adobe. Beyond these again were the tents for the convenience of the more hardy travellers, who, with their cars parked outside them, were busy with primus stoves, or at the roughly brick-built open-air fireplaces, with frying pan and saucepan and kettle.

A group of tents was visible near where David had parked the car, and Mark Teckler, clambering out, eyed them suspiciously.

"I hope you're not expecting me to sleep in one of those," he said belligerently.

"Oh. no. If you'll come with me, I'll show you," said David. "Our accommodation is in the bungalows," and he consulted the paper just given to him and shepherded his small flock towards one of the rows of terraced huts. "Let me see. Yes, these are for you, these three," opening one of the doors to reveal the small, white-washed interior, bare but very clean, with two camp beds, a table to act as dressing-table, a portable iron wash-stand with metal jug and basin and, across one corner, a curtain concealing hooks for hanging clothes.

It was spartan but sufficient, and Domini had already noted, with surprised satisfaction, a board nailed to a tree giving the information that the arrow pointed the way to hot and cold baths.

But Mark Teckler was not at the moment concerned with baths.

"Three?" he echoed. "Three rooms for six people? But that is absurd. I am certainly not sharing a room with anyone."

David stilled a sigh. What trick of Fate had given him this particular individual on his first trip into the Game Reserve?

"I'm sorry, Mr. Teckler," he said firmly, "but the rooms are all the same, all double rooms, so if you and Mr. Craye—oh," breaking off with a little frown and consulting his list again as he realised that by rights a double room should be shared by Mr. and Mrs. Craye, but that would leave this Mr. Teckler and one of the other three women to share a room!

Rowena solved that problem, anyway.

"We'd better make the best of it," she said decisively. "How about doubling up with me, Mrs. Ellman? It's only for a few nights, and I don't snore," and she turned and walked into the first of the three double rooms.

Domini followed, glad at least that she would not be condemned to sharing a room with the austere Miss Koetse, who seemed to be receiving the situation with equanimity and had turned to Yvonne.

"That leaves us to share another of the huts, Miss Dubois," she said composedly. "Do I call you Miss, or would you prefer to be called Mademoiselle Dubois?"

The girl gave a little laugh.

"I'd much rather be called Yvonne," she said. "It will appear to be as friends. I will not mind at all to share this little room with you, Miss Koetse, if you will not mind."

"It seems it would not be much good minding," said Miss Koetse in her stern fashion, "though I think we should have been informed, young man, of this necessity," fixing the luckless David with her cold eyes before marching off into the second of the huts.

Francis Craye smiled and picked up the one case he and Rowena had brought.

"That rather settles us, Teckler," he said. "I'll take my stuff out and bring you the case, Rowena."

Mark stood his ground, clutching in one hand the considerable paraphernalia of his cameras and in the other his suitcase.

"I want a room to myself," he told David, his chin high.

"I'll go and see what I can do," murmured David and went off to find the authorities, knowing quite well that there was little he or anyone could do.

Francis Craye grinned and went into the third hut, took out his few belongings from the case, closed it again and went along the outside passage to Rowena, who was making up her face in front of the small mirror by the aid of the somewhat inadequate electric light hung in the centre of the hut.

Domini had gone to assure herself that there really were hot baths to be had.

"I've brought your things," he said to Rowena.

"O.K. Put the case down," she said without turning. "Is the Teckler resigned to his fate yet?"

"No. He's standing there, looking furious, waiting for David to find him a place to himself. Ridiculous, of course, at this time of year, with the camp crowded out." He hesitated, and then added, "You going to be all right here?"

She turned her head, the lipstick arrested in mid-air in her hand, a look of surprise in her eyes which at once gave way to studied indifference with him.

"Of course," she said. "Anyway, why should you mind? You got us into this ridiculous situation, so I suppose it is what you want."

He set the case down and sat on the side of one of the beds.

"Can't we call some sort of a truce whilst we're in here?" he asked. "It seems a bit fantastic to keep our—quarrel going when we've more or less cut ourselves adrift from civilisation."

"Who said it was a quarrel?" she asked indifferently and went on shaping her lips, her back to him.

He rose to his feet again.

"No, I suppose it isn't," he said curtly. "It's just—nothing," and he went out.

Rowena put down the lipstick and set her two hands on the improvised dressing-table and looked at herself in the small square of mirror fastened to the wall.

"What's the matter with you, Rowena Craye?" she asked herself. "Are you really up-sides with life, or merely plain cat? Why can't you be friends with him if that's what he wants?"

Domini came back with the cheerful news that there were really baths – proper baths with actual plumbing, and real hot water.

"I met David," she added. "If we're quick, we can snatch a bath. I've turned one on for you as well, as there are not many bathrooms and I thought you might not get one."

"That was nice of you," said Rowena, and congratulated herself again on having been quick enough to pick Domini for a companion rather than either the forbidding Miss Koetse or the little French girl, who was too dewy-eyed and innocent-looking to be interesting to the worldly Rowena.

"David's in a flap," went on Domini, unfastening her case to produce sponge-bag and toilet case. "Mr. Teckler is being obstructive and demands a room to himself, and how can the poor boy produce one if there isn't one?"

"I should let him sweat," said Rowena inelegantly. "Tell him he can have the whole of the Reserve to himself outside the gates if we're not good enough company for him. He's quite an unpleasant customer, isn't he? Wonder who and what he is? Self-made, I imagine, and not too well made either!" with a laugh. "Coming?"

The two made their way towards the baths companionably, passing the still indignant Mark, to whom David was trying patiently to explain that there *was* no other accommodation for him than the second bed in the room occupied by Francis Craye.

"As a matter of fact, through some mistake there is actually no bed for me at all," added David shortly, "so I am a good deal worse off than you."

Unexpectedly, Mark Teckler's face changed.

"No bed? You mean nothing at all? You haven't anywhere to sleep?" he asked, and Craye, overhearing it, came out to join the two men.

"That's a bit thick," he said. "What will you do?"

David shrugged his shoulders.

"Sleep in the car, I suppose," he said.

"But, man, you'll never get any sleep like that! There isn't room for you to stretch out, unless the seats come right out. Do they?"

He was perturbed, stirred out of his customary lazy nonchalance. Teckler stood listening silently.

"No, but I shall manage. It's a bit cold for sleeping in the open or I'd do that. I may do it yet, if they can find me a few blankets."

Teckler put in his word.

"How is it you're not provided for?" he asked testily. "If there is one thing I cannot understand or excuse, it is inefficient organisation. Who is to blame?"

"I don't know. Just some slip-up somewhere, either in the office or here," said David with studied impartiality. "Anyway, there's nothing to be done about it, so I must make the best of it."

The three men strolled over to the big car and agreed that it would make a very uncomfortable bed even for a shorter man than David. To the surprise of the other two, it was Mark Teckler who suggested an alternative.

"You'd better come in with us," he said gruffly. "Can't sleep in that and too cold to sleep out. If we put the two mattresses on the floor, the three of us can make shift; and I've brought a rug."

They stared at him. After all the fuss he had made about having to share a hut, it was unbelievable that it was he who was making the proposal to give up even part of his bed.

"I couldn't make you as uncomfortable as that," said David. "I'll manage," but they would not hear of it, Francis eager for the arrangement now that Mark Teckler had snapped the tension by proposing it.

Domini and Rowena came back from their baths, casually arrayed in dressing-gowns with their hair twisted up on top and their faces bare of make-up. In the dimness of the African night, lit now only by the stars and a crescent moon, they looked young and fresh and, Francis thought looking at Rowena, as if the years had been rolled away and given her the virginal, untouched look which once had enchanted him.

They stopped short at the door of the men's hut, astonished to hear the talk and laughter, the directions being given, the grunts as mattresses were being lifted and furniture dragged aside.

"What on earth is happening?" asked Rowena. It was then that Francis, looking up at her over the table he was carrying caught that echo and shadow of the past.

He explained the position, and the two women put down their towels and toilet packs and helped to make the unwieldy bed on the floor with the two mattresses and the combined bedding.

"You'll need another rug," decided Rowena. "Miss Koetse brought one. I'll borrow it," and she sailed off, leaving the other four looking at one another doubtfully.

Rowena knocked at the fast-shut door of the second hut. Yvonne ran to open it, but Miss Koetse prevented her.

"Certainly not," she said. "We don't know who it is and I am in my underskirt."

Yvonne spoke through the door.

"I'll ask her," she said doubtfully to Rowena outside. "Miss Koetse, it is Mrs. Craye. She desires that you will lend your travel rug for the gentlemen, who must sleep together," her demure voice breaking into a ripple of suppressed laughter at the way in which Rowena had explained the situation.

"Indeed?" asked Miss Koetse. "I do not see that that is any reason why I should lend them my personal property. Have they no bedding provided?"

Yvonne went to the door again and had another whispered colloquy with Rowena and returned to her companion.

"Mrs. Craye says there is no bed for David—" she began.

"Do you mean Parley, the driver? I think it is an unnecessary familiarity to call the young man by his Christian name."

Yvonne flushed.

"Yes. Yes," she said. "There is not a bed and he sleep in the hut with Mr. Craye and Mr. Teckler and he has no blanket, so Mrs. Craye ask—"

"That I should lend my rug?" interrupted Miss Koetse coldly. "Certainly not. Every member of the party could have been as well provided as I, and if this young man has not made proper provision for himself, I see no reason why he should make himself comfortable with my private property. Please tell Mrs. Craye to convey that to him," and Miss Koetse turned her ramrod of a back on the girl.

Yvonne's eyes flashed and her mouth set in a mutinous line. Going to her own bed, she dragged off one of the two blankets with which each was provided, opened the door a little and pushed the blanket through.

"He can have this," she said, and shut the door again and turned defiantly to find Miss Koetse looking at her, her pale eyes cold, her thin lips tightly compressed.

"That was an extremely foolish thing to do," she said tartly.

"Well, it was my own blanket. I could do that I wished of it," said Yvonne, her usually excellent English getting muddled as it had a habit of doing in moments of stress.

"Naturally. You are not, I trust, counting on having the use of my rug? I anticipate that it will be very cold during the night, and I shall certainly need the rug as well as my two blankets. It was precisely for that reason that I brought it."

"I desire not your rug, Mademoiselle," said Yvonne with pride. "I shall be very nice with one blanket," and she began rapidly to undress, not attempting to preserve the old lady from the shock of seeing what a minimum of fragile lingerie she wore, but getting as quickly as she could into gay pyjamas with little dancing figures scattered over them, and climbing into the bed, in which she was quite well aware she was going to be very cold.

Still, David had her blanket.

That was the thought that was going to keep her warm, or at least provide the illusion of warmth.

David received the blanket doubtfully.

"You'd have lost your bet, Mr. Craye," he said. "It isn't the rug. But she's given me one of her blankets. Evidently a soft heart beats under that rather forbidding exterior."

Rowena looked at him and smiled. Should she, or should she not, tell him that it was little Yvonne who was going to be cold so that he might be warm? Better not, perhaps. He would only insist on returning the thing and there would be an acrimonious discussion, possibly, with the formidable Miss Koetse. She might tell him in the morning. After all, if the little French girl had fallen for him and wanted to have a few days of fun whilst they were isolated like this, why not?

She thought of the days when life had been fun for her and Francis. Unconsciously she sighed and Francis caught the sound and looked at her quickly. Instantly she brought the mask down over her face again, turned and walked out into the darkness.

Domini followed her, calling a laughing goodnight over her shoulder to the three men.

It was a night, of splendour, the sky purple-black and yet with the soft brilliance of a myriad of stars and the silver boat of the moon. Most people had retired into their huts or tents, and those who remained outside were silent, or speaking with muted voices as if on them too the peace of the African night had laid its spell.

It was peace, and yet not a silent peace, for from the jungle beyond the boundary came the sounds of life still in the primitive, a rustle amongst the trees, the sound of a snapping branch, and, as the two women stood there silent, a roar in the near distance which made them turn their heads to look at each other.

"Really lions?" asked Domini, her spine crinkling.

Rowena nodded.

"Our first home was further north, in Nyasaland," she said. "The lions do more than roar in the distance there. They used to prowl round the house when they were hungry. We could lie in bed and hear them at night, and once, even in broad daylight, I came upon a pride of lions stalking in single file across the stoep!"

"Whatever did you do?" asked Domini, fascinated with fear.

"Well, I moved pretty quickly! I dashed into the house and shut the door and yelled for Frankie."

"Frankie?"

Rowena drew a sharp breath. It was years since she had used that name for him, a name he had hated from anyone else, but had accepted from Rowena because it was a name spelt by her love for him. What on earth had possessed her to use it again, like that, without thought, just because she was recalling those old, dim days when there had been passion and laughter and tenderness between them?

"My husband," she said slowly. "Francis, I mean. I used to call him Frankie then—oh, just to tease him, really. We had not been married long."

They were silent again. Each felt that intangible, inexplicable attraction towards each other, something utterly different from the attraction of man and woman, a sense of trust, of shared experience, of the understanding of another woman's mind.

Rowena spoke suddenly.

"I wonder why you've come on this thing alone, Mrs. Ellman?" she asked.

"My name is Domini and I know yours is Rowena. Will you mind if we use them? But you asked me something, didn't you? Why I came alone."

"Forgive me," said Rowena quickly. "It was inexcusable."

"No. I came because I wanted to—be somewhere where I can stand a little way from life and have a look at it, see where the road leads, if I can, and—whether I am going to take it."

She spoke slowly, softly, rather as if she were talking to herself, than to a woman who, only a few hours ago, had been unknown. Yet Rowena knew that she was aware of her, drawn to her by an incomprehensible bond. They had started to walk away from the huts and tents, and the smouldering fires tended now and then by the native servants, fires which served the twofold purpose of conveying a warning to animals prowling too near the camp and as cooking facilities for the more hardy campers. They reached the outer boundary and stood there, too far now from the muted sounds from other campers to reach them.

"Does that mean that you're not happy in your marriage—either, Domini?" asked Rowena after a pregnant pause.

"I sometimes wonder if there is such a thing as happiness," said Domini, not so much with bitterness as with despair.

"There isn't in marriage, anyway. I wonder how long human beings are going to hang on to marriage as a convention? It doesn't fit into the modern way of life."

"How long have you been married?" asked Domini.

"Eight years. And you?"

"Ten, nearly eleven."

Rowena gave her bitter laugh again.

"They say the first seven are the worst, and we've both had those. The thing is that I don't want another seven."

"You want to break up your marriage?" asked Domini. There was regret and compassion in her voice. Possibly there was not very much difference in their ages, yet she, Domini, felt so immeasurably the older. It seemed endless years since she had had in her eyes that gaiety which, at sudden, unexpected moments, could still leap into Rowena's eyes. Also she had seen the look that had been in Francis's once, when he had glanced at Rowena and had not known himself observed. What was the matter with this marriage? Surely something that could be put right, if he could look at her like that still.

"I want to, but Francis intends to hang on to it," said Rowena shortly.

"Because he still loves you?"

Rowena laughed.

"Heavens no! All that finished a long time ago. As a matter of fact, he never was in love with me. I wanted him and chased him and got him. He knows all about that. He reminded me about it only this morning, before the car came for us."

"You know, I shouldn't have thought of him as an unkind person," said Domini not quite knowing what to make of this too-frank confession, nor how to reply to it. "Just now, for instance. It was a very kind thought to go to all that trouble, and to make himself (not to mention Mr. Teckler!) so extremely uncomfortable so that the driver should have somewhere to sleep."

"That? Oh, that wasn't Francis who suggested that. It was Mr. Teckler."

Domini turned an amazed stare at her.

"Mr. *Teckler*? Surely not! That quite unbearable man?"

"I know. Surprising, isn't it? But that's who it was. David told me so himself. Francis only acquiesced. That's an excellent word to describe Francis's usual attitude to life, by the way – to all of life but me, that is. He *acquiesces*! I wish to heaven he'd acquiesce about giving me a divorce if I leave him."

Domini touched her hand briefly.

"Don't think too much along those lines, my dear," she said. "If he wants to keep you, it can only mean one thing, that he really does care for you. And you know you couldn't have obliged him to marry you if he didn't want to. There must have been something on his side, then at any rate."

"Something? Oh, the usual thing, I suppose. He wanted to sleep with me and I should probably have let him if it hadn't been for my mother. I was quite crazy about him, crazy enough to do anything. My mother kept ramming it into me that once I'd slept with him, he wouldn't want to marry me, and somehow or other I managed to keep off it until he did actually marry me. After that, of course—well, it would have been much better if Mother hadn't interfered. We'd both have got over it, and been none the worse for it. Now we're tied together for life, since Francis won't let me go and I haven't a bean of my own and precious little prospect of being able to earn any. Besides, to be quite honest about it, I don't want to start earning my own living. So you see how things are."

"I'm terribly sorry, Rowena."

The girl laughed her bitter, ironical laugh.

"Don't be," she said. "I'm not worth it. How about turning in? Can you believe that in order to hunt for lion, we're going to get up at half-past five?"

Domini laughed.

"You go in," she said. "I think I'll stay out here for a little while longer."

Rowena realised that the whole conversation had been concerned with her and her affairs, that very little had been said of Domini's.

"Are you going to be miserable, out here by yourself?" she asked, her voice quite different in its gentleness. "Because if you are, I'd rather stay with you until you're ready for bed."

"No. You go in. I shall be all right. But I've only got these five days for thinking, and I shan't do much of that whilst we're looking for game and I've got to do it sometime."

"You won't be long? I shan't like the thought of you here by yourself with thoughts that I feel are not any happier than mine. Your marriage isn't happy, Domini, is it?"

Domini sighed.

"No, but for quite different reasons. If we start on that now, we shall neither of us get to bed, so goodnight, my dear, and don't stay awake for me."

"Goodnight – but I probably shall," said Rowena and left her.

Domini put her hands on the top of the high iron railing and laid her forehead against them, closing her eyes.

She had wanted to be alone, needed to be alone, and yet with the aloneness came a sudden rush of panic quite foreign to her. To be alone, to be always alone, to have no one but herself to think of and for—

She lost count of time and had no idea how long she had been standing there, her head bent and her eyes hidden against her gripping hands, before she realised that she was not alone, that near her in the starry darkness someone else was standing, that the scent of pipe tobacco was mingling with the indescribable, unforgettable smell of Africa, a smell compounded of herbs and aromatic trees, of burnt, dusty earth, of the smoke of wood fires and of just sheer native. She lifted her face and turned her head.

It was Mark Teckler who stood there, his pipe in his mouth, his deep-set eyes fixed speculatively upon her.

Chapter Eleven

Domini's first instinctive feeling was of resentment, as if he had deliberately intruded on her privacy and forced his way into her thoughts.

Something of this was in the look she gave him, because at once his face relaxed into the semblance of a smile. He took the pipe from his mouth, and knocked out the dottle against the iron railing before putting it back in his pocket.

"You've no call to look at me like that," he said, and she noticed that his North Country accent was stronger, as if he no longer tried so hard to hide it.

"Like what?" she asked without reflection.

"As if I was intruding on you. You've only to say the word and I'll go."

"You have as much right here as I have," she said, collecting her somewhat scattered thoughts.

"Ay," he agreed. "Fence is as much mine as thine. Listen to that now!" as, from somewhere not far off, the deep, baying roar of a lion came to their ears.

"Lion," said Domini.

"Ay. To think as it should be me, Mark Teckler, standing here listening to a lion roaring in his own jungle! Ay, to think of that."

She felt his hand on her arm.

"Coom away, lass. It's noan too good for yo' to be here alone. Coom, lass," and she found herself obeying the light pressure of his hand and going with him away from the edge of the camp and the sights and sounds of the jungle.

119

"Have you come out here because you're finding the situation in your hut impossible?" she asked with a little smile.

To her surprise, he returned the smile. She thought how greatly a real smile changed his hard, rugged face and softened the grim lines of his mouth and jaw.

"No, though of course it's a bit of a crowd like. No, I thought I'd come out and take a look at this whilst I've got the chance. It's all a bit new to me, something I never thought to do. There's people from my young days I'd like to see me here now, in an African jungle hearing lions roar and not just zoo lions, but real ones. And to be with someone like you," he said, adding the last clause with an odd, almost boyish shyness.

She gave him her friendly smile. She was still finding it difficult to realise that it was actually Mark Teckler, 'that most objectionable man', who was out here with her and talking in a way so inconsistent with the impression he had so far given.

"Why someone like me?" she asked with that smile.

"Well—look here, Mrs. Ellman, I know what I am, and I know who I am – Mark Teckler, with a bit o' brass and nowt else but a damn fine opinion of himself! Now you – you, Mrs. Ellman – you're a lady—"

She made a little deprecatory gesture.

"Oh, please, please! That makes me sound – how shall I put it? Out of some other world, when there is no other world. I'm a worker like yourself, Mr. Teckler."

He gave her a look of surprise and interest.

"You're a worker?" he asked. "Why?"

She shrugged her shoulders.

"Needs must. My husband and I came out to this country thinking, as so many other ignorant people do, that there is plenty of easy money to be made out here and that the natives do all the work whilst the white overlords rake in the money. We have had to buy our knowledge of how wrong we were, again as the other ignorant people have had to do, and we know now that to make money out of farming, even to make a living out of it, means work and hard work and plenty of it."

"Yes, but why you?" he asked in his blunt fashion.

"Well—I suppose I am a natural-born worker for one thing, and for another, my husband is not very strong."

She spoke with careful precision, and he felt that she had had to choose and select her words. There were few things that Mark Teckler despised more than the kind of man who would *let* a woman earn his living for him, leave alone oblige her to do so.

"If I had a wife, I'd see to it that she didn't have to work for me," he said gruffly.

"Haven't you ever had one?" asked Domini.

"Yes. Yes, I've had one," he said grimly. "She's dead, poor thing. I killed her."

Domini gave a startled gasp and stared at him.

"You—did what?" she asked blankly.

"Oh, nothing they could hang me for," he said, "though I killed her just the same. Poor thing. Poor Lizzie. I've got a cruel streak in me, a hard, cruel streak. That was what she came up against. Dolled herself up, tried to make up to me, thought I'd still got in me something of the thing that brought us together and got us wed, just the physical thing. I hadn't. That was dead. Had been a long time. I told her so, brutally. I've told you I've got a cruel streak in me. They call it being a sadist nowadays, don't they? I didn't mean to. I didn't think it would matter. In fact, I never thought anything about her, except to give her everything she asked for – not that that meant anything. I was making my brass fast by then. No, she didn't want things, poor Lizzie. She wanted a bit o' love. But I'd gone past all that. And it killed her. Not right away. Not in those few minutes. But she had a sort of fit. A stroke. She never got over it. Yes, I killed her all right. Poor Liz. Poor girl," and he let the long monologue, in which he seemed almost to have forgotten his listener, die away into silence.

They paced the hard ground beyond the rows of huts, the few tufts of dry, brown grass worn by countless feet, the flickering flames from the camp fires adding to the eerie sense of unfamiliarity. The camp was very quiet by now, and even in the tents very few lights still showed.

She did not speak. For one thing, she could find nothing to say, no answer to that bitter self-immolation which she had felt to be uncomfortable and unnecessary.

As if he divined her thoughts, he gave a harsh laugh.

"I don't wonder you don't say anything. There's nothing much to say, is there? Don't know why I told you. You're the first I've ever told. Strange what a place like this can do to one. Must be the place."

"You know I shall respect your confidence, don't you?" she asked gently.

"Yes. Better forget it yourself."

"And wouldn't the same advice suit you? Couldn't you forget it?" she asked.

"Don't know that I want to. Better for me to remember it all my life. Keep me from doing the same sort of thing again perhaps."

"It shouldn't keep you from marrying again," said Domini, compassion in her voice. "You are lonely. Loneliness makes one hard and bitter when—when loneliness is forced and not chosen."

"Ha!" His exclamation was derisive. "If I could not make Lizzie's sort of woman happy, my own sort and kind, a mill operative like myself, what sort of chance would I have of giving happiness to the only sort of woman I could love now, always supposing I could love at all?"

"I think if you loved a woman, really loved her, she could be happy," said Domini, and though her words were for him, her mind had gone back to Keith, to his ineffectual dawdling at her heels, his incompetence in even the smallest things he undertook, his drifting weakness, his inability to feel strongly about anything, even the Flora Pearces.

She missed Mark's quick glance at her and the quick averting of the glance. He realised that, wherever her thoughts were, they were not with him. He called up again the vision of her husband, the man who was 'not very strong', so that she herself had to carry the burden.

The thread they had spun between them snapped. They were two people again, strangers, ships that were passing in the night.

"I think we'd better go in if we are going to be up early in the morning," he said, and she nodded and walked with him back to the bungalow huts.

He said good night with a return to his gruff, unprepossessing manner, and she turned into her own hut, where the light still burned.

Rowena was sitting up in bed doing things to her face, the bed strewn with little pots and tubes. She looked at Domini with bright-eyed interest.

"You've been a long time," she said. "Were you with someone? I thought I heard a man say good night. Did you catch something worthwhile out there?"

Domini laughed and began to undress.

"No. it was Mark Teckler."

"Good Lord! What on earth have you been talking about to him?"

"As a matter of fact, he's done quite a lot of the talking. He's quite interesting when you get under his crust."

"Thanks. I wouldn't want to! It's too crusty a crust for me. Don't tell me he's fallen for you! You be careful, Domini Ellman. He's probably got a thoroughly respectable hard-working, chapel-going wife tucked away somewhere in Lancashire whilst he's gallivanting round Africa."

"No. As a matter of fact, he is a widower," said Domini.

"Oh, so you got as far as that? And what about you? You know, you're a dark horse, Domini," laughed Rowena, carefully creaming her now thoroughly cleaned face with the aid of the mirror, which she had unscrewed from the wall and propped up against her knees. "Do you want the mirror, by the way?"

"No. I've got past thinking I can do anything about my face. I'm afraid Africa's got it for keeps. It looks rather like the veld now!"

"It's a mistake to let yourself go, especially at your age. Put this cream on instead of water. Here, let me do it. Sit down here on the bed. Tilt your head back a bit and don't smile!"

Domini was glad enough to have got away from the subject of Mark Teckler, and by the time Rowena had done all sorts of things to her face, they were both tired and glad to settle down in silence with the lights switched off.

Domini did not find it too easy to compose her mind to sleep. Her thoughts passed from Keith and her unsatisfactory life to which, as she saw it now, she must return, and flowed from him to Mark Teckler, so utterly different in every way – poor Mark, who was carrying about with him that burden of guilt towards his wife. He had not actually been responsible for her death, of course, she thought. Obviously she had been a poor thing, if a pathetic one, quite the wrong type for a man like him. He had said that they had come together in the first place only through physical urgency, which had not, on his part at any rate, persisted. Poor Lizzie, to have gone on wanting him, probably loving him, trying pathetically to re-enchant him, and able to make no impression at all on the hard shell he had become!

That must be the tragedy of all tragedies for a woman – still to love and desire her man, but to be spurned by him.

Her mind came back to Keith. Were things the other way round with them? Did Keith still love and want her, so far as he could love or really want anything? And did he suffer as poor Lizzie Teckler must have suffered, by the knowledge that she had no longer any love or desire for him? If that were so, what was there that she could do about it? Nothing. Nothing at all. She knew that the passionate love she had had once for him was dead, and that there is nothing as dead as a love that is over. If she went back to him, it must be with that knowledge.

And suddenly, overwhelmingly, she resented it. She was still young in years, only thirty-three, and an endless stretch of life seemed to lie in front of her – and what could it bring her that really mattered? That she would be able to count as worthwhile when she came to the end of things?

She knew herself to be far more deeply capable of loving than she had been when Keith Ellman had captured her girl's romantic dreams. Her spirit rebelled against the thought of the empty, cold years, the loneliness of body and heart which Keith could never fill. Was this all? Had she had all the gifts life was prepared to give her from its grudging plenty?

She slept at last, but awoke unrefreshed from muddled dreams which had no coherence or meaning.

Rowena was sleepily struggling into her slacks and jersey, grumbling that she had never known such an hour as this existed, and why should she get excited over the possibility of seeing a lion? And, anyway, everybody said it was most unlikely that they would see any.

Domini laughed. She always woke in a cheerful frame of mind, even from such a troubled night as she had had.

But she was anticipating with some interest what it was going to be like to meet Mark again after the revelations of last night. Had he bitterly regretted them?

When they met at the door of the car, it seemed so. His face was like a thunder-cloud and he was evidently having a bitter argument with Francis Craye, who, immaculate as ever in spite of the early hour and the wild confusion of the bungalow, was standing with one foot on the running-board in the open doorway.

"I'm sorry to insist, Mr. Teckler," he was saying, "but I'm going to. It's definitely your turn to sit in the back seat."

Yvonne and Miss Koetse joined the party at that moment.

"Mr. Craye, I do not object, I assure you," said the girl quickly. "I am the smallest. My legs have the room there, you see. It is quite comfortable for me."

Francis gave her the special smile he reserved for nice children and all dogs.

"That may be so, but you're going to sit in the front, my poppet," he said. "In you hop, and you, Mr. Teckler, will get into the back and like it! You can choose any of the ladies to share your discomfort – excepting the small mademoiselle, of course, of whom I have already disposed."

"Oh, I'll sit at the back," said Rowena disgustedly. "If we don't get going, there won't be much point in going at all. Come on, Mark," with an impudent smile at her familiarity. "Let's get in, and if we don't see any lions for you to photograph, you can hold my hand."

He did not reply except with a sour look at which she grimaced impishly, and clambered in after her, grumbling to himself, but audibly, that, of course, it would be impossible to use his camera from that seat.

"Then you can take ravishing pictures of me," said Rowena cheerfully. "Pick up your camera and hold it, will you? Half this seat belongs to me."

Miss Koetse had been uncompromisingly firm that Francis should have the other corner seat, so they arranged themselves in that way and set off. The most contented people in the car were undoubtedly the two in front, David and Yvonne.

"Do you want to take photographs?" he asked her.

She smiled up into his eyes, thinking how blue and sunny they were.

"No, I have no camera, but I am happy just to look and to remember. Oh, I do hope we shall see some lions!"

"I've ordered some specially for you," said David, "but they don't always arrive to time. Look! There's something for you, anyway," as, close to the road, ceasing to graze and looking at the car with startled eyes, was a large herd of the lovely, fawn-like impala, perfectly camouflaged against their background of brown tree-trunks and lighter brown earth by the pale fawn of their legs and under-bodies with the darker saddle of their backs. They stood quite still, but every nerve ready for instant flight if the danger near them became imminent. It was clear that, they recognised the car as in some way an enemy, and a moment or two later one of the leaders, a long-horned male, gave the signal which sent them all on swift, slender, flying legs into the safety of the bush.

The occupants of the car had watched them, fascinated, but Rowena, casually sprawling across Teckler, had balanced her small camera on the ledge of the open window and contrived to take a snapshot of the herd.

"That ought to be a good one," she said. "Why didn't you have a go, Mark?"

"I was not given much chance, *Mrs. Craye*," he said unpleasantly, emphasising her formal name.

She laughed.

"Well, the next lot may be on my side and then you can get your own back," she said. "Have I hurt you?" seeing that he was ostentatiously rubbing the knee on which her sharp elbow had unconcernedly rested.

"Oh not at all. I like it," he snapped, and David decided it was time to move on again. If they were lucky enough to see lion, his contentious passengers might be induced to forget how much they all seemed to dislike one another.

"Now," said Rowena, irrepressible now that she had found someone to bait, "all your eyes out on stalks to see lion, and the first one to sight any can have the reward of sharing this seat with Mark, whose gay chatter makes the heart rejoice!"

Mark's face grew even more sour. Francis could not resist turning his face round to grin at his wife. He knew what a devil of mischief she could be when she liked, and could feel sorry for Mark Teckler. Still, he was a disagreeable swine, and deserved to be baited for his attempt to get out of taking his legitimate share of the uncomfortable seat.

Rowena caught his grin and almost unconsciously returned it and then sat back, looking out of the window and reflecting on how long it was since she had exchanged a look like that with her husband.

And suddenly it was Yvonne who cried out "Lions!" so that David slackened the slow speed of the car and began to manoeuvre into position in accordance with her excited, whispered directions until the great beasts came into view.

There they were, a few yards from the road, almost invisible against the background of winter foliage and tall, brown grass even though they were only a few yards away. There was a pair of them, the lioness crouching, her lord with his great tawny mane towering over her protectively, the sleepy brown eyes of each fixed on the car for the few minutes until they decided to move off into the protective cover of the trees, where, just visible, they stood regarding the still unsolved riddle of a car, which obviously they did not associate with human beings or any of their lawful prey.

Those not busy with cameras sat in fascinated silence, scarcely believing that they were looking at lions in the wild – free, untamed, magnificent in their young splendour.

On the back seat, Rowena and Mark were half-squabbling, half co-operative as they manoeuvred for the best positions.

"I've half a mind to get out," she said. "Look how docile they are! They have not the least hostility towards us."

David turned round in alarm. Apart from the strict ruling of the authorities that no person must be on foot within the Reserve, he had been given very specific instructions from his employers to that effect, and he did not intend to jeopardise his job.

"Please, Mrs. Craye, don't do anything of the sort," he begged her.

"But, David, look how peaceful they are! They don't mind us a bit, and I could get a perfectly marvellous picture if I stood on that little mound."

"Don't be a fool," snapped Mark, but he prefaced the noun with an adjective very rarely heard even in impolite circles.

Miss Koetse sat up very straight, whilst Domini flushed and Francis Craye gave a grin. Rowena hesitated and then laughed.

"Well, after that," she said, "I guess I'll just stay put. Though actually it's a lot more dangerous in this car than out of it!" she added. "Mark, if I may be allowed to say so, you are definitely a one! There now. Look, they're moving off. They must have heard what you called me, Mark, and decided that this is no place for well-bred lions."

They watched until the magnificent pair had padded off out of sight, and then David decided it was time to return for breakfast.

After the meal, plentiful and well-cooked, served to them in the general dining-room of the camp, Domini was surprised and not too well pleased to find Mark beside her. She was going to the 'shop', where all sorts of curios, skins and postcard views were sold.

"When we get in the car again, will you sit in the back with me?" he asked her in a low voice, managing to cut her off from the rest of the party, who were all going in the same direction.

She gave him a cold look. She thought he had been behaving very badly, exhibiting an unpleasant temper with unparalleled rudeness which had wiped out the better impression she had had of him the night before.

"I shall sit where Mr. Craye tells me to sit," she said.

"What business is it of his?" asked Teckler, bristling with aggressiveness.

"It's better for someone to take charge of the seating arrangements so that everybody has a fair share of comfort and discomfort," she said and turned away from him to look at a beautiful *kaross* of cheetah skins displayed over a chair.

She asked the shopkeeper the price, which was twelve pounds, and was considering whether or not to indulge her wish for it when she saw Mark Teckler calling the man aside. She left them to it and went on arguing with herself against the advisability of buying the *kaross*, finally deciding that she would for once be extravagant and buy it.

She turned to find the fur mantle had gone from the chair.

"Have you another one like the one that was here?" she asked the storekeeper. "I think I should like to buy one."

With a smile and a bow, he produced from under the counter a parcel which he handed to her.

"This is the *kaross*, madam," he said.

She looked surprised.

"But—I have only just asked for it. How did you know I wanted to buy it?" she asked.

The man's smile broadened and he looked meaningly at someone standing behind her.

"The gentleman paid for it and asked me to wrap it up for you," he said.

She had begun, automatically to take the parcel from him, but she let it fall from her hand to the counter as she turned swiftly to face Mark Teckler, the colour hot in her cheeks and her eyes angry.

"That was an unpardonable liberty," she said and walked past him out into the camp.

A moment later he was beside her, walking with her.

"Please don't take it like that," he said, and his tone was apologetic to actual humility. "I didn't want to offend you. It was meant as a peace offering. Won't you accept it?"

"Certainly not," she said. "It's unthinkable. You cannot possibly imagine that I would accept a present from you? Why should you give me anything?"

"I've told you. It was a peace offering. A—sort of apology," he said, still in that humble tone that made her the more angry because it threatened to break down her defences. This man, she knew, was a stranger to humility and apology. It must be costing him very dearly to offer it.

"There is nothing for which you need apologise to *me*, Mr. Teckler," she said brusquely.

"You are thinking about how I've been this morning? To the rest of them?"

"Of course. Though it's nothing to do with me and I don't know why you are making it a personal matter. Hadn't you better go back and get the *kaross* you appear to have bought? I see that David is waiting for us."

"David? You can say David about the driver, but you call me Mr. Teckler," he said.

She did not deign to answer that, but walked steadily on towards the car, and again she had that queer tug at her heart as he turned and went back to the shop to collect the fur mantle, which he probably did not want at all. She ought to feel she had scored one over him, of course, but she felt nothing of the sort; in fact, she felt that by the simple dignity of his act, he was taking the lead and making her feel small.

The party had not sorted itself out before he returned, the clumsy parcel under his arm. Francis Craye was consulting the list he had made, more in fun than seriously, of the seating arrangements. Miss Koetse majestically climbed into the middle seat.

"I am too tall to sit in the back," she said, and even Francis quailed beneath her eye and did not argue with her.

"You've done your bit in the back, and the front, Yvonne," he said and the girl laughed and hopped in beside the old lady.

"I want to take photographs," said Rowena, and calmly filled the third seat, leaving only the front and the back for the two men and Domini.

"Like to have a turn at the front, Domini?" asked Francis. "Is it O.K. to call you that? It sounds more friendly than Mrs. Ellman."

She smiled. She liked Francis Craye.

"Of course it is," she said, and was about to go to the other side of the car to take the front seat when Mark interposed roughly.

"It's about time we men had our turn in the front," he said. "After all, we've all paid the same, and there's no reason why the women should expect special treatment. You have your go there, Craye. Domini can sit in the back with me."

She stopped, flushing with annoyance whilst Rowena chuckled audibly.

"Seems that we've changed bosses in this outfit," she said.

"If you feel like that, you go and sit in the front and I'll go in the back with Domini," said Francis. "You'll have to get out, Rowena, so that we can get in."

"You've been at the back," said Mark. "Here, Domini. Get in or we shall never get started," and to her own surprise, Domini found herself meekly setting foot on the running board to obey him, whilst Francis, with a shrug of his shoulders, left them to it and got in beside David, who was looking harassed over the business.

Domini felt hot and annoyed, and kept her head turned away from her companion.

She heard his voice speaking to her, too quietly to be heard by the others.

"Are you still angry with me?"

"Yes."

"Because I got my own way? I usually do, you know."

The old arrogance had come back. She preferred it to his humility.

"It is often possible to get one's own way by rudeness and a complete lack of consideration," she said coldly.

"Well, you never get on in this world if you always stand aside for other people to pass you and get what you want," he said. "In this case, why should Craye have got what I want? He wouldn't have appreciated it himself."

"It didn't occur to you that I might like to sit in the front?" she asked. "I've already had my turn here, you know."

"There will be other opportunities," he said calmly. "I had to have a chance of talking to you."

"Why?" she asked, giving him a frosty look.

"Because we've got to understand each other."

"I can see no necessity for that," said Domini and turned to look out of the window again.

She was feeling oddly disturbed, unwillingly conscious of him. He was everything she disliked, ill-mannered, boastful, pretentious, inconsiderate, selfish, arrogant. Why, then, should she feel that odd, illogical resentment that was so near to attraction?

"We'll talk about that later," he said. "Hold this for me whilst I get my cine-camera fixed, will you?" pushing into her hand unconcernedly one of the various expensive gadgets he used. "Ever done any cinematography? Very interesting. Much more use than the stills. I've got a colour film in here. If I can get it developed properly before I leave the country, I could arrange for you to see it."

She gave in. What possible line could she take with a man who simply could not be quelled? He seemed impervious now to her attempts to crush him.

They were out of the camp by now and at once there began to be cries from the others, as herds of animals appeared amongst the trees, the graceful impala predominating and sufficiently unafraid to do no more than move off warily for a short distance before they grazed again, enabling Mark to get what he said should be an excellent shot. To get it, he had to lean over Domini, one elbow digging into her knees to steady the camera on the window-ledge.

Coming from a water-hole were a dozen or so of wildebeest, more wary than the impala and keeping their distance, whilst flashes of black and white showed where the zebra, usually to be seen with the wildebeest, made off into the bush.

David proved an excellent custodian of the party, driving the big car slowly and quietly so as not to disturb the animals, his eyes quick and alert to discern them in spite of their perfect camouflage. It was he who sighted the spotted hyena, which slunk along, trying to get away from the following car and at the same time to cross the road to the water-hole. With its body low to the ground, its tail drooping, its head turning sideways, its small, mean eyes glancing furtively to the right and the left, its fur scruffy and coarse-looking, the creature presented a mean spectacle after the grace of the impala, the upflung head of the wildebeest and the wild dash of the zebra.

"Nasty beast," observed Rowena after taking a photograph of it.

Francis turned his head.

"Remember what he looks like next time you call me one," he said, but there was sly amusement rather than malice in the words, and the smile which accompanied them and they all laughed, including Rowena.

"Giraffe," observed Miss Koetse, in the calm serenity which it seemed little could disturb, and they saw a procession of the lordly creatures walking, one behind the other, the tall male leading them, their incredible heads amongst the branches of the trees, nibbling as they went.

"How beautiful they are, seen like this instead of in a little pen in the zoo!" said Domini. "Look how they walk, more like ships on the sea than as if they moved over rough ground. Oh Mark, look! Get them from here now! They're just going to cross that bit of open ground!" and she squeezed herself as far into her corner as she could, to give him room.

When he had finished, and the car was moving on again, his arm still lay across her knee, though there was now no need for him to steady the camera.

She knew that he was looking at her, but she could not meet his eyes and looked instead out of the window. She was still crushed tightly back into her comer. She was remembering what she had said to him, that she had used his name in the excitement of the moment.

"Thank you, Domini," she heard him say very quietly, and she knew he was not just thanking her for enabling him to get such an excellent picture.

She could think of nothing to say, and he spoke again, "Is it over?" he asked. "Am I forgiven?"

"Oh—I suppose so," she said in a low voice.

"Good," said Mark in such a satisfied tone that at once she regretted having yielded to him. He was a hateful man, she thought, but when the next moment she felt his hand touching hers, gripping it, she made no immediate movement to draw it away. It might have been that she was too much taken by surprise. She felt something of the tremendous strength of him – physical strength as well as mental. It seemed to flow into her from his fingers, the thick, square-tipped fingers of the manual worker, though the skin was now as smooth as her own, the nails well tended, the flesh soft but firm, a hand that could be cruel, but which also could be exquisitely tender.

She checked her thoughts, astonished and a little dismayed. This was a man to whom it was impossible to be indifferent – impossible, at any rate, for a woman in whom he displayed an interest. Such a woman must either hate him or – love him.

She thought of his dead wife, poor Lizzie, who had loved him after he had ceased to want anything of her. Poor Lizzie whom he had never loved as probably he could have loved.

Unaccountably she gave a little shiver and withdrew her hand from his and sat up straighter.

"Are you cold?" he asked, for there was a fresh little breeze blowing in at all the open windows of the car.

"No," she said.

She would not meet the eyes she knew to be fixed on her face.

"You shivered."

"It wasn't anything."

"If you're cold, I'll shut the window."

"You couldn't take your photographs then."

"That wouldn't matter, not if it makes you cold to have it open."

She had to look at him then, her eyes wide, surprise and a little laughter in them, perhaps the friendliest look she had yet given him.

"That would indeed be a triumph," she said.

"You don't think I ever think of anybody but myself, do you?" he asked.

"Well—do you?"

There was still that faint laughter in her eyes and in her voice, but there was no malice in it and he knew it and his hard face relaxed almost unconsciously.

"Yes. I'm thinking of you at this moment," he said, his eyes holding hers. "In fact, I've been thinking of you ever since I first saw you. Your husband was—kissing you."

She was annoyed with herself for the flush that came to her cheeks. She looked away from him again.

"Did you want him to kiss you?" he persisted.

She glanced at him and then, nervously, at the three women on the seat in front of them, especially at Rowena, who had sharp ears and a mischievous mind.

"Please," she asked him in a low, urgent voice.

He smiled.

"Afraid they might hear? All right. Will you come out with me this evening again, Domini? After dinner, when the camp has settled down?"

"I shall be tired," she said.

"You're hedging. Come even if you are tired."

"I told you you never think of anyone but yourself."

"And I told you you're wrong, because I'm thinking of you. I'm thinking all the time of you, Domini. Do you mind?"

She made a little helpless gesture with her hands. The whole situation was so absurd. This rude, ill-bred man – what could they possibly have in common that she should be expected to make an assignation with him? Agree to go out to meet him in the darkness and the silence of the jungle night?

Suddenly she was afraid.

"I can't meet you," she said in a swift, tight voice, and looked away from him.

"Why not? Why not, Domini?" and when she did not answer, "You will, you know," he added and was silent again until someone sighted a wart-hog and they all discussed the peculiar ugliness of the creature.

Francis turned to Rowena again.

"Have a good look at him," he said. "It'll be so much more effective than the hyena when you're really furious with me!"

Oddly, she found herself smiling, and not with the bitter, hating smile which had become usual between them. Then she pulled herself up with a jerk and looked away from him, back at the wart-hog with its hideous snout and ungainly body. Her eyes no longer saw it. She was looking within herself, looking back at the past, remembering all the disillusionment, the bitterness, the ugliness that had so incredibly come out of their early raptures when they had been happy and in love. In love? Had Francis ever been truly in love with her or she with him?

She tried to fix her attention on the things of the moment. The wart-hog had shambled off into the bushes, and following it had come the stately kudu, not venturing too near the road and yet appearing not to notice it but passing with slow, measured steps in front of a line of bushes, the males with their great, curved horns, the females less spectacular, well guarded by their mates, which kept between them and the open veld from which danger might come.

Wearily Rowena dragged the scene into her consciousness, thought how much simpler and easier was the life of these creatures. She heard Miss Koetse's precise voice asking David a question: "I have been told that though the lion scents and finds the prey, it is the lioness who makes the kill. Do you know if this is so, Mr. Parley?"

She alone amongst the little party had not started to use Christian names, but still stood on ceremony with all of them. It set her apart even more than her age did, and in return they all treated her with an aloof respect.

"I am not sure about that, Miss Koetse," admitted David. "Has anyone else heard that?" to the company in general.

They were making their way now to Skukuza for lunch, after which they would look for hippo at the hippo pools and then go northwards to Satara for the night.

"I also have been told that is so," said Yvonne, who had been very quiet all the morning, obviously occupied with her own thoughts when they were not actually observing the game.

"It's the lion who tucks in first, anyway," said Francis. "Then his wife and kids have a go, and after that the jackals – or is it the hyena? – and finally the vultures. It would be in keeping with the rest of Nature for the female, to get her talons in first, anyway."

Rowena looked steadily out of the window. Though there had been several occasions on which they seemed to be meeting on something like the old ground, when he spoke like this, back they came to the place on which they fought as enemies. Or had she just been stupid and credulous to think there was anything different about his attitude to her? In the way he looked and spoke to her?

Her mouth set into the grim hardness which had become habitual to it.

Chapter Twelve

After lunch at Skukuza, David took the party to the pools where the hippo spent their days, wallowing in the cool water and as unconcerned about the human watchers as any of the captive fellows in a zoo. The party scrambled carefully down the sloping banks to the water's edge and Rowena turned to Domini.

"Have you had any chance to use your own camera?" she asked, glancing meaningly at the back of Mark Teckler, who had taken, the most advantageous position and was setting up the more elaborate of his cameras, a large cine on a stand.

"I don't think it's much good," said Domini. "It seems to stick when I turn the film, and I don't believe it's actually turning at all. I've decided not to bother with it, but shall have to content myself with bought photographs."

Mark turned his head briefly.

"I've told you I'll show you mine," he said.

"That won't give me anything to keep," said Domini, conscious that Rowena was watching and listening with her mischievous mind alert and receptive.

"I'll have a look at your camera this evening, when the light has gone," he said and returned to his own affairs.

Rowena deliberately caught Domini's eyes and smiled.

"You seem to have tamed the bear," she said, and though she kept her voice fairly low, it reached Mark's ears and he listened for the reply.

"Only temporarily and partially, I think," said Domini, and the two laughed a little as they moved off down the bank.

Mark pursed his lips angrily. So she laughed at him, did she? He forced his mind back to the focusing of his camera, but realised that, unusually for him, he could not give it his whole attention. He was thinking of Domini, of everything about her, her soft, smooth hair which he had wanted to touch, her brown eyes which could snap with anger at him and yet which last night had been soft and starry bright by turns, and this morning cold with dislike. He thought of the slender grace of her, the sureness of her movements. He would not turn his head to look at her, but he could picture her, moving with purpose and ease whilst Rowena Craye scrambled uncaringly and dangerously ahead.

He bent his attention sternly on the job in hand. Tonight he would see her again. Though she had refused him, though she was determined that she would not come to him as he had bidden her, yet she would come. He knew his own strength and his power to dominate. She would not be easy to command. The knowledge brought a swift breath of satisfaction to his lips. No, she would not be easy. She was giving her friendship so grudgingly, fighting all the way, but that was how it should be, how it must be for him. He had never wanted the easy things. He wanted to fight and conquer, not to have anything given to him on a plate.

He did not ask himself yet what he wanted of Domini Ellman. He could not define it —would not, even if he could. He only knew that he wanted her to come out to him in the darkness tonight, to come of her own free will, not just to be found there as he had found her last night, by chance. He wanted the triumph of knowing that she came to him because he demanded it of her, because she had no strength to pit victoriously against his own.

Rowena's voice came up to where he stood, David and Yvonne not far away and too deeply engaged in conversation and in their young laughter to be bothering much about hippo.

"David, would it be all right if I went round to the other side of the pool?" asked Rowena. "I could get a marvellous shot over there."

"No, please don't, Mrs. Craye," said David quickly in alarm. "It would not be safe."

"But look how peaceful and stupid they are! They're all asleep, all except those two little ones tumbling over each other in the water."

"That just makes the danger, Mrs. Craye. Hippo can be very dangerous when there are young with them, and though they're so huge and clumsy, they can move with terrific speed when they're roused. Please stay on this side."

"But I won't go too near," she urged and put a tentative foot out towards a sort of natural causeway which would give access to the other side of the big, natural pool in which some twenty or thirty hippo lay wallowing, most of them motionless and like great lumps of grey rock, their submerged snouts occasionally blowing up water, their tiny, wicked-looking eyes blinking with drowsy, deceptive contentment as their young tumbled about them.

David made an instinctive gesture, but Francis was quicker and took the bank in a couple of leaping strides and caught Rowena by the arm.

"Don't be such a little idiot," he told her angrily. "Haven't you any savvy at all? Of course the brutes are dangerous, and we're only allowed out of the car if we keep to this side."

She tried to shake off his grip but he would not relax it.

"Good heavens, why is everybody in such a dither?" she asked. "I should be perfectly safe, and of course I could get away from great, clumsy brutes like that even if they did come after me. How could they get across that, anyway?" indicating the narrow, rocky causeway.

"Whether they could or not is beside the point," said Francis, holding on to her grimly. "The thing is that though they may look like animals in a zoo, they're not. They're wild and free, and if they wanted to, they could swim much more quickly than you could get across here again. You're not going to risk your silly little neck."

Their eyes met, defiantly, in dire enmity. Then she gave in.

"I didn't think you cared," she said, but her tone was full of cynical bitterness.

"I don't," he told her curtly. "I'm thinking of David, who has for his sins to be responsible for what happens to us all, including you. If everybody's finished, shall we move on, David?"

David had been only too glad to leave the issue with Rowena's husband. What had happened between these two, he could not begin to guess, but obviously they were out of love with each other, though it was a good thing for him, David Parley, that Craye still considered himself responsible for whatever foolish things his wife wanted to do.

Then he forgot Rowena and looked down at little Yvonne beside him, her face still frightened, her dark eyes with their pupils contracted, her small hands gripping the folds of her heather-brown skirt.

"Oh!" she breathed. "C'est terrible! J'ai peur – j'ai peur!"

Instinctively he put out a hand to touch her arm and at once, without her own volition, her own hand came to meet it, whilst her eyes were lifted to his face. His heart gave a jolt. What a sweetheart she was! So small and sweet and sort of pathetic, though why on earth he should think suddenly that she was pathetic, he did not know.

He smiled at her reassuringly.

"It's all right," he said. "He won't let her go. I don't think she really meant to. I think she wanted to scare us."

"Or—so that *he* should have fear?" asked Yvonne in a small whisper.

David nodded thoughtfully.

"Yes. Perhaps you're right. I think somehow you *are* right. Knowing little thing, aren't you?" and in the moment in which their eyes met, blue looking into brown, something sparked and lit between them, something which dazzled them, made them suddenly afraid and yet, as suddenly, wildly happy.

He still held her hand tightly in his, hidden by the pleats of her skirt, as they turned to go back to the car, Rowena propelled sternly and inflexibly by Francis, Domini following them up the steep bank, Mark Teckler hesitating as to whether he would be met with a rebuff or not if he managed to extricate a hand from his mass of cameras and stands in order to offer help to Domini, but deciding in the end that she would not welcome it.

Miss Koetse, being already at the top, reached the car first and settled herself in a corner of the middle seat with her usual serene disregard for the rights of the others, and when the Crayes arrived. Francis pushed Rowena with scant ceremony into the seat next to her.

"I want to sit in the corner so that I can use my camera," said Rowena defiantly.

"You sit in the middle where you're out of mischief," he told her calmly, and she pursed her lips and sat still. If she tried to retort, the idiotic tears would start again. For some reason or other, she felt upset far beyond the natural reaction to their little contretemps. She was remembering his tone and look when she had taunted him and he had said that he did not care.

Francis was looking at David and Yvonne as they walked up to the car. They did not know that the radiance of that moment was still in their faces, in their eyes and hovering about their young lips.

"Poor, silly young fools," he thought, but when they reached him, he smiled at Yvonne, the special smile she seemed able to evoke from all of them, except possibly old Miss Koetse, who never smiled at all.

"You sit in the front with David, Yvonne," he said.

"But it's your place," she said.

"I'm going to sit with my wife – and keep her out of mischief," he said, without looking towards Rowena, and when Domini and Mark had climbed into the back seat, he slipped into the window corner next to his wife, who studiously avoided looking at him. She felt sore and humiliated, knew she had acted foolishly, but would not for the world have let him know it. Actually she had had no intention of crossing the hippo pool. Yvonne had been quite right in her suggestion that the real idea had been to frighten Francis. It was irritating to realise that all she had succeeded in doing had been to make herself look a fool.

It was dusk, the short twilight of the sub-tropics, by the time they reached their next rest camp, Satara, and for one reason and another, they were all glad to get out of the car.

There were no bungalows at Satara, but only *rondavels* and tents, and as soon as he saw the lines of tents, Mark began to assert himself again.

"I'm not going to sleep in a tent," he said to David. "You remember that I asked you about that before we left Johannesburg, and you said there would be no tents."

David sighed, but his innate courtesy upheld him. He was going to be glad when this first trip of his to the Kruger Park was over – until he remembered that with the end of this would come also the end of his knowledge of Yvonne Dubois.

"There will be *rondavels* for you all, Mr. Teckler," he said, and went off to find the office to see what had been arranged.

Mark caught him up.

"I'd like to have one of these things to myself," he said.

"I doubt if that will be possible," said David. "The camps are all full up at this time of the year, but at least I'll see that it isn't as uncomfortable for you as last night."

But when he had been to the office and studied the arrangements, he came back with a face full of foreboding.

"Well, what have you arranged?" asked Mark from amongst the group of the six of them gathered about the car still. "I hope you're giving me one of these round things to myself."

"I'm afraid that's not possible, Mr. Teckler," said David. "In fact, the camp is so full up that—that I'm sorry to say the four ladies will have to share one *rondavel*, and you and Mr. Craye the other."

There was a gasp of dismay from the women.

"Four in one *rondavel?* But that's positively indecent!" cried Rowena. "How could they get four beds in, even if we could all breathe?"

"There are four in most of the *rondavels* tonight, they say at the office," said David apologetically. "I'm terribly sorry, but you understand that this is the best they can do, with so many to accommodate."

"Any objection to our dragging our beds outside?" asked Rowena. "How about you too, Domini?"

"I'd much prefer that," said Domini, looking at David. She had no wish to add anything to his obvious worries with his difficult charges, Mark looking like thunder, Miss Koetse with her face even more severe and forbidding than usual, only Francis Craye and Yvonne taking the situation without comment or obvious annoyance.

Francis interposed calmly.

"You're not sleeping outside, Rowena," he said.

"What's going to stop me if I want to?" she demanded.

"I am."

"Why?"

"Because it gets very cold in the night at this time of year in the Transvaal and you're not used to it, and I don't want the bother and inconvenience of having you ill," he said with complete calm.

"Well, if you think I'm going to share a *rondavel* with three other women, or even with two, you've got another think coming," said Rowena furiously.

Francis turned and began to walk away.

"Suppose we discuss it in rather greater privacy?" he suggested, and after a moment's hesitation, she went with him.

Miss Koetse and Yvonne went with David, peering with him at the numbers on the *rondavels* to find the one allotted to them, and for a moment Domini found herself alone with Mark Teckler.

"Do you really intend to sleep outside tonight?" he asked her with a little frown.

"Yes. I shall prefer it. I could not agree more with Rowena about four women in one *rondavel!*"

"But if it's too cold for Rowena outside, it will be too cold for you," he said.

"No. I'm used to it."

They were walking slowly after the other three. Behind them they could just catch the low voices of the Crayes, and though the words were inaudible, the tones did not suggest any friendly discussion.

Rowena and Francis joined them, Rowena obviously in a very bad temper, Francis as imperturbable as ever. Three beds were arranged in the *rondavel*, and though David was still not happy over the arrangement, the fourth was made up outside for Domini, set in the most sheltered position against the white-washed wall and provided with extra blankets.

"How about you? Will you be all right?" asked Mark of David before he set off with Francis to find their own quarters.

"Yes. I'm sharing a tent with one of our other drivers," said David. "I think perhaps we'd better go and get dinner before we unpack. By the way, there are baths and plenty of hot water, even if we're going to be a bit crowded."

As seemed to be usual in the camps, a good meal was provided in the dining-room, and afterwards the little party disbanded to unpack, to find the promised baths and, since after dark there was nothing to do and only swinging oil lamps for light in the *rondavels* and tents, to go to bed.

Domini managed to elude Mark, who, she knew, wanted to press again his invitation to her to meet him before going to bed.

Over their baths (she and Rowena found cubicles next to each other and could talk across the partition) Rowena, who had come out of her bad temper, asked: "Are you going to dress again?"

"I think I'd better put on most of my clothes, as I'm going to sleep out. I dare say it really will be cold."

"I'm doing ditto," said Rowena.

"What do you mean by ditto? You won't want much on, sleeping with two more in that *rondavel*!"

"I'm not going to sleep with them," said Rowena calmly. "I told one of the native boys to move my bed out alongside yours."

"But Francis—" began Domini anxiously.

"Francis is an old woman – and anyway, my life is my own."

"Not to risk, my dear," said Domini.

"Who says it would be risking it? Anyway, I am definitely not going to sleep with two others in any *rondavel* tonight, and that's that," said Rowena blithely, and Domini did not feel she had the right to go on arguing about it, though she hoped that Francis would be able to prevent it.

Presently the two of them, their dressing-gowns over the very feminine underthings which would give them very little warmth, strolled back from the bath-house to the *rondavel*.

Rowena exclaimed with satisfaction, for her bed had been moved out beside Domini's.

"I'm rather worried about your doing this," said Domini with an anxious frown. "It isn't just the cold. I know that won't hurt you. It's this heavy mist that seems to come up with the morning. I know, because I sleep out so much and in all seasons."

Rowena laughed and patted her arm affectionately. "You ought to be somebody's mother, Domini," she said. "What a honey you are! Oh, damn! I forgot to clean my teeth. I shall have to go back across the waste desert spaces."

"Shall I come with you?" asked Domini.

"No; but lend me your torch, will you? It may save me from falling over the guy-ropes quite so often."

When she had gone, Domini stood still for a moment, wondering whether there was anything she could dispense with so that Rowena could be warmer. Then, as she had done on the previous night, she realised that Mark Teckler was close to her.

There were little clouds scudding over the moon tonight, and the light was fitful, but she felt that she had needed none of her material senses to know that he was there.

"Is it you?" she asked, though she knew the answer.

"You wouldn't come to me, so I had to come and fetch you," he said. "Come away from all this rabble," for the camp was still alive and lively, people talking, laughing, preparing food, even the radio in some car pouring out dance music, to which some young couples were dancing between the *rondavels*.

She felt his hand on her arm, drawing her away, and she made no attempt to escape, but went with him almost against her will.

"I'm in my dressing-gown," she protested as she went.

"Who's going to mind about that?" he asked, and he thrust his hand now under her arm and held it strongly against him as he led her away from the lights, from the sounds and the sight of other people, through the maze of lanes of short, sunburnt grass between the *rondavels* and out to the boundary of the camp.

Then he stopped and turned her to face him. Her hair was still damp from her bath and waved loosely about her face, with a curved tendril lying on her cheek. She looked very young, almost as if her sweet girlhood lay still untouched about her.

He put out his other hand and very gently took the soft brown tendril of hair from her cheek and let it curl about his linger. For a moment they stood there, motionless, and then he let his hands fall from her and turned away a little. She thought she heard him catch his breath in a sigh. She felt oddly shaken, disturbed as if something had fallen into a still pool and sent its ripples ever wider and wider until the whole surface was moved.

When he, spoke, it was with disconcerting abruptness.

"Do you dislike me very much?" he asked.

"I? Dislike you?" she echoed, astonished. "But—why—no. What makes you think I do?"

"Of course you do. I'm everything you aren't and never could be. If I had any sense at all, I should keep away from you, but I can't. For the first time in my life, I'm saying those words about something I want to do. I want to keep away from you, but I can't."

She had never before felt so tongue-tied, unable to form even a coherent thought. In the shifting light, she caught a glimpse of his face, its ragged strength softened and unfamiliar, his eyes searching for hers in the darkness, and she put out her hand and it touched his.

"Mark," she said.

His fingers held hers strongly, hurting her by their grip.

"Domini, tell me one tiling. This husband of yours. Do you love him?"

"Don't ask me that. Please, Mark, don't ask me that," she whispered, shaken.

"That means that you don't, so you need not tell me," he said.

There was quiet triumph in his voice and she shivered a little. His sureness of himself and of her was inexorable. Of what use to try to evade him? Or ever to resist him?

"But I do," she said vehemently. "I do love him. That was not why I said you must not ask me. It was—that I am so confused, so uncertain of values."

"Be honest with both of us," he said. "You don't love him. How could you? Something splendid and free like you, and that poor tool of a man who lets you work for his living."

"I've told you. He's not strong," she insisted, but he gave a short laugh.

"Rubbish. If a man can walk to his gate, he can work for his woman. He's not crippled, is he? Or blind? Or bedridden with some illness? Sitha here, lass. I'm noan a one to tek another's wife, but he doesna tek yo' hisself," and before she could have any idea what he meant to do, he had caught her into his arms and strained her against him. "My lass," he whispered thickly, "my lass, I'm droonk wi' the beauty of yo' and the longin' for yo'."

In the darkness he found her lips. His were firm and hard against them, and though for the first startled second she struggled instinctively, in the next second she had surrendered to his arms and lay against him, aware in every fibre of her being of his strength, the domination of his possessive character which demanded from her the response of her own long-dormant desires. Vaguely she heard his voice whispering to her, his speech so broadly dialectal that she could not have understood the words even had she wanted to do so. The tones of that soft murmuring were enough for her, their tenderness, their adoration. Her arms held him, her mouth possessed his with parted lips, her eyes were closed to shut into the close warmth of their embrace all rapture and all delight.

He kissed her closed lids, and now that he had freed her mouth, she could hear something of what his own lips said.

"I have had that. I have had that of you, Domini," and he was consciously slipping from his own native accents and words to those of the world he had forced to adopt him, her world, though his voice would remain rough, uncultured, harsh in its ugliness. "I have had this of you, Domini—and this—and this," kissing her eyelids, her hair, her throat, "but I want more. I want all of you, all the woman of you, in my arms without all this junk between us."

His hands pulled roughly at the opening of Keith's old gown, and he stood looking boastfully, exultingly, from her half-shamed eyes to the uncovered whiteness of her throat and the cleft between her soft breasts.

He bent his head to kiss them, but suddenly she found herself again and pushed his head away and dragged the gown back across her throat.

"No! No!" she said, gasping. "Let me go. Please let me go, Mark. I can't let you kiss me."

He laughed. The sound added to this strange, sudden terror of him. He knew that she had surrendered herself. In his mind was the certainty that when he called to her again, she would come, she must come. He had claimed her and set his seal upon her.

"Please let me go, Mark," she said again, in a low, shaken voice, and without another word, without trying to hold her, he let her go.

She fled from him, wildly, tripping over tent-ropes and all sorts of domestic utensils as she went, not choosing her way and getting so completely lost that it took her a long time to find her way back to the *rondavel*, which was now in darkness, the two camp beds just discernible in the shadow of the wall.

They were both flat and unoccupied, and she paused a moment, frowning because Rowena had not yet come to bed. Where was she and what was she doing? It was still early by ordinary standards of time, but here in the rest camp, it was night and the time for sleeping. They would be up again very early the next morning.

Then she shook herself. After all, Rowena Craye was not her responsibility, but Francis's, and as she sat down on the edge of her bed to take off her shoes, she realised that she was desperately tired – tired not with the business of the day, which had been no more than being driven about in the Reserve, but exhausted by the emotional upset that had followed it.

She lay down in the bed and pulled the covers up to her chin and closed her eyes, though she felt that sleep was far from her. Her whole body still tingled and glowed with the wild uprush of her response to Mark Teckler's rough love-making, his arms crushing her against him, his hands tugging at the neck of her gown, his lips pressing hers open and forcing his tongue between them.

She put up her hands to her hot cheeks and felt miserable and ashamed and yet knew that deep down in her was the memory of all delight, that she had responded to his demands on her, had known a need of him just as she had felt his need of her.

She thought, too, of Keith and his Flora Pearce whom she had so self-righteously despised. How much different was she from Flora Pearce, except in the actual fulfilment of the act which, hot-cheeked now, she knew her mind had conceived in his embrace.

She turned on her side, away from the moonlight which now glimmered clearly and calmly over Rowena's empty bed. She told herself that she must compose herself and get some sleep, and with her eyes closed, she tried out all the well-known and seldom-effective remedies for sleeplessness.

She was beginning to feel drowsy when at last she heard careful movements and then the creaking of the other bed. She turned sleepily without opening her eyes and stretched out her hand across the narrow space between the two beds.

"Rowena?" she said sleepily. "About time you came."

A hand came at once to meet hers, and immediately she was galvanised into full, startled consciousness. It was not Rowena's small, soft hand. It was the large, blunt-fingered, hand of a man – Mark Teckler's hand.

She jerked her own hand away and sat upright, pushing the hair out of her eyes and staring at him, angry, incredulous and yet forced to believe.

"What are you doing here?" she asked in a furious whisper.

"I'm going to sleep here," he said calmly.

"But you can't—you can't stay here—and what about Rowena? Where's Rowena?" she asked almost incoherently.

"She's where she ought to be. She's in the *rondavel* with her husband, and if he's got any sense, she's in his arms at this moment," said Mark calmly.

"Is that true? Is she really with him?" demanded Domini, realising that if that were so, she was trapped beyond possibility of escape. She could hardly pick up her bed and take it somewhere else, and even if she could, there was nothing to prevent his following her, quite apart from the commotion any such undertaking would cause in the quiet of the sleeping camp.

He had been lying down. Now he propped himself on one elbow. He was clad in loudly-striped pyjamas, good, homely pyjamas of some sort of flannel. The sight of them should have comforted her, for surely no intending philanderer would appear before his anticipated partner in those? But they did not comfort her. Instead they seemed to add to the strength of the bond he was forging between them. In those pyjamas, he might have been married to her for years!

She could see his face in the moonlight, grave, calm, with no particular expression on it. His hair was tousled and stood up in points absurdly. Even more absurdly, she felt a stab of something very much like tenderness at the sight. For the first time she had a vision of him as a small boy.

"Listen, lass," he said quietly. "I shall never say anything to you that's not true. Don't you know that?"

She sat looking at him and could not know that with her ruffled hair and her wide eyes he was seeing her, too, as a child.

Slowly she nodded her head.

"Yes. Yes, I do know," she said, "but—you shouldn't have come here."

"Where else was there for me to go? You know for yourself there aren't any more beds. If you feel so nervous of me, though, I'll drag this off somewhere where you won't be able to see me or hear me – though I don't think I snore."

She had to laugh, though it was a quavery sound. It *was* absurd to think of him dragging his bed away, for he would still be in the camp, still able to get to her if that was what he meant to do.

Then she met his eyes again and a deep peace and sense of safety flooded through her. He would do her no harm. She was in his protection. She could sleep there beside him and know herself secure.

She smiled at him, gravely, with the trusting smile of the child she seemed.

"Well?" be asked. "Satisfied?"

"Yes," she said, and slipped down beneath the blankets again and lay there staring up into the night sky, velvety purple, the stars shining with a brilliance she had surely never seen before, even though the African nights were no new thing to her.

His hand came to seek hers again and she gave it to him.

"Don't ever be afraid of me, lass," he said in that quiet, tender voice which, for all its rough edges and uncultured accents, might have soothed and comforted an unhappy child. "I'll never do you any harm, never force you to give me anything you don't want to give, though I want you and I'm not going to say I don't. I love you, Domini, and I've never loved a woman before and I think you love me too."

She was silent, their linked hands a bridge by which they seemed to pass into each other, neither wanting to return.

Did she love him? Was this compelling force within her love? Could she dislike so much about him, despise him, fear him, even hate him at times – and yet love him? Or was it only the thing that had drawn her, ignorant and innocent, to Keith all those years ago? Drawn her to him and inevitably failed to hold her there?

She felt a surge of fear run through her and tried to draw her hand away, but he held it.

"Don't, my darling," he said. "Let me at least lie with your hand in mine. Are you afraid of me, Domini?"

"No."

"What of, then? Yourself?"

"Yes—I think so."

"Because of loving me?"

"Yes."

"You don't want to?"

"No. No!"

"But you love me already, so why be afraid? You can be afraid that something *may* happen, but you can't be afraid of it when it has happened. You do love me, Domini. I felt it and knew it when I had you in my arms just now."

"No, Mark!"

There was sharp distress in her denial, though they kept their voice to quiet whispers in the still night.

"Why don't you want to admit it?" he asked.

"Because of—Keith. My husband."

He gave a short sound of derision and gathered her hand more closely into his, engulfing it in his strong fingers as if they held her very being.

"He's nothing to me. He's nothing' to you any more. Some day you will be as sure of that as I am, and some day very soon, very soon, my love, my love," though his voice dropped instinctively and inevitably into the old, softer accents and he called her 'ma loov, ma loov', and she felt strangely soothed and as if she drifted, in utter safety, on the bosom of a wide, calm sea.

Tears pricked her eyes and she closed her lids over them.

"You are tired, my love, and worn out," he said gently. "Go to sleep. You are safe with me."

She nodded and turned her head away so that he should not see the tears that forced their way beneath her eyelids.

He kept her hand in his until her quiet breathing told him that she was asleep at last. Then, very gently, he released her and drew the covers over her without waking her.

Chapter Thirteen

Domini Ellman and Mark Teckler were not the only two members of David Parley's *safari* to be wandering about in the camp in the darkness.

David was disinclined for bed and, in any case, he was to share a tent with another driver with whom he had very little in common, and if he could manage not to return to their sleeping quarters before the poker game was over and the players disbanded, so much the better. It was not that he had anything against a gamble, and he was an excellent poker player when he chose, but just now he did not choose. He was more and more determined that somehow he would get together enough money to start some sort of business on his own, either getting a car to take his own private parties about the country, or by going in for the trucking business, which just now was booming.

He stood with his arms folded ever the bonnet of the car and looked out into the mysterious night with no appreciation just then of its mystery. He was back in Johannesburg in spirit, wresting a living from the City of Gold.

A sudden movement and a little cry startled him, and he went instinctively to the aid of the shadowy, small figure stumbling over some obstruction, the torch slipping from the hand that had instinctively grabbed at the back of the car for support.

"Are you hurt?" he asked, and then realised that it was Yvonne Dubois, in a short, gaily flowered kimono over pyjamas.

She scrambled to her feet, laughing softly. He thought it about the most seductive sound he had ever heard.

"I went to clean me the teeth," she said, "and I go back to the *rondavel*, where Miss Koetse will think I have been eaten by wild creatures."

"May I escort you back to the *rondavel* and Miss Koetse? Because it's quite in the other direction."

She lifted surprised eyebrows.

"Is it? But I thought I came in this path."

"If you had, I should have seen you or—sensed you," he said, turning and beginning to walk with her in the other direction.

They laughed again, softly and like conspirators, for the camp was quiet except for occasional bursts of laughter from the tents with their hanging oil lamps. The *rondavels* were some distance away and their occupants more discreetly protected by solid walls.

She realised that they had been walking for some minutes and that the collection of *rondavels* seemed to be further away instead of nearer.

"You are well sure that this is the way?" she asked him.

"No; it isn't. It's the other way, over there. Do you mind? It's such a lovely night, and my tent is occupied by a crowd of men playing poker."

"What is that game?"

"Oh, just a gamble. Good fun if you feel like it, but I'm not in the mood — and I can't afford to lose."

"You lose much at this game pokaire?"

"Might do. It's all right for them. They're content to stay in their jobs and let the future look after itself, but I'm not," and somehow he found himself telling her about his job, about his dissatisfaction with a life of working for someone else, about his very faint hope of getting a car or a truck of his own.

"I'd rather do the trucking, though it's harder work. There is such a shortage of transport. Everybody, businesses, Post Office, railways, are crying out for someone to take their stuff, and if only I could get enough to put down as a deposit on a truck, I could make twenty or thirty pounds a week, perhaps more."

"Poor David," she said softly. "How much money will you need to have for this truck?"

"No good buying a cheap one. Have to be really reliable. Not less than three hundred pounds to put down on it and the rest on hire purchase," he said gloomily.

Three hundred pounds, she thought, and roughly converted into French francs. Such a little sum, really, when one thought of all the money in the world – of what Jean Lafitte had, for instance. She had begged before leaving France for this holiday that she should not be openly affianced to Jean, not until she came back, but he had insisted on taking her to a jeweller's shop, asking to see engagement rings, picked out for her approval one that would cost more, much more, than the equivalent of David's three hundred pounds.

"Something smaller and not so expensive," she had pleaded to Jean, and he had laughed and smiled his wide, fat smile at her and nodded his head until his big, flowing moustache had waggled and told her approvingly that she would make a wife who was both charming and thrifty but that yes, that was the ring he would buy for her when she consented to be affianced, to him.

And she would have to wear on her finger something whose value could have given this nice David his heart's desire and all the future of his life! Things could be very unfair.

"You're very quiet," he said. "What are you thinking about?"

She told him, quite simply and frankly.

"And you mean you're actually going to marry this fat old man?" he asked disgustedly.

"He is not really old. Fifty, I think," she said.

"Well, isn't that old? Good heavens, Yvonne—"

He stopped, embarrassed, and she lifted her charming face to him again.

"Yes?" she asked.

"I'm sorry. I apologise," he mumbled, flushing.

"Why? Because you call me Yvonne? But that is my name and they all call me that."

"Yes, but they're different. They're passengers. I'm the paid driver," he said with a touch of bitterness.

He had taken his hand from her arm. Now she deliberately put it back there.

"Don't be foolish," she said. "What is it, one and another? We are the same."

"Only you're going back to France to marry a rich old man, and become a grand lady and I'm going to stop here and drive people about and hope for tips," the bitterness now keen.

She pressed his arm against her.

"Poor David," she said softly. "Do not then let us think of those things, but only of this what we have now. Look up at the stars. Are they not beautiful?"

But he looked at her face,

"You. You're beautiful," he said.

She lowered her eyes to his face, flushing, adorable.

"Am I? To you, David?" she asked.

They stood looking at each other, young, impressionable, ready for loving and being loved, and for those few moments all the barriers which life can erect had no meaning for them.

"What if I fell in love with you, Yvonne?" he asked. "I could, you know."

For an enchanted moment, life stood still for them. Then, with a little quivering sigh, she let her eyes fall from his and moved so that she no longer held his hand beneath her arm.

"Don't. Please don't," she said shakily.

"Don't what? Don't fall in love with you? Or don't tell you that I have done so already?"

She shook her head and kept her eyes turned from his.

"You must not. Me, I have my life made."

"With the fat Jean?"

"It is not that I should have told you he is fat," she said. "He is very good, very kind."

"And very rich," added David bitterly.

"I do not love him," she said with simple sadness.

"Then why are you going to marry him? It's a sin."

"In France it is the way we make marriages," she said in that simple way which he had decided was part of her charm.

"But do you mean that because you've been told by your parents to marry him, you'll do it, just like that?" he asked.

"But yes. He will make me a very good husband and I shall be a good wife," nodding her head sagely.

"But it's archaic. It's criminal."

She sighed.

"It is what we do and it makes good marriages and much that is happy," she said.

"But don't you want to be in love?"

She hesitated. Perhaps by her very race, she felt wiser than he, older, better able to accept the inevitable.

"It is better not, for the woman," she said at last. Suddenly he put his hands on her shoulders and turned her to him. He was on fire for her, for the feel of her young, light body in his arms, for her innocent mouth, for all the untouched and unaware loveliness of her. And she was going to be sold to some fat old Frenchman! He was going to buy all that with his filthy riches! And Yvonne would submit and never know what she had lost.

"It's not better," he said. "How could it be? Why should you be cheated out of the best thing in life?"

She stood quite still, afraid and yet thrilling to his touch, knowing that there was only one wise thing to do, since her destiny had to be fulfilled, and that was gently, oh quite gently, to draw herself away from him and slip back through the darkness to the *rondavel* and to the safe keeping of old Miss Koetse.

"David," she breathed, her lips parted a little, her eyes starry, her breast heaving softly with the quick beating of her heart.

"My little sweet," he said shakily. "I *am* in love with you. May I kiss you, Yvonne?"

She closed her eyes and swayed towards him.

"Once. Just once," she said, and he took her wholly into his arms and kissed her, but gently, tenderly, controlling the passion rising within him.

She drew herself from his arms at last.

"I must go," she said unsteadily. "Please, David, take me back," and he turned without a word and with the mere touch of his hand beneath her elbow and led her back to where the light still shone in the *rondavel*.

Outside it, the two empty beds still awaited their occupants.

"Good night, my small love," said David very softly.

"Good night," she whispered, gave him a fugitive smile and opened the door of the little round bungalow, whilst David slipped away into the darkness.

Miss Henrietta Koetse, a marvellous figure done up for the night, sat up in bed and looked at the girl accusingly. She wore a prim nightdress, long-sleeved and high at the neck, made of thick white silk without one shred of lace or one stitch of embroidery, whilst on her head she were a tight-fitting cap of white net like a bathing cap, enclosing every strand of her grey hair.

"Are you not cold, child?" she asked, and Yvonne felt a sudden little warmth at her heart because the words were not the expected question and reproof.

"No. It's not cold," she said, and because there had been no reproof in the old woman's voice, she said suddenly, "I've been talking to David."

"The young driver? Like that?" asked Miss Koetse, and now the disapproval was there.

"I didn't think about how I was dressed," said Yvonne quite truthfully. "We just—talked," and to cover her momentary confusion, she surprised herself by telling Miss Koetse about David, about his longing to be able to buy a car or a truck.

"Just imagine, then! All he needs to have is three hundred pounds, but he says he might want the moon with as great sense, the poor David."

She threw off the kimono, stretched her small, lithe figure for a moment, and then climbed into bed, hopping out again as she remembered the lantern, which hung from a nail on the central post which supported the thatched roof.

With the ease and resilience of youth, she was soon asleep, even though at first she had thought she must lie awake all night with the remembrance of David's kiss on her lips, the first kiss she had ever received from a man.

Henrietta Koetse did not find it so easy to sleep. Three hundred pounds.

And for David Parley, they were as unattainable as the moon, though to her, Miss Henrietta Koetse, they meant little or nothing. She could draw a cheque for three hundred pounds from her current account and feel its loss no more than the Standard Bank of South Africa in Commissioner Street would feel its withdrawal.

But, of course, one did not go about giving cheques for three hundred pounds to strange young men who happened to drive one's car. Of course not.

She slept at last and had no uncomfortable dreams.

Meantime in the other *rondavel*, which Mark Teckler should be sharing with Francis Craye, husband and wife faced each other sitting on the edges of the two beds, the lantern swinging gently when the light breeze blew in at the open window.

Francis was his usual calm self, his face expressive of no emotion, of no thought other than a faint, half-amused curiosity; Rowena looked sulky and sat swinging one of her legs, trying not to obey the overwhelming impulse to look at him. She had come into the *rondavel* to find a pair of stockings which must still be in the case, and as she had been about to go, having found the stockings, she had heard her husband's cool, casual voice behind her. Until she was about to leave, he had apparently taken no notice of her.

"Just a minute, Rowena," he said and instinctively she paused and turned, and then, realising it, moved towards the open door again.

Francis stretched out a long arm and shut it and shot the bolt into its slot.

"What for?" she asked.

"I'd like to talk to you. That's all. Do you mind?"

She shrugged her shoulders and stood waiting.

"Does it make any difference whether I do or not?" she asked with the touch of insolence in her manner which she knew had more power than anything else she could do to infuriate him.

"In this case, yes," he said. "I'd rather like you to *want* to hear what I have to say, and perhaps throw me a few odd words yourself."

"All right," she said indifferently.

"At least sit down," he suggested, and she dropped down on the other bed and sat there, one leg swinging, one hand tracing the pattern of the Indian blanket, her eyes avoiding his.

"What do you really think of me, Rowena?" he asked, the question so unexpected that for an unaware second she glanced at him and then away again.

"I don't," she said.

"Never? Because that rather cuts away the ground over which I had hoped we might tread, oh very carefully and slowly, to reach some no-man's-land where we could perhaps meet and talk. You see I am not any more pleased with the position between us than you are. The only thing is that we want to do different things about it. You want to cut loose."

"Well, don't you?" she snapped at him.

"No. At least, not yet. You see, there is a fundamental difference between us and always has been. My original desire for you was entirely carnal. Now yours, on the other hand, was primarily to secure the sort of husband you and your mother thought a good catch."

"Oh!" broke in Rowena indignantly, furiously.

"Yes, my dear, that is the plain truth, and you know it, so why not be as honest as I am being and admit it? I wanted to take off your clothes and make love, so-called, to your body, but you wanted a suitable husband – that is to say, one who had enough money to keep you in comfort, not to say luxury, and who could also be presented to your friends as the prize you had secured. Very well. We struck our bargain. You gave me the right to do what I liked, within reason, with your lovely white body, and I set that said lovely white body in a suitable environment of good clothes, comfortable home, expensive friends and the rest. Well, I'm going to do something I am sure you never expected me to do. I'm going to admit that I drove a bad bargain. So, my sweet, did you. We both got what we thought we wanted, only they turned out to be not at all what we really wanted. You wanted to flit between hotels in London, Paris and New York, whilst my idea of comfort was a home in the country, and I admit that I over-persuaded you to come with me to Rhodesia. So you didn't get what you thought you were going to get. I was luckier in a way.

You gave me your body to play with, and you gave it so delightfully and so entirely without reserve or scruple that I, poor fool, was actually deluded by the belief that you—well, shall we say, cared for me?"

She made a movement, a little sound, and he put up a protesting hand.

"Don't, my dear. Let me have my say, even if it's unconscionably long and tedious. As I say, I deluded myself and that was the beginning of the real trouble between us, because I found I could not be content with what you had bargained for. It was really that that made me play on you the sorry trick of carting you out to Rhodesia. I gave you all the things you had bargained for, so far as a very new country can supply them, but I will own now that one of my chief reasons for bringing you out here was because I thought – hoped – that if I separated you from friends and conditions which I thought were bad for you, you would let me count for more in your life. You see what a complete idiot I made of myself? Are you smiling, Rowena, my sweet?"

"No," she said, the sound barely reaching him.

"Well, you can. It's a laughable matter."

"You're not trying to make me believe that you are – or were – in love with me?" she asked, and it was because she wanted to keep her voice steady that she made it very hard and curt.

"Were, perhaps. Not now. Not any more. I've seen the error of my ways and realised that unless a man intends to remain a complete idiot and debase himself beneath even his own estimation of himself, he had better stop fooling round in his mind with a wife who not only dislikes and despises him and likes to sleep by herself, but who also has an occasional flutter with other men."

He heard her sharply caught breath, but did not give her time to frame any words.

"You see, my dear," he went on smoothly, "I knew about your affair with Gil Clarkley, knew about it positively. I saw you come out of that shady hotel in a street off the Strand with him, each with a suitcase and a furtive look, that Monday morning when you had gone off, almost in tears, to the bedside of a sick cousin of whom until that moment I had never heard. I stood and watched you. I admit it. I just stood there. I'd just come up from the Underground station. Do you remember that the car was in dock that week-end? I stood there and watched you, saw him get you a taxi and put you into it, heard him say quite loudly to you, 'You've been so wonderful to me!' and I could quite well believe that you had. I know all your little tricks, my sweet, and how beguiling they can be to a mere man. It was when I actually saw you with Clarkley and heard what he said and knew the reputation of the place to which he'd taken you (he might have done you better than that, darling!) that I knew I had not been mistaken the other times, the times of which I had no proof and had been glad that I hadn't proof."

He broke off, and they sat there in silence. She had nothing to say. How could she begin to explain? How could she hope ever to make him see what had prompted her to do the things she hated now to remember? How could he understand what she had been looking for in these other men? That they all had in common the one thing Francis never gave her or tried to give her, for all his lavish gifts? Tenderness. Admiration without which few people and certainly no woman can be happy. Gentle ways and a belief in her. He was telling her now that he had loved her, but he had never told her so. Certainly he had made ardent love to her, if the satisfaction of his physical senses could be called love. But he had never *loved* her, and it was for the shadow of that love, though even at the time she had known it to be false, that she had had these affairs, the last one with Gil Clarkley having sickened her so much that she had sworn she would never have another.

And Francis knew about it, had known about it ever since, known and never said a word – only since that time, he had not offered her any serious love-making, had taken her at rare intervals in a brutal way which had hurt her spirit even more than her body, taken her like that but had never told her why.

"Well?" he asked presently, when they had sat in silence a long time.

She looked across at him. He could read no more in her eyes than she in his. For once there were not even the tears which enraged them both.

"You knew all that, and yet you brought me out here to South Africa, and you still refuse to let me go. Why? Why didn't you divorce me then? You could have done. I played right into your hands."

"Yes. I wonder why I didn't? I think the chief reason was that my pride would not have let me admit to the world that a clot like Gil Clarkley could take you away from me. I should have been the laughing-stock of all our friends, and quite reasonably so. Also he would not have married you, my dear, even if you could have borne to be married to him."

"I knew he had a wife somewhere," she said. "I never wanted to marry him. It wasn't anything like that."

"No? Then what in hell's name was it?" he asked, and for almost the first time since she had known him, rage broke, through his careful calm and glowed in his eyes and spoke in his voice.

"I don't know," she said, but she did know and could not tell him, could not possibly have told him that she had ached for tenderness, for the almost womanly tenderness of Gil. A psychoanalyst would probably have told her that she was suffering from the lack of love her own mother might have given her had she been of a different calibre.

Then "What are you going to do about it? About us?" she asked after another pause.

"At the moment, nothing. We'll see this thing through – this trip, I mean. It hasn't worked out the way I thought it might. I thought being off the earth like this, out of the ordinary world, cut off from normal contacts, we might have—found something, I don't quite know what. Well, we haven't, have we? I told you before we left Jo'burg that I was not going to give you a divorce, but I see now that I was wrong. I *will* give it you, my dear, be the perfect gent, and take all the blame and so on, but—*but* on my own conditions."

"And those are?" asked Rowena not quite steadily, her eyes fixed on the fingers which still restlessly traced the pattern on the blanket. She felt very cold, though her hands and cheeks burned.

"Only that you find yourself a really suitable successor to me, a man who can keep you decently and of whose ousting of me I need not feel to be derisively humorous amongst our friends. In short, a man, not a bleating sheep like poor Gil Clarkley. Rowena, why in hell's name did you have to go off with *him*? Surely you could have found something better, if all you wanted was a sex orgy? I wouldn't even have thought Gil had got what's necessary, though you'd know that, of course."

She rose to her feet, her face flaming.

"I hate you when you're so coarse," she said.

"My sweet, you hate me, anyway, so why should I not be my own natural self with you? By the way, don't go. You can't, you know," as she went towards the door again.

"Who's going to stop me?" she demanded.

"As the mere tool of a stronger force, I am. You've got to sleep in here tonight. Oh, don't worry! I'm not going to touch you, if that's what you're afraid of! I feel as pure and unemotional towards you as a babe in arms, and far more pure than, a crystal-voiced chorister in the choir stalls. You can strip yourself stark naked and parade before me, but all I should think would be, 'She's still the same luscious shape, I see' and I should turn over and sleep. No, my lovely, I have no designs on you. I'm merely doing a good turn to old Teckler."

Rowena turned at that and stared at him.

"Teckler? Mark Teckler?" she echoed. "But what on earth has he to do with us? What business is it of his where I sleep?"

"Oh, he doesn't care where you sleep, sweet, nor with whom, so long as you leave untenanted the bed outside the other *rondavel* next to Domini Ellman's."

"Good Lord! So he's that sort, is he?" asked Rowena furiously. "Well, I can tell you and I could tell him that he won't get any change *there*. Domini Ellman is about the most decent and honourable woman I know."

"Well, you should be in a position to recognise them," said Francis. "However, set your heart at rest. He has no evil intentions towards her."

"Then why does he want to sleep with her?" demanded Rowena scathingly.

"Technically, he doesn't. That is to say, he merely wants the somewhat unsatisfying delight of sleeping *next* to her, which is quite a different thing from sleeping *with* her. You may not appreciate the fine distinction, but he gave me his solemn assurance (though I pointed out to him that it was his affair and hers, but not mine) that he meant no harm to her and would not in any way force himself upon her. Of course, if she edges over in the night and says, 'What about it?' I have no doubt she'll find him gratifyingly ready, but—"

"She won't," snapped Rowena. "I've told you she's decent and – and good," with a little gulp.

He made an expressive gesture with his hands.

"All right. There's nothing for anyone to worry about, then, but at least give them their chance."

He glanced at his watch.

"I should say it's a bit late now to do anything about it, anyway," he said, "and you can hardly go and rout a man out of his bed, or anybody else's bed, because you won't sleep in the same *rondavel*, in utter purity, with your own husband, can you?"

She stood uncertainly, frustrated, knowing herself beaten. Then she turned slowly, threw off her dressing-gown and got into bed, turning her face towards the wall.

Francis blew out the lamp and she heard him chuckle softly in the darkness.

Chapter Fourteen

The next day, David was to take his party into elephant country.

"We'll get up early again," he had told them, the night before, "so as to get a chance of finding some of the game we've missed so far – buffalo, perhaps, and possibly more lion. Of course, if anybody prefers to stay longer in bed, we can all meet at breakfast here, and as I suggest that we also come back for lunch here and go on towards Olifantsriver this afternoon, anybody who wants a really long lie-in can meet us at lunch!"

They had all laughed and said they would make the early start, but when Domini woke and looked at her watch to see that it was half-past five, and time to think about getting up if she were joining the before-breakfast party, she glanced at Mark in the next bed and smiled at the profundity of his sleep.

She left him sleeping and unaware of her, but she knew herself to be utterly aware of him, to be unable to cast the thought of him from her mind. What was it she felt for Mark Teckler? Though she had to hurry over a brisk wash, and scramble into her clothes in the bath-house rather than go into the *rondavel* and disturb Miss Koetse, who had said she would not join the early party, she found that her thoughts were busy over things which needed time and care, so that when she returned to the waiting car, she felt confused and restless.

They were waiting for Rowena, who had not scrupled about waking Miss Koetse and was dressing in the *rondavel*. David, with little Yvonne pattering about helping him, was carrying round cups of coffee. Domini and Francis Craye sat on the edge of the running-board drinking theirs. She had instinctively looked for Mark when she came to the car. He was there, the disreputable sun-hat perched sideways on his bullet head, his face grim, his mouth in a hard line.

She smiled at him. To her embarrassment and chagrin, the smile was unrequited, from set mouth and steely eyes. She felt as if he had struck her in the face, and, flushing a little, she turned again towards Francis and engaged him in animated and, for her, somewhat foolish conversation about nothing.

Mark came round from the back of the car with his empty cup and gave it to Yvonne with a curt "Thanks" and Francis looked up at him with raised eyebrows.

"What's bitten *you* this morning?' he asked. "Had a rough night?"

Domini's flush deepened. He knew – of course he must know – that if Rowena had been with him for the night, there was only one place in which Mark Teckler could have been – namely, in the bed intended for Rowena, and that bed had certainly been next to hers, Domini's, in the morning. It was still visible from where they sat. For the first time – though, of course, it should have occurred to her at the outset – she realised the position in which Mark had put her and she felt the more angry and incensed by his attitude this morning.

He glowered at Francis.

"I hate people who're so damned chatty first thing in the morning," he growled.

"Then how you must love yourself!" said Francis, grinning. "Ah, here's my loving spouse rushing to greet the morn," getting up to stroll in his leisurely fashion towards where Rowena was coming over the grass in slacks and jersey, a coat trailing on the ground from her hand.

Automatically Domini and Mark looked at each other. Her eyes were frosty. She saw his soften a little.

"Will you sit with me?" he asked:

"I don't think so. Francis!" calling to the retreating back. "Francis! Would it be all right if I sat in the front for the trip?"

He had turned.

"Yes; I should think so. Yes, of course, Domini. It must be your turn by now," and she smiled her thanks and walked away, leaving Mark standing discomfited.

She saw very little of the game which the others sighted and pointed out, returning to the camp for breakfast after a vague impression of giraffe, zebra, wildebeest and kudu returning from their morning drink. Her thoughts had been too deeply on Mark, and on the shock and confusion of his changed attitude. What was the matter? It was hateful to her, but inescapable, to wonder if it were the result of disappointment, if he had actually planned the arrangements of the night before in the hope and expectation of making her his mistress.

She had left the other four to arrange themselves as they liked. It resolved itself into Rowena and Mark sitting in the middle seat, with a corner each, whilst Francis tucked in his long legs beside Yvonne on the back seat. Obviously, thought Domini, listening to the arrangements without turning round, whatever had transpired between husband and wife during the night, the morning left them still at variance with each other.

When they returned for breakfast, Mark contrived to seat himself as far from her as possible, and she certainly did not make it difficult for him, but when later on they gathered round the car again, she found that she was to occupy one of the window seats in the middle, with Mark sitting between her and Yvonne. Francis sat in front with David, and, rather to the surprise of all, Miss Koetse herself had suggested that she should take a turn in the back seat, shared with Rowena.

"Shall we see elephants this morning, David?" asked Rowena.

"We might do, but we certainly shall this afternoon, when we get nearer to Letaba. The camp is on a cliff that overhangs Olifantsriver, and you can always see elephant coming down there at sundown, even if you don't see them before that."

"I want to get some really good shots of elephant, so would everybody be agreeable to my having a window seat not at the back after lunch?" asked Rowena.

They were all understood to agree, though Mark growled something unintelligible and obviously not complimentary. Domini gave him one of her coldly impersonal looks and turned her whole attention to looking out of her window. She still felt faintly sore, but had forced herself to accept the position vowing in her mind that he would not get the chance again to humiliate her.

As the morning wore on, however, and they were afforded more than casual glimpses of many kinds of game, including the troop of baboons who came right up to the car and took biscuits, sweets and fruit from their hands, it was impossible for any of them to keep up a grudge. They were all talking and laughing together, leaning over one another at impossible angles with their cameras and giving one another quite superfluous advice of which none of them took any notice.

Mark seated at a disadvantage in the middle, but refusing Yvonne's repeated invitation to change seats with her, leaned over first one side and then the other, his movie-camera resting on the window-edge, it was whilst he was taking shots of some vultures sitting in hideous conclave on the low boughs of a tree that Domini suddenly exclaimed in excitement.

"Elephant!" she cried. "Mark, quickly! This side!" and as David put the car into reverse and became extremely wary, they saw the great beast, some distance off, but making its leisurely way towards the road ahead of them, its grey back almost indistinguishable against the background until it lifted its trunk and tore at a leafy branch.

They watched in breathless excitement as the elephant came nearer.

"Change places with me, Mark," said Domini, but he refused.

"I'm all right here if I may lean across you," he said , and as he did so, one arm resting on her knees to steady the camera, he turned his head to meet her eyes. In his was the look which so completely disarmed her, pleading, almost humble, a look which in some inexplicable way hurt her as his bad temper of earlier in the day had not been able to hurt.

Almost against her will her mouth relaxed and she smiled. At once into his eyes leapt enormous relief and for a brief second his hand touched hers. Instantly there leapt through her a wild, unreasoning response, and she turned her fingers so that they locked in his before she released him.

"Domini," he said in a quick whisper. "My dear."

Then he gave all his attention to the great lumbering brute as it came crashing through the undergrowth, making straight for its objective without being diverted by anything in its way.

Rowena sat in the back bewailing her misfortune in not being able to get any satisfactory sighting for her camera.

"Give me the camera," suggested Francis, but she shook her head.

"You're such a fool with a camera," she said, but there was no ill-nature in her tone. "You'd get me a lovely view of the surrounding country, but not even a smell of elephant. Now if I could change places with you."

"Please don't think of it for a moment, Mrs. Craye," said David in quick alarm. "It would be most unwise to get out of the car."

"But look what a long way off it is!" she objected. "I can nip out and in again in no time."

"You stay where you are, my adorable idiot," said Francis. "It wouldn't be only you, but all the rest of us if you want to get out of the back seat."

"Oh, all right, but I'll get a jumbo before we leave the Reserve or die in the attempt," said Rowena.

"So long as we don't all die in the attempt," remarked Francis. "Look out, everybody. Any minute now," and a moment later there was a crashing and rending in the bushes and out he came, tremendous, taking no notice of the car, forging across the road, awe-inspiring in his freedom and in the knowledge that he could crush the car and its occupants as easily as a man could tread on a beetle.

After lunch at Satara, they strolled about the camp whilst David filled up with petrol, and Domini found herself with Mark.

"Will you sit with me at the back this afternoon?" he asked her in a low voice.

"What about your photographs?"

"It's more important to make my peace with you, Domini."

She walked beside him in silence, wondering a little uncomfortably whether they were being conspicuous to others as well as to Rowena, whose mischievous eyes missed nothing and who was enjoying the situation, though she thoroughly disliked Mark Teckler and thought it was sheer impudence on his part to aspire to Domini.

"Will you?" he asked again.

"Will I what? Sit with you, or make my peace with you? I thought we did that this morning," she said, not looking at him.

"When you let me touch your hand? Did that mean that it was all right between us? That I am forgiven for my bad temper?"

"You really were impossible, you know."

"Yes, I do know. I'm a bad-tempered brute, Domini, and if you cut me off, it will be no more than I deserve, but that's the way I'm made. I always have been like that first thing in the morning and always shall be."

"You sound as if you are very well satisfied to be so," said Domini, turning her head to see his face for a moment.

He was not smiling. He looked grim, chin up, eyes like polished steel, not a man to be soft about, she thought, and inwardly smiled a little rueful smile, for she knew how easy it was for her to be soft about him, even when she had good cause to be angry with him.

"I'm not saying that I'm satisfied, but that if a man's made that way, he can't help it, and that's that."

"And that other people have just got to accept him – or not?"

"Yes. I'm not likely to change, Domini."

"I might think that a pity."

"Why? Do you want me to charge? Do you want me to be different? Because there are other ways in which I'm not likely to change. About you, for instance."

"About me?" she echoed, knowing that they were about to step on very thin ice, but unable to draw back to avoid it.

"Yes. You know I love you, don't you?"

She drew a swift breath.

"No, Mark! No, you mustn't," she said.

"No good to say that, lass. It's happened – and I don't change about that any more than anything else. I didn't think ever to say that to a woman and mean it, but I'm saying it now. I love you, my darling."

The endearment came out with difficulty. She guessed that it was the first time in his life he had said those two words. It made them the more potent, and she stopped and looked at him, helpless and without word. What did one say to a man like this? How was she to meet it?

As it happened, she was saved from the need to find words, for they heard a call coming to them from a little distance away. It was Rowena.

"Domini! Mark! Where are you, you two? We're loading up."

"Coming!" called Domini, and set off in the direction of the car, thankful for the reprieve, but knowing that she had only delayed the inevitable.

There was a little friendly altercation over the seating arrangements, Rowena insisting on a window seat and Francis haggling with her until she cut short the argument by calmly seating herself next to the driving seat.

"You can sort yourselves out now," she said.

Yvonne caught David's eye. She had wanted to sit there just as much as he had wanted it, but he could not say so. As he opened the door that gave access to the middle and back seats, however, he managed to whisper to her.

"Tonight? After dinner?"

She nodded, all her world radiant again.

It proved a disappointing afternoon, for though they were very obviously in elephant country, which meant that there were few other animals at large, they saw nothing but the traces of the passage of large numbers of the creatures, the bush-veld torn up and devastated, the enormous footprints wherever the soil was damp enough to take their imprint.

They turned at last towards Letaba, the last of the rest camps. Tomorrow night they would be out of the Reserve and back in civilisation. Life would meet them again, and it seemed to the Graves that it would be more or less where it had left off.

Rowena sat staring in front of her for the last few minutes before the car turned in at the gates of Letaba Rest camp. She had not planned this excursion in to the Reserve and she had not wanted it, but she knew now that deep within her there had been the faint hope that something would come out of it, some change, anything that would vary the dull, hopeless mess in which she and Francis seemed to have become involved.

Well, she thought bitterly, perhaps the change would show itself when they got back home, if indeed they were both going there. Her mind was filled again with the memory of the things he had said the night before, of the way in which he had told her that he had known all along about Gil Clarkley and the others. She was filled with a deep, biting sense of regret for all that. How had she been so insane, as to get herself into such things? Looking back at them, she realised how small and worthless had been her gain, and in that doubtful gain she had lost Francis for ever.

One of the startling things to her was the discovery that the loss mattered so much to her, that Francis himself still mattered, that she would give everything she was and had (so pitifully small these assets!) if she could go back to the time when all that foolishness had started – for she could not even now think of them as more than foolishness. They had meant so little to her, these men, those casual week-ends, but the price she had paid for them was the man she still loved and wanted. Well, it seemed that after all this trip out of civilisation had done something for her. It had shown her where they both stood, she and Francis – and they stood as the poles apart.

David went to the office to check up on the accommodation and came back to them with the papers in his hands.

"Well, we've got a mixture of things here," he said in his cheerful fashion. "Some *rondavels*, some tents."

"No tent for me," put in Mark Teckler quickly.

"No. I've managed a *rondavel* for you to yourself," said David. "There's a double *rondavel*, another single one, and a tent for two, so will you sort yourselves into those?"

Though he managed to speak cheerfully, be was not very sanguine about the happy disposal of his party, for none of them would like the tents and yet somebody – two, in fact – would have to accept them.

Francis Craye was the first, as usual, to help him to smooth out the difficulties.

"I don't mind the tent," he said, "so if it's for two, Rowena and I will take it and leave the *rondavels* for the others."

"I have no intention of sleeping in a tent," said Rowena calmly. "I'll share the double *rondavel* with Domini."

"Leaving either Yvonne or Miss Koetse to share the tent with me?" asked Francis with a grin. "How about it, ladies?" and his cheerful *bonhomie* was so infectious that for once even Miss Koetse's stern face relaxed into a stiff smile.

Rowena looked annoyed.

"Don't be so idiotic," she said. "I suppose I shall *have* to sleep in the tent with you, Francis. Please take the case."

"Don't worry, my sweet," he said to her, turning to pick up the case and speaking so that no one else could hear.

"You're just as safe as Miss Koetse would have been, and a lot more safe than Yvonne would have been."

She gave him a scornful look.

"Of course I'm safe," sire said. "Do you think I don't know how to take care of myself?" and she stalked in front of him towards the rows of tents.

Domini spoke to Miss Koetse.

"It seems that we three women have a double and a single *rondavel* amongst us," she said. "I expect you would like to have one to yourself, wouldn't you? I will share with Yvonne."

But to her surprise, Miss Koetse shook her head and gave the French girl a singularly sweet smile.

"Unless Yvonne finds me too trying, I would prefer to have her with me," she said. "She has been very kind to an old woman so far."

Yvonne returned the smile.

"Of course I'll stay with you, Miss Koetse," she said. "I like to be with you."

"So I am going to be in state on my own," said Domini with a smile. "What is my number, David?"

He gave it to her, but when she stooped to pick up her small case, she found that Mark had it in his hand.

"The single *rondavels* are over here," he said, and they went together, whilst the others were escorted by David.

Mark opened the door for her with the key David had given her and she stepped inside.

"But this is a double one!" she said in surprise.

"Yes. So is mine next door. They all are," said Mark calmly.

"But—then there was no need for anyone to sleep in the tent. Rowena could have come in here with me and Francis with you."

"Don't you think they're better together?" he asked.

"I'd like to think so, but did you see the way she looked at him when she was practically forced into the position of sharing the tent with him?"

"Well, that's up to them. Anyway, I've had enough of sharing a room with a man – and of sleeping in the open."

"Weren't you comfortable sleeping in the open last night?" she asked. "You were very reluctant to get up, anyway."

They were inside her *rondavel* and he had lit the lamp and hung it from its peg on the central pole. He turned up the wick carefully and did not look at her as he spoke.

"You know quite well that I was not comfortable, Domini," he said.

"Well, I was," she said cheerfully.

He finished with the lamp and put an arm round her shoulders and drew her down to sit beside him on one of the two beds, stretching out a foot meanwhile to make the door close.

"Don't let's waste time pretending to misunderstand each other," he said. "I was uncomfortable not because I was in the open but because I was near you and not near enough. I've told you that I love you, Domini, and that I shall never change," and he pulled her wholly into his arms and held her there until her resistance broke and she lay against him, her heart beating madly.

He kissed her, his mouth as hard and ruthless as the man himself, until she cried out in protest as well as she could against his lips.

He released her, but held her only a few inches from him.

"What's the matter?" he asked.

"You hurt me," she said, and he saw a tiny point of blood against her rubbed lipstick.

"I wouldn't hurt you for the world, my darling," he said, and kissed her again, tenderly and with an exquisite gentleness that drew her heart from her body. "Do you love me, Domini? You must. What I feel for you must have its answer in you. Tell me. Tell me just that. Do you?"

He read the answer in her eyes and bent his head with its thick, grey hair and laid it against her breast in an attitude of utter humility which brought sudden tears to her eyes. That he of all men should feel humble at a woman's love!

She set her hands about his face and lifted it and of her own will gave him her lips and let him see the tears that made her eyes more starry.

"Tell me, Domini," he said again.

"I love you, Mark."

He smiled.

"You say it as if you are sorry, and your eyes are wet. Are you sorry, love?"

She shook her head.

"Not really. Not—with all of me."

"But with part of you. What part?"

She looked away from him.

"The part that—belongs to Keith," she said slowly.

"No part of you belongs to him any more."

"He is my husband, Mark."

"Only in name, and only until I take you from him. Can I, Domini? Shall I?"

"Oh Mark, I don't know. I don't know! I'm all confused. I came on this trip to give myself a chance to sort things out and decide what I want to do and must do, and now I'm in a worse state of chaos than ever."

"Through me?"

"Yes."

"Look here, love. In a few minutes they'll be routing us out to have dinner. Will you come back here afterwards so that we can talk?"

She had to smile a little at that.

"Talk?" she asked.

"Aye—and make love. I want you. I want you more than I've ever wanted anything in my life. Let me kiss you again. You're like fire to me."

"And what do you think you are to me?" she asked quiveringly against his lips.

His arms tightened about her.

"I've got to have you, Domini. You belong to me and I to you. I'll never let you go, never in this world."

He left her to go to his own *rondavel* and she sat there, motionless, afraid and yet wildly exhilarated and exultant. This, she knew, was love, this rushing, tearing torrent that filled her body with its urgency and yet so strangely brought an unknown peace to her spirit. This was her mate, destined for her as she for him.

Yet presently when he came to take her to the dining-room at the far side of the camp, there was no suggestion in the manner of either of them of the tumultuous emotion of half an hour ago.

"Ready, Domini?" he asked and waited outside for her.

"What will it feel like to wear other clothes again?" she asked. "This is our last night in a camp. Tomorrow night we shall be in a good hotel with carpets on the floors and running water in our rooms!"

"I shall miss what we lose by the transfer, though," he said, and took her elbow in his hand to pilot her across to where the line of lights showed the position of the dining-room.

Dinner tonight was a more protracted affair than it had been on the other nights. They all felt that they would miss something when they returned to the outside world, and at least one of them, Rowena, was afraid, though she was the brightest and gayest of the party.

Nothing alcoholic could be bought anywhere in the Reserve, and Mark had already exhausted the small store he had brought with him, so that toasts had to be drunk in lemonade and grenadilla, but the absence of more potent drinks did not seem to affect their spirits. Domini, looking once at Mark, though during the meal she had avoided his eyes, became suddenly grave. He was looking at her, a strained, impatient look in his eyes.

He wants me, she thought, and felt her pulses beginning to throb again. He wants me and – dear God, what am I going to do about us all? About myself and about Mark and about Keith?

The meal ended at last, and the party adjourned to the store with talk of buying keepsakes and souvenirs.

Mark spoke quietly to Domini.

"Will you let me buy you something now?" he asked.

"Something small," she said.

"Does that matter? Some day I am going to buy you diamonds," and he waited in the store whilst she chose an ivory elephant, tiny and exquisitely carved and fitting into an ivory case of the shape and size of a walnut.

"That all?" he asked with a rueful smile, and when she nodded, he bought the thing and tucked it into her bag.

They walked out of the store, and she knew that he was turning their steps towards her *rondavel* again when Yvonne came innocently to join them.

"They say there are lots of elephants down in the river now," she said. "You come to see?"

He gave Domini a look of martyred resignation.

"All right. We'll come. I could not bear to miss elephants," he said, and Domini laughed.

"You won't stay too long?" he asked her in a whisper, but she pretended not to hear and went on with Yvonne, who sensed that she had walked into something without realising at all what it might be.

Yvonne was feeling light-hearted and light-headed. Though there could be no future in it, she was going to meet David by the barrier set high above the river as soon as he had finished the accounts and report which were part of his day's duty. Jean Lafitte had receded so far into her background that she could almost forget him – almost, but not quite. In any case, there would be time enough to remember him after tomorrow.

Tomorrow!

It had come so quickly, this last day. They were not to be in Johannesburg until the following day, Friday, but this was their last day in the Reserve and tomorrow would so quickly be like any ordinary day.

They stood in a bunch by the railing, watching the herd of elephant which had come down to the river to drink, one great brute actually on the bank just below them, but calmly oblivious of them as he first munched great mouthfuls of the lush grass growing at the water's edge, pulled a few leafy branches to go with it, and then proceeded into the water for a long drink and a shower-bath. On the opposite side of the water, narrowed down to a small stream by the long months of drought, the rest of the herd fed, bathed and disported themselves, their great grey bulks outlined against the setting sun, the quiet of the evening broken by their trumpeting.

Domini realised that Mark had come without a camera and commented on it.

"I can't be bothered just now," he said, and she hesitated and then laughed a little.

"Because of me?" she asked.

"Of course."

"I am indeed complimented, taking precedence over your cameras!" she teased him.

But he was not to be diverted, and she knew that his attention was not on the elephants, in spite of their being one of the prime attractions of the whole expedition.

He managed at last to detach her from the others.

"Haven't you seen enough of them?" he asked, his voice slightly testy, and she smiled at him for the little boy most grown men can become at times and let him draw her away from the crowd still hanging over the rail of the camp boundary.

Slowly, his arm through hers, they walked amongst the trees whose deep shade defeated the lingering twilight, short though it would be, and enfolded them in silent peace. Voices came to them as no more than distant, indistinguishable sounds mingling with the soft murmuring of the jungle beyond them, the night wind stirring the leaves, the cry of a jackal.

He turned and drew her closer.

"Domini, what is it to be?" he asked. "Will you come to me?"

She felt a sudden sense of helplessness, not so much of drifting as of being forced into the irresistible current – to what end? His hands held her. She was aware of their sinewy strength, strength typical of the man himself, the man who by his own admission had been ruthless in getting what he wanted, never admitting the possibility of denial or defeat. Her mind went back to Keith, the husband who had failed her, had leant on her own strength and forced her to be stronger than surely nature had intended her to be. Keith, who was her husband – and Mark, who would be her lover.

She shivered a little, and his hands tightened, though still his arms did not hold her and she knew that at this moment, and perhaps only at this moment and never again, she could free herself by the lightest gesture.

She knew she would not make that gesture. The old, almost forgotten excitement was surging through her. Unconsciously she swayed towards him. In the darkness, he could see the shining look in her dark eyes.

"Domini, will you come?" he asked again.

Again the little shudder passed through her, but he knew it was not from the chill of the night, for she was warm beneath his hands, her light breath was warm, and the scent of her hair.

"Mark, how can I?" she asked, but there was longing in her voice.

"Do you want to, love?" he asked her very gently. "Look, I'm not holding you if you want to go. You can leave me and I won't follow you. But if you stay, love, I'll never let you go again. You know that? Domini, do you want to stay? To be mine for all the rest of time? I know I haven't the right, except by loving you. You're so far above me. You belong to another world. I don't talk your way or think your way or know how to behave your way. I'm rough, Domini, and I haven't learnt the things people of your sort learn – things about music and painting and books. But I'd learn, love. I'd make myself know all these things so that you'd never need to be ashamed of me, love."

His voice had slipped again into the accents of his youth. It caressed her. It offered her a subtle comfort ever, whilst it excited and entranced her.

"Mark!" she whispered. And again, "Mark!"

His arms drew her now, and she let herself slip into them and after a moment or two her own came about him, her arms linked at his neck.

"Do you love me, Domini?" he insisted.

"You know I do."

"You'll come to me?"

"You mean—leave Keith?"

"Ay."

"I don't know. Mark – I could never make you understand. He is so – dependent on me."

He gave a short, derisive sound.

"Dependent on you? A man on a woman?" he asked. "He's no man. No man for you. Domini. Why did you ever marry him?"

She sighed.

"I loved him," she said.

"You thought you did perhaps, but a weak thing like that is no man for you, and you know it. You're strong and you're full of pride and you hold your head high and you try not to let anyone see that in your mind there's—what is there, love? Sadness and sorrow and pity for this poor thing who is your husband. Come to me, Domini. Let me show you how to live life. I'll work for you and worship you all your days."

"Oh, Mark, I don't know! I don't know! It's true that I don't love him any more, I know that I haven't for a long time, but—he needs me and I married him and made vows to him and—when you promise something, it doesn't mean that the promise only holds good when it suits you. Mark, I don't think I can leave Keith, ever," and there was a deep despair in her voice and she let her head drop to his shoulder and so she stood, leaning against his strength and yet all the while refusing it.

His hand stroked her hair with rough tenderness. Then he lifted her head and kissed her mouth.

"I shall never give you up," he said, and again that surge of gladness swept through her because she knew his strength and her own helplessness to stand against it. What if somehow, some day, he made that come true? What if he really did refuse to let her go? How could she or Keith or any convention or promise or law stand against him?

Darkness, black and complete, had fallen, over the camp and people began to return. Voices and laughter invaded their solitude and she drew away from him.

"We shall have to go," she said. "Kiss me again—my dear."

He kissed her, lightly and perfunctorily, and she frowned and wondered if she would ever understand him. Where, in an instant, had gone all that fierceness of desire, that tenderness of acceptance?

But when, later, she returned to her *rondavel* from, her bath she knew why he had not lingered over that parting kiss.

He was there, sitting on the edge of her bed, waiting for her.

She drew back with a sharp sound of dismay, but in an instant he had risen to his feet, had drawn her inside, had shut the door behind her and taken her into his arms.

"If we are to have nothing else, give me just this, Domini. Just this one night, love—my dear love."

For a single instant she tried to resist him, fought wildly against him and against herself. Then suddenly she went limp in his arms and her mouth clung to his and her arms went round him.

"Just tonight," she whispered and closed her eyes to feel the more intensely his kisses on her lips. "Just tonight, my darling, my beloved. Mark."

Chapter Fifteen

Domini lay awake after Mark had left her, filled with a chaotic mingling of emotions, chief amongst them being amazement at what she had done and a deep, welling tenderness and love for Mark Teckler. This, she knew, was something fine and strong, beyond the mere physical delight which she had experienced with him and never to the same degree with Keith.

She tried to keep from her mind the thought of tomorrow and of all the tomorrows. Last night she had said that she could not leave Keith, that she felt him to be her responsibility and herself bound to him by her vows. But that had been last night, with her passion still unfulfilled and Mark still a separate entity.

At last, with stern resolution and the habit of years, she forced her mind to be composed and still and let her rest, and she dropped asleep with her problem still unsolved, to wake at the first stirring of the camp to the instant memory of Mark and of his love and of the new day which would hold this new wonder.

She sprang out of bed, suddenly afraid lest she miss one moment when she might be with him, and with her towels over her arm, she ran across to the bath-house, hoping for hot water. As she waited for the bath to fill, she stripped and stood momentarily arrested before the long mirror fastened to the wall. Was that herself, Domini Ellman? Loving Mark and being loved by him had transformed her in a few hours. Many of the lines had gone from her face, her eyes were clear and shining, and through her body there rippled a new strength, a re-budding of her youth. She lifted her arms and drew herself up straight and taut and rejoiced to feel the eager life coursing through her.

She laughed, hopped into the bath and hurried so that she might see him the sooner, singing softly to herself as she dried on the rough, coarse towels.

When would she see him? Where? At the breakfast table probably, and though he was definitely not at his best at such an hour, this morning would be different. She hoped she might have just a minute or two with him before they had to meet the others, and as she left her *rondavel* to go to the dining-room, she saw his door opening and paused, her eyes shining, her heart beating quickly.

As bad luck would have it, Yvonne and Miss Koetse emerged from the opening between the two huts at that moment, so that the four of them were face to face. It looked as though they might have to go on together when she so urgently wanted that minute alone with him.

She thought swiftly. Yesterday something had happened to the fastening of her case and Mark had said he would fix it for her.

"Oh, Mark," she said, as the four of them came together, "do something to my case to make it shut properly, will you?" and she smiled at him as she said it.

To her amazement, his face wore even more grim and sour an expression than it had on other mornings and he actually scowled at her.

"Oh, anybody can do that for you," he said rudely, and pushed past her – actually pushed past, and strode on in front of the three women in the general direction of the dining-room.

Domini shrank back, frozen with shock, scarcely able to believe that she had seen and heard aright.

"What an extremely rude and offensive man that is," said Miss Koetse in her thin, well-bred voice, and she and Yvonne went on whilst Domini, her knees shaking, somehow got back into the *rondavel* and sat down on the bed.

It could not have happened to her. It simply couldn't.

That was her first thought, and it beat into her brain and she knew that it had happened. All that rapture of the night before, his loving and her wild, glad surrender of herself to it -– it had meant nothing to him, no more than a casual night with just any chance woman. That was all. He had taken her and merely thrown her aside, his purpose and his need of her fulfilled.

She writhed, her head bowed to the pillow, remembering things she had said to him, things she had done, giving herself without reserve and from the deep need of her woman's love to give.

She repeated to herself his words, his contemptuous tone.

"Anybody can do that for you," he had said, and he must have known she had jumped at it as an excuse to have him to herself for a few moments in her room.

What else had he thought before he flung the rude words at her and pushed her aside? That she was contriving another opportunity for him to make love to her? That she could not wait for the coming of another night?

She lay in utter self-abasement and humiliation until Rowena came to find her and tell her they were having breakfast.

"Whatever's the matter, Domini?" she asked in concern when, pushing open the door of the *rondavel* she saw her lying face downward on the bed, her hand gripping convulsively at the blankets. When she raised herself, her face showed chalk-white and her eyes tearless but strained.

"I—nothing," said Domini, dragging herself from the bed and mechanically beginning to tidy her hair.

"But you're ill," said Rowena. "What can I do for you?"

"Nothing. I'm all right, really," said Domini.

"Shall I bring you some breakfast here?"

For a moment she was tempted. It would delay the moment when she must see Mark again. Then pride came to her aid. He should not have the opportunity of thinking that she minded, that last night had meant anything more to her than to him. If he had taken her casually, a light woman, well, she could be that light woman and meet him with an indifferent smile though in her heart was the knife-wound he had dealt her.

"No; I'll come," she said. "I'm quite all right now. Let me put on some more lipstick."

"And just a touch on your cheeks," said Rowena. "Here. Let me," for she saw that the hand trying to apply the colour was shaking. She could not begin to imagine what had happened to Domini, the serene, the poised, the never-flurried or upset. Something had happened, though, and Rowena, skilfully smoothing a touch of colour into the pale cheeks, wondered if it could possibly have had anything to do with Mark Teckler.

With their arms linked, the two went across to the dining-room, where the rest of the party were finishing their meal. Mark was getting up from the table as Domini approached it and for a second their eyes met. His were expressionless and a faint hint of a smile played round his mouth, but she gave him a brief, ice-cold look and went past him.

"Just coffee and—oh toast, biscuit, anything," she said to the native boy who came to serve her, and she had finished it and had joined the others at the car by the time they were ready. She had packed her case before breakfast in order to have more time with Mark!

He was standing at the open door of the car. Francis was in the front seat, explaining that they had decided to cast lots for it on this last morning in the Reserve and he had been the lucky one.

"I put your name in the hat as well, Domini. It was quite fair," he said.

She smiled briefly.

"I don't mind where I sit," she said.

"Can I have one of the window seats today in case we see more elephant?" asked Rowena and hopped into the middle seat and took the far corner as she spoke.

"It is better for me to be either in the middle or in one of the back seats," said Miss Koetse, "as I have no camera."

"You go in next to Rowena," said Mark, and, in a low voice to Domini. "Come in the back with me."

It was an order rather than an invitation, and she did not even look at him, but followed Miss Koetse, leaving Yvonne and Mark to share the back seat.

David realised that though his party had managed to shake down into the semblance of friendliness, there were still the subversive elements which kept them all individuals at variance with one another. He had hoped against hope that Yvonne would be put in the front seat beside him, though he knew it was not really her turn, but not all his mental willing could produce her name from the hat, and she was about as far from him as she could possibly be.

Driving mechanically, and with some part of his physical vision still concentrated on sighting game, he thought about her, of the swift flowering of their friendship, of the fascinating mixture of sober, good sense and mischievous fun of which she was made up and of the delight she was to him.

It was a sobering thought, and the more it occupied his mind, the more surely he realised that if he were not very careful, he would be thinking far too often and too much of Yvonne. And then what? They were both young. They could afford to wait. But she was already engaged to this fat French hog, and that, according to her, was practically the same in her country as being married to him. At any rate, she was quite acquiescent and had no thought that any other course might be possible.

A cry from Rowena behind him brought his whole attention back to the matter in hand.

"Elephant!" she cried.

"Where? Where?" came the excited cries from the others, for they had been driving slowly about for more than an hour without sight of anything more than a herd of impala.

"There! Right close to the car! Oh, David, stop! Back a bit. He's in those bushes and I can get a marvellous shot of him!"

Cautiously David backed the car and then saw the elephant, his great grey back looking more like a huge rock than a living animal as he stood, only a few feet from the roadway, his trunk lifted and swaying as he tore off the foliage and stuffed it into his mouth, his little wicked eyes showing that he was aware of the car and its occupants.

And then suddenly everything happened.

Rowena, moving her camera to get a better view, let it slip from her hand. It rolled into the roadway and before anyone else could do or say anything, she had thrown open the door and jumped down to retrieve it. Quicker than thought, moving with incredible speed, the elephant left the bushes and charged at the car. Rowena thrown to the ground, lay crushed against the running-board whilst the animal lifted its trunk and with an angry bellow brought it down like a flail on the roof of the car, which splintered down in jagged spikes on the cowering, terrified occupants. Moving, the elephant then lifted one huge foot and crushed in the bonnet, trumpeting again with rage.

Francis had been the first to move after the first blow.

"Keep the engine running, but if you move, you'll run over her," he shouted to David against the noise of the animal and the passengers and the splintering roof, and the next moment he himself was out of the car and running along the side towards the back to get to where Rowena lay at the other side.

What might have happened had the elephant decided to continue the attack may easily be conjectured, but he seemed to have satisfied himself by the two blows from trunk and foot, and he lumbered off down the road, trumpeting loudly and making for his original objective, the river.

Francis stooped to Rowena, who was very white, but conscious.

"Are you hurt badly?" he asked her.

"I don't know. I'm afraid to move. I feel numb," she said faintly.

The others joined them, David's face almost as white as Rowena's. The car was smashed beyond hope with that blow on the bonnet, but his immediate concern was his passenger.

"We shall have to move her," he said anxiously, and Francis agreed. They both knew that there was considerable risk of the elephant's returning, perhaps with the herd.

Other cars had heard the noise and approached warily, so that help was at hand, and at the insistence of David and Francis, and of Mark, who by now had joined them, Miss Koetse and Yvonne were put into one of the other cars, whilst another had gone back to the camp for the ambulance and a doctor if one could be found.

"One of the other cars will find room for you, Domini," said Francis as she stooped and knelt beside the now almost unconscious Rowena.

"No. I'll stay with her," she said.

David was looking at the injured woman.

"I think she's fainted," he said, "it might be better to move her to the side of the road before she's conscious again," and they did this, lifting her carefully away from the running-board against which she was crushed and laying her down on a rug from someone's car. Domini took off the jacket of her suit to cover her with, since there was no second rug available, and the three men took up positions from which they could command a view of the probable angles of approach should the elephant or any other animal threaten them. They were all profoundly relieved when the ambulance, followed by a breakdown van, both kept at hand in the rest camps, appeared. Rowena, showing signs of returning consciousness, was lifted carefully into the ambulance and the breakdown van proceeded with, its job of conveying back to the camp what was left of the *safari* car.

A doctor had been found and was awaiting them by the time the ambulance reached the camp and his examination of Rowena established the fact that by a miracle her injuries were only superficial, though her body had been badly bruised by the projecting edge of the running-board, which actually had been the means of saving her from worse injury.

There was, however, no possibility of her being able to be moved for at least some days, and the camp supervisor and his wife were kindness itself in arranging for the party to be accommodated pending the arrival from Johannesburg of another car, and also in putting at their disposal for as long a period as they wished two *rondavels* in the quietest part of the camp.

Domini had volunteered at once to stay with Rowena until she could be moved, and since it was obvious that Rowena was much attached to her, Francis accepted the offer gratefully.

"Will you turn in with her, then, if I take the other *rondavel?*" he asked. "Would that be the best arrangement, do you think?"

"I'm sure it would," said Domini, and when the cases were brought in from the wrecked car, she unpacked for them both and made everything as comfortable as circumstances would permit. Since Rowena was in considerable pain, and was also suffering from shock, the doctor had given her a shot of morphia, and she was sleeping heavily when Francis returned and suggested that Domini take the opportunity of getting a breath of fresh air. Though the *rondavels* were white-washed inside and out and had thick walls and good-sized windows, they were very hot in the middle of the day, and she accepted gratefully.

The camp was very quiet, since, except at meal-times and at night, everybody was out in the Reserve, and she wandered towards the high bank overlooking the river, watching with mixed feelings the enjoyment of three or four young elephants at play in the water, their dams looking on and occasionally heaving themselves down for a splash or a drink with their monstrous children.

She could shudder still at the feeling of trapped helplessness when the elephant charged at the car, with Rowena lost to sight and the roof splintering down on them. She felt she would never hear a more hideous sound than the angry trumpeting which accompanied the destruction of the car, nor see anything more petrifying than that great grey bulk looming over them and lashing out with trunk and foot. It was a miracle that Rowena was not only still alive, but comparatively unharmed.

She heard someone approaching, and turned to find Mark near her. Instantly her mind and her face froze and she turned back to her contemplation of the elephants at play.

"Look harmless enough from here, don't they?" he asked in an easy conversational tone which amazed her with its effrontery. Could he possibly imagine they were going to renew their former association?

She did not reply, but kept her back turned to him, and he came nearer to her and stood close beside her.

"Can't we be friends again?" he asked. "I'm ready to be."

She turned to him at that. Her eyes were cold.

"My dear Mark, you surely cannot imagine either that I would lay myself open to a repetition of this morning's humiliation or that—that—there could be any occasion for it."

His brows knitted in a closer frown as he looked at her.

"Humiliation?" he asked, and his voice was gentle now. "Why use that word, lass? I wouldn't humiliate you—nor I couldn't, from the height above me that you are," he said simply.

Unconsciously her eyes softened.

"But you did humiliate me," she said. "To speak to me like that, to be so—so uncaring, after the night—to make me feel that you regarded me as just—one of the women you can spend a night with and then forgot or ignore. To be no more than that, cheap, giving myself lightly to a man—oh Mark," and she broke off and turned her head away from him.

She felt his hand groping for hers, would not make any movement to contact it, but did not resist it when his fingers linked strongly into hers.

"Domini, I don't know what to say except that I'm sorry. I am sorry. I wouldn't hurt a hair of your head. You know that. It's just that that's the way I am. You'll have to get used to me and take me like that."

"You mean you're satisfied with yourself as you are and don't think there is any need for you to try to alter?" she asked, stung, still wrestling with herself against that insidious enemy within her that wanted to forgive him and let herself love him in spite of everything that should have prevented it.

"No; not that. God knows I'm nothing to brag about, not when I'm with you and think of you. But I'm a rough man, Domini, rough and hard and uneducated and ignorant in the ways you're used to. I'm too old to change. It's too late for me to be any different. You'll have to take me as I am and not get what you call humiliated and mad with me because – well, because I'm bad-tempered sometimes."

She stood silently thinking not so much about what he was saying or what he was implying. How could she take him, no matter what his temper?

"Domini?" he said gently.

She turned to him.

"Mark, even if I forgive you for this morning, even if I could be satisfied to 'take you as you are', as you put it, what's the use? We have been mad, my dear. There is no future for us – together, I mean. We have had all there was for us."

His fingers tightened their hold on hers.

"No," he said. "That is one of the things we are not going to accept. I never shall, and I am not going to let you. We're of different worlds, Domini. I shall never be your equal in some things, and we both know it and it's too late for me to try, though I'll do my best not to offend you in—well, in behaving at the table and opening doors for people and so on, if you think those things important. But we belong to each other, lass. Last night taught us that if nothing else could do. I'll make you happy. I've got plenty of this world's goods and they are all for you. I may not be your equal, but I can give you a home and a setting worthy of the highest in the land. You've got to come to me, Domini."

"How can I? I'm married. There's Keith," she said, troubled, unhappy, and yet thrilling at the knowledge of his complete subjugation to her, as any woman must thrill. She had a moment's passionate rebellion at the hold Keith had on her and then forced herself to recognise and accept it.

He pushed aside the thought of Keith as negligible. "Him? A poor thing that can't even keep you, or won't? If you ever had any liability to him, you've discharged it long ago, I'm coming there to see you, Domini. I'm not going to lose you, I want you, and I've always got what I wanted out of life."

She felt a little shiver run through her at the tone of his voice, masterful, self-confident, so utterly sure that what he willed should be. She longed wildly that it might be so, even whilst her common sense warned her that in this instance he might have come up against the invincible thing, the one thing he could not get out of life. How could she leave Keith? What would happen to him without her? Taking on the responsibility for another person's life, transporting him to another country, as she had done Keith, asking him to live a life completely different from the one he had originally chosen for himself and just because she had married him and linked their two lives – all this could not be ignored and pushed on one side, regarded as no longer her affair. She could not agree that she had discharged her liability to Keith nor would ever discharge it.

Miss Koetse came across the grass to them, walking in her prim, dignified way and not beginning to speak until she had no need to raise the tones of her quiet, ladylike voice: "Mrs. Ellman, I came to tell you that Mrs. Craye is awake and would like you to go to her if you can."

"Oh, thank you, Miss Koetse. I'll go at once," said Domini, feeling that help had come at the crucial moment.

Miss Koetse lingered when the younger woman had gone, and though Mark Teckler felt he had nothing to say to her, even he could not very well leave her abruptly, and he stood at her side looking down at the elephant pool.

"Make a nice picture from here, don't they?" he observed.

"Yes, though without my glasses I am not able to see very well," she said. "This is a rather awkward accident, is it not?"

"You mean about Rowena Craye? Yes. Could be damned awkward if any of us had to get back in a hurry," he agreed. "Are you in a hurry, Miss Koetse?"

"No. No, I do not think I am ever in a hurry," she said thoughtfully. "I have reached a time of life when I find I am very well content to let life pass slowly if it will, though I find in actual fact that it passes far too quickly."

Looking for almost the first time directly at her, seeing her thin, pale face, to which she added none of the usual artifices of modern womanhood, her spare, unfeminine figure, her spartan grey suit and flat-heeled shoes, Mark was conscious of a sudden stab of pity for her. He knew that she had never lived, that through her allotted span she had merely existed, being in the world but never of it. Seen against the colourful, fighting background of his own life, hers looked drab in the extreme, drab and purposeless.

"You find it goes too quickly?" he asked, with the least and unintentional emphasis on the first word.

She nodded her head.

"I think that, for almost the first time, I should like it to stand still," she said, rather to his surprise, and then she turned to him. "Mr. Teckler," she said, "you are, I think, a rich man. Do you spend all your money on yourself, or save it?"

He looked as much surprised as he felt.

"Well—well, yes, reckon I do," he admitted.

"And do you feel that it gives you all the satisfaction you need?"

"Well—yes, in a way," he said. "Not that I never give anything away, I give to the chapel, though I don't know as I hold with it."

"I don't mean that. I mean private gifts."

"Christmas and birthdays and so on? Well, now that my wife is dead and as I haven't any children or other relations, I don't reckon much about those things," he said grimly.

"No. I did not mean quite that, but other gifts, quite large ones. A gift, for instance, to help someone in life and with no possibility of its return. I have been a hard woman, Mr. Teckler, as I think you have been a hard man. I am, of course, many years older than you, but looking back, and even looking forward, I do not see anything that has justified my long life. I have not added anything to it."

He was surprised and rather embarrassed by this unexpected approach. Secretly he was as much afraid of Henrietta Koetse as he was likely to be of anybody, and he kept his prickles sheathed, but handy.

"Yes, I suppose it looks like that to most successful people," he agreed. "To make success, you've got to walk over somebody."

"I do not think I have 'walked over' anybody," she said severely, "and I have not had to make my success, as you phrase it, but I am beginning to feel I have not made anything else either. Perhaps there is something in the strange atmosphere of the Reserve. One is so much cut off from ordinary life, and it is very strange for me to be living a communal life of any sort, having to share a *rondavel*, and with not even electricity nor running water, I wonder if perhaps it has made us all more—human, Mr. Teckler?" her face relaxing into the strained, difficult smile which transformed it, but made it unfamiliar.

He smiled and nodded and looked into the distance.

"Yes. Happen it has," he agreed.

Chapter Sixteen

It was three days before matters could be cleared up and David free to leave the Reserve in the other car which had been sent out to him from Johannesburg, three days of this strange captivity in a jungle camp, unreal and yet to some at least of the captives days in which for the first time, possibly the only time, they became their true selves, all the artifice and the barriers between themselves and reality torn down.

For Yvonne and David, they were days snatched from the heaven they might not enter in their real lives.

It had begun for David the first time the little French girl had looked at him and smiled and told him she had been waiting for him.

Had he? All his life so far? His affair with Elissa now looked to him just that and no more – an affair. It was difficult to believe that she had once meant so much to him, or had appeared to mean so much. His feeling for Yvonne was something completely different. It lacked some quality of excitement which had kept him restless and on edge, constantly expectant, all the time he had known Elissa, but he knew that the lack was a good one, for in its place was a feeling of contentment and fulfilment when he was with Yvonne.

Yet what was the use? What possible end could this have but parting? She had told him frankly about Jean Lafitte and her future and that she intended to go back to her own country when this holiday was over and meekly acquiesce in this abominable plan made for her by others.

He thought of her attitude as 'meek acquiescence' without having the least idea of the tumult of rebellion within her, the misery of the thoughts which came to her when she was alone. For the first time in her life she was unable to sleep, but tossed about half the night and spent the other half with dreams from which she woke unrested – dreams of David receding from her, always just eluding her grasp, with Jean Lafitte's broad, red, good-humoured face become that of a Mephistopheles.

She tried to feel suitably sorry for the accident, for Rowena, who, if not badly hurt, was in considerable pain, for David, who felt sure he would be blamed for allowing the thing to happen, though nobody who had actually witnessed it could believe that he could have either foreseen it or done anything to prevent it. Yet overriding the sympathy she felt was the joy of being given this extra time with him. She had been able to send a telegram of reassurance to Marie, after which she had given herself up to the enjoyment of these unexpected days.

With nothing to do whilst he waited for the car to be sent out and the various enquiries made into the accident, David could spend the time as he liked, and he and Yvonne naturally gravitated together, watched with something like compassion by the others. They were so young, so obviously in love, and even if there were no future for them (they all knew by now of the future mapped out for Yvonne and that David would possibly not even have a job after all this), their youth and gaiety and effervescent happiness bubbled up in them like bubbles in a champagne cup.

But on the very last evening they were to spend at the camp, since David had received word over the emergency telephone that the second car would be there the next day, it was not easy for them to keep their happiness.

After dinner that night, Yvonne wandered off as she had done each evening to their special spot, a corner which overlooked the river, but which did not afford a view of the elephants and which accordingly seldom invaded. David was making his last visit to Rowena, as he had done each night, and seeing that all the other members of the party had as much comfort as could be got in the camp.

She heard him coming over the dry grass to her, but did not turn her head. When he slipped his arm about her, she leaned against him, her face pressed to his shoulder.

"Well, my sweet," he began after a long silence, but she put up a hand swiftly to his lips.

"No. No, don't say it, David."

"You knew what I was going to say?"

His lips caressed her hand.

She nodded without looking at him.

"Yes. The last, time," she said shakily. "Oh David—David—*bien-aimé*," and now the tears came.

He held her tightly and looked out over her head, the dear dark head which had come to mean so much to him that it was impossible to believe that life could go on without her, and yet it must go on.

"Don't, sweetheart," he said. "It hurts me terribly to know you're unhappy and I can't do anything about it."

"Aren't you unhappy too, David?" she quavered.

"Yes."

There was a concentration of bitter wretchedness in the one syllable, and she lifted her head to look at him.

"David, isn't there anything?" she asked desperately. "Isn't there anything at all?"

"Well, nothing that I can see, darling," he said. "After all that's happened, I don't expect I've even got a job."

"But it was not of your fault," she insisted. "They see that, of a truth."

He smiled even in his unhappiness. Part of the dearness of her was her funny little expressions, so earnestly spoken.

"Of a truth, I don't for a moment think they will, my sweet," he said, "and there isn't much I can do but understand and drive cars, and I've about as much hope as a snowball in hell of finding the money to start on my own. Yvonne – Yvonne, darling – are you beginning to think that if I could, if I could somehow make a decent living, enough for us to start a home on – you would?"

She clung to him.

"It would be so terrible a thing to do, I know, but it is that I cannot never to see you again," she said wildly.

"You'd stay here? Tell them in France that you're not going to marry this man?" he asked, his heart leaping in spite of the hopelessness of the thing. "You'd really do that?"

"I don't know only that I cannot to part from you!"

"If only all this accident thing hadn't happened, I should at least have had a job," he said miserably, "but as it is, without a job and with not a penny saved – darling, I can't ask you to wait for me. I can't even keep myself, let alone you."

The iron of despair sank into his soul, and when at last she told him she must go in as it was very late, he held her in a close, fierce grip and without a word took her back to her *rondavel* and left her. There was nothing else he could do.

Miss Henrietta Koetse had grown accustomed to the light, broken sleep of the elderly, and she had been aware of the change in her young companion, who at first had dropped off at once into the deep, solid sleep of the young, but who for the last few nights had lain awake, tossing and turning, for long hours at a time, and then had slept restlessly, murmuring even in that sleep.

The oil lamp still burned when Yvonne returned, and by its light Miss Koetse had caught a glimpse of David Parley's tall figure and the glint of his fair hair, and before Yvonne had turned away from the light, her tear-stained face had told its own poignant tale.

Miss Koetse lay and thought. She had been thinking quite a lot lately, unaccustomed, unfamiliar thoughts which were not of herself. When her parents and her brother had died, though she felt sorrow for them, she had also felt a sense of relief since she was at last alone, responsible for no one and with no one on whom she need any longer spend the money she loved.

Yes, she had come to a realisation of that unpalatable fact; she loved her money – her house, her car, her possessions, all the beauty and value with which she could surround herself and which she liked to enjoy alone.

She was thinking of that when Yvonne had quickly undressed and put out the light and hidden her small form in bed, her face in the pillows which did not entirely conceal her tears.

Miss Koetse knew what the trouble was. The girl was to go back to France after this holiday in South Africa and marry a man – a quite worthy man, according to Yvonne – who was her parents' choice. It was, Miss Koetse thought, quite a sensible arrangement, much better than the haphazard way in which people of some other countries entered into marriage. There was sufficient evidence even in this small company of the foolishness of letting young people choose their own mates, with no more wisdom in selection than animals. Look at the Crayes, for instance.

The more she thought about it, the more sensible she thought the plan which would give this little Yvonne a husband chosen with the heads and common sense of the people who loved her and wanted to ensure her happiness.

And yet—

The smothered sobs made a pitiful background for her thoughts.

Miss Koetse thought about David Parley. A nice young man. A steady, reliable type of man, not one of these fly-by-nights who did not care what they did nor whom they inconvenienced so that they themselves might have what they called a good time. He had showed her, Henrietta Koetse, courtesy and attention, considering her comfort in every way, treating her as very few of these modern young men thought it worthwhile to treat a woman of her age.

Yes, definitely a very nice young man, and Yvonne, even though she was French and therefore somewhat beyond the pale in Miss Koetse's opinion, was a very nice girl.

And suddenly, amazing herself, Miss Koetse made up her mind.

"Yvonne," she said, sitting upright, a gaunt, unlovely figure in her prim nightgown, her grey hair twisted into paper curlers, her face shining with the cold cream Yvonne had persuaded her to use at night whilst the atmosphere was so dry.

At the sound of her name, the girl sat up, pushing the hair from her eyes. They were barely visible to each other in the light from the window, across which the elder woman always primly insisted the curtain should be kept drawn.

"You speak?" she asked, struggling with, her tears.

"Yes. You are unhappy, child?"

"I am sorry. I keep you from to sleep," said Yvonne confusedly.

"That doesn't matter, but why are you crying?"

"I—it is nothing. Nothing."

"That, of course, is not true. A girl does not cry for nothing, and I have known for several nights that you are not as happy as you were at first. Tell me. It is David Parley?"

"Y—yes," admitted Yvonne reluctantly, battling with fresh tears at the sound of the beloved's name.

"You are in love with each other?" demanded Miss Koetse.

Yvonne nodded in the darkness and her silence was taken for affirmation.

"What about this man in France whom you are supposed to marry?"

"I know. It is that I am so—confuse. It is wrong that I love David— but I do, I do!" And her voice broke again in fresh sobs.

"Now come, come," said Miss Koetse briskly. "Nothing was ever put right by crying about it. Can this be put right? Is there any way? Are you forced to go back to France to marry this man, or are you still legally free?"

Yvonne made a great effort and managed to pour out the full story, much of which Miss Koetse knew already and much that she had guessed.

"So," she said when the girl had finished, "the facts seem to be that though you are under a sort of obligation of honour to go back and marry this Frenchman, this Jean, as you call him, you are still legally free to marry someone else, and if David Parley could improve his prospects if he could start this—trucking, did you call it?"

"Yes," said Yvonne in a sad and doleful voice, as one without hope.

"If he could start this, he would be in a position to give you a home and marry you?"

"Yes," agreed Yvonne again.

"And if he had three hundred pounds, he could start this trucking?"

"Yes," said Yvonne a third time, and heaved a sigh. "But where would he get three hundred pounds from?"

"From me," said Miss Koetse calmly, though as soon as she had said it, burning her boats, she felt panic-stricken, scarcely able to believe that she had come to such a decision, let alone make it already irretrievable.

Yvonne stared at her in the darkness, unable to see her face, seeing only the outline of her gaunt figure bolt upright, her head bristling with the curl papers.

"You—what is it you have said?" she asked wonderingly.

"That I will give him the three hundred pounds – or more if he needs it," said Miss Koetse, reckless now that it was too late to draw back her first offer.

Yvonne left her bed in a rush and was on the other bed, her arms around the stiff, unyielding form, her cloud of soft hair brushing her face and then her warm young lips pressed to her cheek.

"Oh, thank you, thank you a thousand million times. You are too good, too wonderful. The good God will reward you ..."

It poured out, a spate of French, with no attempt now to try to find the English words, and if Miss Koetse did not understand, it was impossible to mistake the meaning and the rapture and the passionate gratitude.

For a few moments she let the flow of words and affection flow about her. Then she pushed the girl away and put up her hands to ascertain how much damage had been done to the curl papers, but her gesture was of embarrassment rather than the annoyance she tried to show. There was a strange feeling about her heart, as if the ice were cracking around it after encircling it for years. The girl's warm arms, her cloud of soft hair, her kisses, her broken, unintelligible thanks, made her wonder why she had never done anything like this before. After all, three hundred pounds, possibly even five hundred – what were they? She could take them out of her current account and scarcely even know that they had gone.

But of course she *would* know. She kept in her current account only enough for the needs of the household and herself, for her insurances and taxes and estimated outgoings, and the rest of her substantial income was invested immediately, after consultation with her broker, who was also her tried and trusted adviser on all financial matters. What on earth would Mr. du Toit think of her, and possibly say to her, when she told him, as of course she would have to tell him that she had given – no, *lent* – no, *given*, three hundred pounds to a strange young man who drove cars for his living and now wanted to buy a truck on hire purchase to enable him to marry a young French girl who was already affianced to someone else?

All these thoughts rushed through her mind in the instant it took her to push Yvonne away.

"Now, that's enough," she said severely. "Go back to bed and go to sleep and let me do the same. All this fuss and nonsense, indeed!"

Yvonne laughed, her volatile spirit up in the clouds again from the depths to which it had sunk only a few minutes ago.

"Sleep? How can I sleep when I am so happy?" she cried.

"Rubbish. A moment ago you could not sleep because you were unhappy. There is no satisfying some people," but behind her stern tone was an undercurrent which belied it.

"To think that I must wait until the morning before I tell David?" said Yvonne tragically. "He will not be able to sleep also, my poor David, for to be unhappy – and all the time if he know, he could be happy like me!"

The older woman could not miss the longing, appealing note in the young voice.

"You want to go and tell him, I suppose?" she asked harshly.

"Would it be very terrible?" cooed Yvonne.

"Yes. It must be a long time past midnight. Go to sleep and wait until the morning."

But sleep would not come to either of them: Yvonne because she had so much to think about, so much to plan, a letter to write to her parents, perhaps even to Jean; Miss Koetse because she had to reconcile her calm, everyday mind with the wild impulse, so foreign to her, which had robbed her, yes, actually robbed her, of three hundred pounds! Three – hundred – pounds.

But when she spoke, it was with the mind that had prompted that impulse and not with the one that was regretting it.

"If you cannot sleep," she said tartly, "then I cannot sleep either. You toss and turn too much. Do you think this young man will still be awake?"

Yvonne sat up.

"David? I think he probably will," she said wonderingly.

Miss Koetse was climbing out of bed.

"Light the lamp," she said. "Since it seems I shall not be able to sleep until you have seen him, and since you cannot possibly go alone, I will go with you. Light the lamp!"

Quite sure that she was asleep and dreaming, Yvonne scrambled out of bed, lit the lamp and saw that Miss Koetse was getting into her dressing-gown, a substantial affair of heavy brown tweed, man-tailored and designed to last a generation, as it probably had done already.

"Get into something warm, and as decent as possible. I suppose you know where this young man sleeps?"

"Yes. In a tent, with another driver," said Yvonne, and though she was still sure she must be asleep, she went through the motions of scrambling into her dressing-gown and slippers and then dived under Miss Koetse's bed to retrieve that lady's substantial no-nonsense shoes.

Thus attired, the two of them crept out of the *rondavel* and towards the rows of tents, Yvonne with laughter bubbling within her, the laughter of pure happiness, and Miss Koetse realising that her life had been a very solemn affair and this the most extraordinary thing for a lady of her years and tendencies to be doing.

Light showed in the tent David was sharing with a friend, and the shadows of the two men could be seen quite clearly as they sat on their beds playing cards with a stool between them.

"All right. I'll see you," said David, and at that precise moment there was a tap on the canvas and Yvonne poked her head in.

The two men jumped up, startled, upsetting the stool and scattering the cards.

"Yvonne! What's wrong?" asked David at once, hurrying to her and drawing back again, unable to believe his eyes, at sight of the girl's happy smile and of Miss Koetse, incredible vision, behind her.

"David, nothing is wrong, but nothing!" cried Yvonne. "It is all so very, very right. David – *chéri* – it is Miss Koetse. She will give you the money, the three hundred pounds. We have come to tell you."

Bewildered and unable to take anything in, he pulled back the canvas flap of the tent.

"Please – won't you come in? Yvonne? Miss Koetse? Dick, these are – two of my passengers."

He made the introductions awkwardly, but Yvonne was much too excited to feel any embarrassment and in spite of the presence of a stranger, a young man whom she knew vaguely, having seen him during the evening, she poured out her story with laughter, something that was almost tears, and a passionate gratitude to Miss Koetse, who stood there in uncomfortable silence, wondering what madness had overtaken her to bring her into such a situation in the early hours of the morning.

Dick Braddon quickly grasped the main essentials, being more or less in David's confidence, and he stooped down and produced a bottle half full of gin from his rucksack on the floor.

"I think this calls for a drink," he said. "Can we rake up four things to drink out of?"

"Not for me," said Miss Koetse severely, eyeing the bottle with alarm.

"Oh come! As the fairy godmother, you can't leave yourself out," argued Dick blithely, not feeling for her any of the awe in which she was held by her own party. "We've got two tumblers, and what did you do with your ice-cream carton, David? Oh, here it is. I'll wash that out for a third, but where can we find a fourth?"

"David and I will share," said Yvonne, and in spite of her refusal and protests, Miss Koetse presently found herself sitting on one of the beds with Dick Braddon, she with a tumbler in her hand and he with the ice-cream carton, whilst on the other bed Yvonne and David, their arms entwined, drank from the second tumbler the almost neat gin served to them by Dick.

"The only thing to dilute it with is the water from this," he had said, lifting the tin jug which was part of the portable washing equipment. "If I don't put much of it in, the gin will be able to stand up to the bugs and kill 'em. Here's to you, Yvonne and David, and here, with my hand on my heart, is to you, Miss Koetse!"

She drank the contents of the tumbler in sips at first, but presently in gulps as the unaccustomed liquid ran through her body, and by the time she had emptied the tumbler she was aware that the world was a very pleasant place with very pleasant and happy people in it. In fact, she was one of the happy people herself, and she laughed with the sound of a creaking gate at even the most outrageous of Dick's jokes until they were interrupted by the sound of a voice outside and the sight of a head poked round the opening in the canvas.

"Not wanting to be a spoil-sport, I'd still like to know how long it will be before we can get to sleep," said the visitor mildly.

"Sorry, old man. Packing up right now," said David, disengaging himself from the clinging sleepiness of Yvonne and getting to his feet. "Come on, ladies. I'll take you home."

Miss Koetse rose majestically to her feet, only to find that her knees at once bent and refused to bear her weight, so that she collapsed in a heap on the bed again.

She stared at the others, who were regarding her with mixed feelings, Dick wanting to roar with laughter, David feeling that things had gone too far. He had been dubious about it when he saw the tumblerful of nearly neat gin gradually being emptied.

"I—I am not feeling—quite well," said Miss Koetse, still struggling to maintain her dignity when she had struggled to a sitting position once more. "It is—very hot in this—this tent," getting the words out with difficulty.

Yvonne giggled and was instantly suppressed by David's warning hand on her arm.

"Yes, it's very hot," he agreed. "You will feel better when we get into the fresh air. Let me help you," and as Yvonne was only a little merry and inclined to giggle, since she and David had only shared their drink, the two men between them hoisted Miss Koetse to her feet, led her to the doorway and, one at each side, conducted her safely back to the *rondavel.*

"Can you manage her?" David asked Yvonne in a whisper when they had got her into the *rondavel* and sat her down on her bed, from which place she continued to smile and nod at them.

"Yes. You go," said Yvonne, and when they had gone, chuckling as they went, she contrived to get Miss Koetse out of her gown and slippers and safely tucked up in her bed.

It was some little time after that the old lady suddenly sat up in bed again, looked across at the quietly sleeping mound that was Yvonne, and gathered her senses together again.

"I've given away three hundred pounds," she told herself incredulously, "I've sat in a tent with two young men in the middle of the night in my dressing-gown with my hair in curlers – and I've been drunk."

Having assimilated that thought, she lay down again, and very gradually it began to dawn on her that she was feeling no intense regret or remorse for any of these things, not even for the fact that undoubtedly she had been the worse for drink and had had to be helped back to her room, and put to bed.

"It must be the Reserve," she said. "I've been told before that queer things can happen to people in here. Now I know," and presently she drifted off to sleep from which eventually she woke with a splitting headache and a taste like that of old rubber boots in her mouth.

Chapter Seventeen

Domini was with Rowena when the car left to take the remaining passengers back to Johannesburg, so though she had said goodbye to Yvonne and David, who had told her what Miss Koetse was doing for them, and to Miss Koetse herself – a changed and much softened Miss Koetse – she did not actually see them go. She was, therefore, astonished when a perfunctory tap at the open door of the *rondavel* preceded the entrance of Mark Teckler.

She glanced warningly at Rowena, who had fallen into an uneasy, drugged sleep, and when he made a sign to her to come outside, she felt obliged to do so rather than risk waking her patient.

During the past day or two she had seen very little of him, partly through her own choice, but also because Rowena, suffering now from delayed shock rather than from any specific injury, could not bear her to be out of her sight. It had, however, piqued her that Mark was apparently going to make no attempt to see her before he went – went out of her life for ever, she told herself. Yet she had just managed to persuade herself that it was the wisest thing he could do when she looked up to see him there.

"Hasn't the car left yet?" she asked him when they were outside.

In spite of herself, in spite of the severity of her self-discipline in keeping away from him, in spite of her constant reminder to that traitor within her that Mark was not for her nor she for him, her heart had given a jump and refused to settle down again.

"Yes, it's gone," he said.

"But you—why are you here then?"

His steely eyes looked out at her from their deep setting with the steady, intense look in them against which she was never proof.

Beneath that level gaze, she knew herself to be weak and yielding, whatever her mind demanded of her.

"You know why I'm here," he said. "To be with you."

She made a little helpless gesture with shoulders and hands.

"Oh Mark – what's the use? It's just prolonging the agony. It's putting off the adjustment you know we've got to make, the—final acceptance."

"I don't agree that that sort of acceptance is necessary or even possible to us, and as for prolonging the agony – is it such agony to be with me, Domini?"

A little shudder ran through her. She was afraid of his strength and his indomitable will. Why, when she had nerved herself to the parting, had accepted the position of not seeing him again, was he here with he still? With all the struggle and the inevitable parting to be gone through again?

"We can't discuss it any more, Mark. It's over and finished. You know it as well as I do."

"I don't know it, because it is not true. A thing like this between a man and a woman can't just be finished like that, put aside to be forgotten like—like last year's summer or an old suit of clothes. It's us, Domini, you and me, and what there is between us is a part of our lives for ever. I'm not going to give you up, and the sooner you accept that fact, the better."

Her pride of character came to her aid, belatedly, perhaps, but giving her strength to resist him.

"No, Mark," she said quietly. "I have not to accept that at all. I belong not to you, but myself, and I have the right to decide my own future. I am going back to Keith and to the job I undertook when I married him. It was for better or for worse, Mark, not merely as long as it suited me and provided that it turned out for—better."

She was turning to go back to Rowena when he caught her arm and held it, turning her to him.

It was early afternoon, and the sun was blazing down from a cloudless sky on the dazzling white of the *rondavels* and their brown reed thatch and the burnt, dry veld grass. No one in the camp was astir. Thin spirals of smoke went up from the many fires, but the natives whose job it was to tend them were asleep beside them, their heads bent on their folded arms, the inevitable brown blankets heaped over their shoulders. Beyond the camp all the rest of Nature seemed to sleep. Not even the leaves stirred nor did a twig crack under a cautious pad or hoof.

"Please let me go, Mark," said Domini in a whisper.

"Presently. I only want you to know that I am here, that I'm staying here so long as you are here, and that I'm never going to let you go because you belong to me and I to you, whatever you may say about belonging only to yourself. I made you mine the night I had you in my arms, and when you gave yourself to me you gave me more than your body. You can never belong to anyone else, not to this poor sap of a husband of yours, not to yourself, not to anyone for the rest of your life, but me—me, Domini. My lass," changing his tone from that dominating one to the gentle voice which could so utterly break her resolve, "don't make it so hard for us both. Why should you? Doesn't it mean anything to you that we love each other? Doesn't it, lass?"

"Oh—Mark!" she said in a broken whisper, and turned away again and he let her go.

Inside the *rondavel*, Rowena was lying with her eyes wide open, and Domini knew from the look on her face that she had heard and seen at least something of what had passed between her and Mark.

She stretched out her hand, and Domini laid her own in it.

Rowena had changed in many ways since she had been carried back unconscious to the camp to start on the weary waiting to become whole and free from pain again. Domini was able better than any of the others, including Francis, to recognise the change, though she did not know what, if anything, it portended for the future.

"You two are in love, aren't you?" asked Rowena. "You needn't be afraid to tell me. I guessed it a long time ago. What are you going to do about it?"

"Nothing," said Domini. "What is there to do? I'm married."

"You're not in love with your husband any more, though, if you ever were."

"I was once – or I thought I was. Do you want to break away, Rowena?"

"From Francis? I don't know. We're miserable together, as you must know without my telling you, but he won't let me go. Oh, what's the use of going over it all again? Is Francis here, by the way, or did he go in the car with the others?"

"No; he's here. Of course he wouldn't go and leave you."

Rowena laughed her hard, brittle laugh which held no mirth.

"No, of course not! Always the perfect gentleman to do the right thing! What a quartet we are, Domini – Francis and I hating each other and staying together, you and Mark Teckler loving each other and having to part. Why are you so determined to part from him, Domini?"

"I happen to want to do something quite old-fashioned," said Domini with a slightly derisive smile. "My duty."

"A cold thing to hold husband and wife together."

"Possibly. But I think it's better than breaking the contract and parting. Can't you sleep again, my dear? That stuff the doctor left for you ought to have put you out for much longer than it did, and you so badly need sleep. Try to relax."

When eventually Rowena had drifted into the state of half-sleep, half-consciousness which was the best she could achieve, Domini left door and window wide and lay down on her own bed, not to sleep, but to think.

Was there any alternative for her but to go back to Keith, feeling as she did about marriage and its responsibilities? Her whole being craved for Mark, for his strength against Keith's weakness, for his love against her husband's light infidelities, for the blessed relief it would be to be able to lay down the burden of planning and providing for herself and for Keith, who seemed her child rather than her husband. Looking back, she realised that that was what he had always been, from the beginning. It was she who had been the deciding factor, she who had planned and dictated, he who had meekly allowed himself to be made the tool of her will. He had not really even wanted to marry her in the first place, she thought with a touch of self-scorn, though she knew that he had been as happy as she in the first few months, possibly even the first year or two, of their marriage. Love had been new to them and they had delighted in its expression and in the discovery of a new delight. How was it that they had lost this delight and the enjoyment of each other? Could any of it be recaptured?

She began to feel restless in her self-imposed captivity, to long not so much to be back with Keith, but to have done with this period of mingled rapture and despair.

Between them, the two men made an effort to amuse her and ameliorate the conditions of camp life. She was more at her ease with Francis Craye than with Mark, though after that first day, the latter seemed, if not to have accepted her decision, at least to be satisfied to postpone the fulfilment of his own. Now and then, however, she would catch an expression in his eyes when he looked at her, a tone of his voice, which told her that he still regarded her as his own.

Eventually it was decided that it would be better for Rowena to be moved from the camp so that she could have the benefit of physiotherapy treatment, but this could not be obtained near their home in Rhodesia, nor was she yet fit enough to make the long journey. Somewhat reluctantly, Domini felt obliged to suggest her own home as the best place in the circumstances.

"It is near enough to Johannesburg for you to go in for your treatments without being too tiring for you, and the country air will be good for you."

Rowena accepted with alacrity. The last thing she could bear to contemplate just now was a return to her own home and the need to try to readjust herself to her life there. Francis's attitude to her since her accident had been exemplary. He had paid her visits frequent enough to be those of a devoted husband, whilst her incapacity and her desire to remain under Domini's care were sufficient reason in themselves to explain why such visits were those of friend rather than husband or lover.

Domini, who had had a faint hope that Rowena might refuse, concealed her disappointment and turned to Francis, in whose presence the suggestion had been made.

"You'll come too, Francis, of course?"

"I'd like to, if I shall not be too much, for you. I shall be interested in a Transvaal farm, which is probably run on quite different lines from my own in Rhodesia. My land is chiefly under tobacco and cotton, with a good acreage of mealies as well, of course. You're sure you can cope with me as well?"

"Quite sure," said Domini quietly.

She knew that Mark was looking at her beneath his heavy eyebrows and guessed what he was thinking, that if she could find room for these two visitors in her small house, it might mean that she herself would be obliged to share her husband's room, a thing which she had told him she had no wish to do.

It was arranged that a car would take the four of them the next day to Magoeba's Kloof, where they could break their journey and spend a night at the beautifully situated hotel – in civilisation again, as Rowena said with mingled relief and regret. On the day following, Domini and her guests would go on to her home, whilst Mark would find his own transport to Johannesburg.

Domini knew that a final meeting between herself and this man who loved and dominated her was inevitable, and after she had seen Rowena settled for the night, she obeyed the unspoken invitation to go out towards the camp boundary, where they would be alone.

For some minutes they stood in silence, looking out over the valley from which now the last of the short twilight had gone, leaving only the stars and the waning moon for light.

It was Mark who broke the silence which had become too poignant for them.

"So tomorrow has nearly come," he said. "You're glad, aren't you?"

His tone was brusque, almost rough, and he made no attempt to touch her but stood beside her, his arms folded, his face wearing a scowl.

"You know I'm not," she said in a low voice. Had they then to part on this note? Would she ever be able to understand him?

"You should be. It's of your own making."

She turned to him appealingly.

"My dear, please don't let us part like this," she said. "Don't be bitter and unkind, so as to make it harder for me."

"Is it hard, then?"

"Of course," she said, her voice now a mere whisper, her hands clenched at her sides.

He unfolded his arms and took her by the shoulders and turned her to him, his eyes searching her face. During these days of waiting, he had not touched her, had not spoken to her one word which the world should not have heard.

"It's your own decision, Domini," he said in the same harsh voice, "but it isn't too late to change it."

"It is," she said, "even if I wanted to change it."

"And you don't? Not even though you know that after tomorrow we may never see each other again?"

She knew he was purposely keeping that tone in his voice to hurt her. She held up her head and though her lips quivered, her voice and her eyes were steady.

"I am not going to change my decision, Mark," she said.

"All right, if that's the way you want it, but you're being a fool, a fool to yourself and to me and also probably to this precious husband of yours. Besides, how do you know he wants you back? He knew as well as you did that you came away on this trip as a sort of testing time, so that both of you could make up your minds. How do you know he has made up his to match yours? That he will be glad to have you come back to him?"

She continued to hold his eyes, steadily, proudly.

"I don't know," she said simply.

His face relaxed a little. He was torn between pity and exasperation. He wanted her and he knew she wanted him, and yet with that and with all his dominating strength, he could not break down her determination to go back to her husband.

"Domini, Domini! What am I to make of you or to do about you? Tell me this one thing. Promise me one thing. If you are not happy— no, I won't put it that way, because you cannot be happy with things as they are. Let me say it this way: if you feel that life is unbearable with him, if you feel that after all he would be as happy without you as with you so that there is no obligation on you to remain with him, then will you send and tell me so? Wherever I am, whatever I am doing, I will come to you. You know that! You believe it?"

She was not proof against this urgent tenderness as she was against his harshness and she turned her head away from him. Her throat ached and there were tears behind her eyes which she would not shed.

"Yes. Yes, I believe it, Mark," she said in a low, choked voice.

He caught her against him and held her in a close, passionate embrace.

"I've got to let you go," he said against her lips. "I know I can't hold you. You've got something in you that's stronger than I am, but it's not love for him or for any living creature is it, Domini? You don't have to answer. I know it. It's part of you yourself. Part of the woman I love and shall always love, wherever I am, wherever you are, even if you never send for me – though I shall always hope you will. And I'll come to you from the ends of the earth. You know that, don't you?"

His words beat into her heart and her brain. Was she right, or terribly, criminally wrong, to spurn this love, to throw it away with so little for memory, and for what? For the sake of her own conscience, her own sense of right and wrong, her obsession towards duty. She thought of Keith and of what Mark had just said. Suppose he were right? Suppose Keith did not, after all, want her back?

The thought that Keith may not want her back, might even now be hating the thought of her return, gave her a queer feeling of emptiness, of being cast adrift and lost. Would she know as soon as she saw him? Would there be something in his eyes, his voice, something he would try to hide from her but unsuccessfully, as he did most things?

She knew that Mark was watching her, that he possibly could form some idea of what was passing in her mind. She tried to draw herself from his embrace but his arms would not let her go and in the end she gave way before his insistence and let herself relax against him, her forehead pressed down on his shoulder, her eyes hidden from that too-sure gaze of his.

"You'll send for me if that ever happens, Domini?" he asked. "If you find yourself free for any reason, or if by coming to you, I can set you free? But, my darling, don't send for me unless you mean me to stay, or to take you away. I don't want to come back to you to be like this, to have you and yet not have you, to part from you again. You understand, my love?"

She raised her head and he looked deeply into the dark pain of her eyes.

"If I ask you to come to me, it will be for the rest of our lives, Mark—Mark, my dearest, my dear love."

Their lips and their hearts and their bodies clung together. He could feel the pliable firmness of her limbs against his own, and he knew that she was his woman, wanting him, seeking him as he wanted and sought for her, and yet refusing that passionate satisfaction they had known together for so short a time.

"Domini – let me come to you tonight," he said, his lips against her hair as her head drooped again after that dangerous embrace.

She shook her head without raising it.

"Don't ask me, Mark. I know what I have to do, and I cannot do anything which will make me too weak. Kiss me again now and let me go. Darling, I shall love you all my life, and remember you and—want you so."

In another moment she had torn herself away and gone back on swift, unrelenting feet to where Rowena slept in fitful discomfort. She undressed and got into bed, but it was a long time before sleep came to her. She was thinking of them both, Mark whom she so deeply loved and Keith to whom she must return – Keith to whom she must return for her conscience' sake.

Chapter Eighteen

Domini had not been, mistaken when she decided that she would know from the look in Keith's face whether or not he wanted her to come back.

There was no mistaking the gladness, the relief, with which he welcomed her, putting his arms about her and holding her to him and kissing her as he had not done for a long time.

"Oh Dom, it's heaven to have you back," he said, and she knew he meant it and determinedly cast from her mind the first irrepressible regret that it should be so.

"It's nice to have been missed," she said gently and gently returned his kisses and drew herself from his arms only when Francis had come up to them, helping Rowena up the two steps to the *stoep*. "Keith, these are our visitors, Rowena, about whom I wrote you, and Francis. You had my letter? I got someone to post it for me when they got outside the Reserve."

"Yes, I had it; and course I'm delighted Domini brought you with her, Mrs. Craye – or may I call you Rowena and Francis straight away?"

"Of course," they both said, and they briefly sized him up, this rather mysterious husband of Domini's who had seemed a rather menacing figure in her background, but who, on near view, looked pleasant and friendly and was certainly glad to have his wife back.

"I did as you said and had the rooms got ready, Domini," he said, with a touch of pride in his voice, as if he felt he had accomplished something of importance. Domini gave him a brief glance of something like wonder. How young and immature he still was, in spite of his thirty-seven years. Coming straight from the lusty strength and dominating manhood of Mark she felt Keith to be even more of a weakling than she had realised, and at once blamed herself for the thought and, in atonement, smiled at him.

"Good. Thank you, dear," she said, and to Rowena, "Come along and let me show you which is to be your room."

She had taken her guest as she spoke along the corridor which ran from front to back of the bungalow, and into a large, airy bedroom.

"Domini, this is your own room!" said Rowena at once. "You mustn't turn out for me."

"My dear, I'm glad to do so. You will spend far more time in here than I should, and the other rooms are too small for anything but the short nights of us farm folk. This is the bathroom," opening a second door, "and beyond that is Keith's room, but he need not use this bathroom, as we have a second one, and you can keep that door locked and feel quite private. Right opposite you on the other side of the passage is the room I'm having, and Francis is next door to it and the other bathroom next door again."

"You're sure you're going to be all right in another room than your own, Domini?"

"I shall be perfectly all right," Domini assured her again, and tried to crush down the knowledge that by this arrangement she had secured some sort of privacy for herself from Keith whilst their guests were with them.

The two bedrooms which she and Francis were to occupy were very small and had originally, she explained to him, been intended for the native servants, but actually they had been housed in a separate, detached building, so that these rooms remained as spare rooms.

As the evening progressed, she was the more glad that she had not had to spend it alone with Keith, who was on his best behaviour and exhibited to their guests the old charm which had captivated Domini herself at their early meetings. Rowena quickly responded to the change of atmosphere after the rest camp and seemed almost herself, with colour in her cheeks and animation in her voice. She even wanted to go out with the two men when Francis suggested they might see something of the farm before it was too dark, but he vetoed it.

"Better go easily, my dear," he said in his carelessly friendly way. "You haven't even walked much yet, and you're up later now than you've been for some time."

She obeyed without argument, but was very quiet after they had gone, and Domini suggested bed for her.

Lying in Domini's comfortable bed with a book, she had no desire for sleep, but heard the two men come in, listened to the clink of bottles and glasses which betokened a final 'spot' and then to the footsteps going to the various rooms, Domini's quiet goodnight to Francis, and the closing of bedroom doors.

She waited perhaps half an hour and then slipped into the satin house-coat which Domini had lent her to replace the jaded one which had done too much duty in the Reserve and opened her door softly and tiptoed across to the room she knew was Francis's.

He looked up as she softly opened the door. He was sitting by the window, in the only possible space for an easy chair, reading. He was in pyjamas and dressing-gown, for the night was too chilly to sit about without a wrap of some sort.

She closed the door as softly behind her and came to him.

He put a book-mark to keep his place and closed the book, but kept it in his hand.

"Hullo, my dear," he said. "Anything wrong?"

"Must there be before I come into your room?" she asked.

He smiled.

"No," he said; "only there's usually some specific reason why you do me such honour."

She felt herself shrink from his tone.

"Francis, I—I thought perhaps we might—talk a little," she said, hesitating over her words.

He raised his eyebrows.

"Isn't it late for you? After eleven, anyway," glancing at his watch.

"I'm not sleepy," she said, and as she waited for him to say something else, they could hear Domini's movements in the next room through the thin plywood partition.

He rose reluctantly and put his book down.

"We'd better not talk in here," he said. "This wall is so thin that we shall disturb Domini. We can go back to the lounge."

"Come to my room. It's just across the passage, and there's a bathroom between it and the next bedroom."

He gave her a quizzical glance which made her flush and feel angry, but he followed her and stood with the door open until she made a movement towards it, when he closed it quietly and with a rather grim look. What was this new game, he wondered?

He watched her, standing quite still just inside the door whilst she moved about in obvious embarrassment, touching things aimlessly, stooping to turn off the electric fire and then to turn it on again.

"She's still very easy on the eye," he was thinking to himself, but thinking it without emotion of any kind or the least stirring of the senses. "Wonder why I can't feel anything about her any more? Most men would give their eye-teeth to be in my shoes just now. It just doesn't register with me any more."

"Can't we sit down?" asked Rowena at last, and indicated the two comfortable chairs drawn up near the fire.

With a slight smile, he moved towards them, waited with his customary punctilious courtesy for her to sit down, and then sat opposite and looked expectantly at her.

"Well?" he asked. "What is the subject of this important talk?"

She flushed. He could so quickly and easily make her angry, and she did not want to get angry.

"Francis, I—I must know something. Is it all finished between us, absolutely finished? Isn't there anything at all left?" she asked jerkily, not looking at him.

He appeared to be considering the question, or perhaps it was his answer which he was considering, for eventually she looked up and found his eyes fixed on her with the familiar, speculative, faintly amused interest.

"I wonder why you are asking that just now?" he asked.

"I don't know what you mean by 'just now', but we haven't had much opportunity for any private talk lately," she said.

"Nor, I thought, any particular desire for it," said Francis.

"Perhaps you hadn't but I had. Francis – this isn't going to be easy for me, and you're not helping me, but—is it any use my saying that I'm sorry?"

"For what, my dear?" he asked blandly.

"For—everything. For the mess I've made of things, for all the beastly business with Gil and—and the rest. Even for doing what you said I did and chasing you until I caught you and made you marry me. You need not have married me, Francis, even if I did chase you."

"No; that's true," he agreed.

"Why did you, then?"

He paused again to consider his reply.

"I'll tell you," he said at last. "It may surprise you. I married you because I was deeply in love with you."

She drew a deep, half-sobbing breath.

"Why have you never told me so, then?" she asked.

"Never? Surely I did at first, just at first. I seem to remember that I told you very soon indeed after our marriage, in the car on the way from the church to the reception, if I remember rightly."

She closed her eyes and let her head sway back against the cushions of her chair. She was remembering that day, though so much had happened since that it was all hazy and uncertain. She did remember, though, now that he had reminded her, that on that short romantic journey she had disentangled one hand from the misty folds of her veil and her chiffon gown and had slipped it into his, and he had patted it and let it go again, but first he said to her in the way he had which at that time she had called 'funny', "You're an adorable bride and I adore you suitably."

He, too, was caught up in the memory of that day, the feeling of panic he had had when he saw her coming up the aisle towards him, looking like a frosted angel under her veil, drifting towards him like something in a dream, as unreal and unsubstantial.

Somehow he had got through the ceremony, had come out unscathed from the performance in the vestry, and was sitting beside Rowena in the bridal car, but Rowena come to life again, faintly flushed, starry-eyed, a warm, living, breathing woman instead of a sugar angel or a drifting cloud.

She had touched his hand and the slight contact had filled him with something of the same panic, the knowledge that she was his, had been given to him by the old parson – how dared he give anything like Rowena to a coarse and beastly man for his delight?

"You're an adorable bride and I adore you suitably," he had said idiotically, of course, but because he had been too much moved, too deeply affected by his realisation of his love for her, to dare to speak seriously – and with all the ordeal of the reception before him.

There would be time to tell her how he felt about her later – plenty of time, all their lives.

And that night he had come to her and taken her in a reverence hitherto unknown to him in his experience with women, and with a sense of his own utter unworthiness made her his own – and had known with a blinding, searing pain that she would never be his own because already some other man, perhaps more than one, had taken her.

When Rowena opened her eyes, there was in them the faint, unbearably sweet vision of that day of her marriage to him, but until this moment she had never known that he had really meant that, when he had told her he adored her. There had been nothing else to remember. He seemed at once to change – or not so much to change as to remain the same, mocking, cynical, never serious, never to be understood.

"I didn't know you meant it," she said.

"Oh, but I did. You really were an adorable bride, Rowena. You nearly lost me right at the very altar because, when I saw you coming up the aisle looking like a snow fairy, I got into a cold panic and wanted to rush out. You see, I thought you could not possibly know what was in front of you, could not conceivably understand the quite revolting and disgusting things that old man was saying. That, you see, my dear Rowena, was where I made my mistake."

She was leaning forward now, her hands grasping the arms of her chair, her eyes strained as she watched him.

"Your—mistake?" she whispered jerkily.

"Yes. You see, you did understand, didn't you?"

"Why— have you never—said this before?" she asked, her voice almost soundless.

"To what end? I had married you. You were my wife. I don't know whether or not there is any law which permits a man to divorce his bride because he finds out on his wedding night that—well, to put it in vulgar parlance, that he has been sold a pup."

"Don't. Don't," she said and shrank down in her chair and covered her face with her hands.

"But, my dear, why all this display now, at this late hour in the proceedings? You obviously felt no shame or contrition on your wedding day, nor on your wedding night either. That surely was the time to feel it, not now, not after eight long years. Is it eight? Anyway, as I have said, I could see no redress save the very unpleasant one of appearing before the world, *my* world, and proclaiming to them publicly that I, Francis Craye, who had always prided myself on my sagacity and cleverness, had been hoodwinked and trapped into marriage by a whore. I am sorry, my dear, if the word offends you, but it should not, since the thing itself did not. You understand now how it was that I was not even surprised when I found that marriage had not made so much difference to you, that you were still able to run several men at once, and that your husband, poor boob, was only one of them – a convenient one since he kept you and you could always come back to him, but only one of them all the same."

His calm voice stopped, and he sat back in his chair and looked at her. She could feel his eyes upon her and at last she made a supreme effort and looked at him.

"Francis, if I admit all this, if I say how sorry, how ashamed, how bitterly humiliated I am, will you put it from you? Can you bear to forgive me and let me at least try to regain something that I lost all those years ago?"

"My dear, what's the good? There's nothing there any more. It isn't a question of forgiveness. It's just that it's impossible to do what you ask."

"Not if I tell you, very sincerely and humbly, that I love you, Francis? Really love you, with the best that is in me – if you can concede me any best!" with a curl of her lips.

He regarded her with the quizzical look she hated and feared. The one thing he could never see in her was any goodness or decency, she thought bitterly.

"You know, Rowena, if it were not in its small way a tragedy, this might easily be a comedy between us, even a farce. I dislike farce almost as much as I dislike tragedy, so let's keep it as comedy, shall we?"

"And its title?" she asked curtly.

He gave a shrug.

"I don't know. I've been told by writers that they do not as a rule find their titles until the book, or the play, is completed so that they can survey the whole story and sum it up."

"And our story is not yet completed?"

"I don't think so."

"What remains, then? Why don't we write 'Finis' and have done with it?"

"I've given you once my reasons for not setting you free legally, though you are free as air in every other way. I don't want to marry again – God forbid! – and I don't see why I should betray my sex so far as to let one of them get into my unenviable position."

"You really mean that you would never divorce me, Francis?"

"You're my wife and I'm prepared to let you maintain that position before other people, to support you, to treat your desires with reasonable generosity, to give you the cover of my name and your status as my wife so long as you do not openly disgrace me. When you do that, then, my darling, you will have to go, but I still should not divorce you – except under the most unlikely circumstances of your being in love, really and honestly in love, with a man who also cares for you, poor brute."

"So you would do it then?"

"Not would – might. I commit myself to nothing. You see, it would be most difficult for me to believe that you could love anyone better than yourself."

She lay back in her chair again. He felt a slight compunction as he looked at her and saw her as she really was tonight, with the flush of anger fading from her cheeks and being replaced by the pallor of the scarcely convalescent, her eyes deeply shadowed, her mouth drooping, her whole attitude one of defeat.

"I'd better leave you to get to bed," he said, changing his tone to his more normal one of casual indifference. "You must be very tired."

He had risen when he suggested her going to bed, and was standing looking down at her.

She took his hand, which was hanging near her, and laid it against her cheek. Why could she not be different? she wondered. What was there in her that made her antagonise him at every turn? Was there nothing she could do to reach him? Surely *everything* that had been between them could not be dead?

Holding his hand, she rose and stood beside him, very close to him, the colour coming softly into her cheeks again, the familiar perfume she used mingling with that from Domini's satin wrap and producing something subtly intoxicating and new.

"Francis, stay with me tonight," she said in a low, quick whisper. "Stay with me."

His brows drew together and his lips were pursed in the surprise of her words, but he did not move or take his hand from hers.

After all, why not? She was his wife and the thing which had passed for love could still be revived within him even though he despised her with his mind.

"Would that sort of thing satisfy you, Rowena? Knowing that it is an empty thing? Just farmyard?"

She quivered and he felt her shrink from him. It gave the sadist in him momentary satisfaction.

"If that's all you can give me," she whispered, not looking at him. "Doesn't it really mean anything to you?"

"Oh yes, my sweet. Definitely. I feel the familiar pricking down my spine even now at the prospect of having you in my arms in bed again, your white body, the soft texture of your skin, your limbs entwined with mine. Come along. For a start, let's have these things off, charming though they are and no doubt designed to give me exactly the sensations I'm at present enjoying," and his hands were busy with the fastenings of Domini's gown, with the fragile fabric of a nightdress

Domini had found for her to replace the now unlovely pyjamas she had brought out of the Reserve.

Rowena gave herself up to him, the satin and the georgette slipping to the ground, her body as slender and beguiling as when he had first seen and caressed it, though he felt a stab of pity when he saw the darkness of the bruises which still showed on the whiteness of her shoulders and her thighs and the tender curve of her breast.

He touched one of the marks with a gentle finger.

"Are you sure I shan't hurt you?" he asked. "Sure that this is what you really want tonight?"

"I know it's what I want, and I don't care if you hurt me."

It was the old Rowena, passionate, demanding and giving, able to satisfy so wildly the urgency of his body. He felt the surge of his desire again, the excitement.

He laughed, and bent his head and kissed her bruised breasts and then picked her up and carried her to Domini's wide, soft bed.

It was Rowena who dropped asleep first, lying with her dark hair tumbled about his shoulder, her cheek pressing the lean, hard flesh, one arm flung across his body, her whole attitude one of contentment and abandon. There was a faint smile curving her lips. His kisses had given them a soft colour more alluring than the bright lipsticks she liked to use. It seemed to him that even the dark bruises on her skin had lessened in the ardour of their shared passions.

Francis, lying wide awake and watching her as she lay in the circle of light from the bedside lamp, felt in his mind a confusion of compassion, remorse, even anger, though the anger was against himself and the compassion for her. He was going to remember with loathing of himself this hour or two of surrender to the worst within him, to the mere animal.

His mind wandered along these lines, growing with every thought further from the woman who lay on his breast asleep. He had never allowed them to have children. It was his reaction to his discovery on his wedding night that she was not virginal, and when in later years she had betrayed him with other men, he had been the more glad that he had not made her body the vehicle for the production of his children. For one thing, he would never have been sure that they were his.

They had drawn the bedclothes over themselves, but in her sleep she had flung them off again. The room was hot, for they had left the electric fire burning, forgetting it in the urgency of their desire for each other. His eyes travelled down the long length of her body, the clean-cut limbs, the flat stomach of a girl, the small, firm breasts. She was physically perfect and designed for a man's delight – or downfall. What cruel freak of Nature had left out a woman's soul, the beauty of fidelity, of tenderness, the essential goodness which holds a man, in spite often of himself, to the end of days?

Moving carefully, he slid his body away from hers, his arm from under her, drew his warm pillow beneath her cheek, gently so as not to wake her from the first deep, natural sleep she had had since her accident. He pulled the covers over her lightly, put on his pyjamas and dressing-gown and tiptoed out of the room, pausing a moment to switch off the light, satisfied that she had not wakened.

When Rowena awoke, daylight was streaming into the room through the blue curtains. She realised her naked state and remembered and laughed, jumped out of bed and picked up the nightdress from its circle on the floor, drew back the curtains and called to Domini, who was in the garden in slacks and open-necked shirt, weeding a flowerbed.

"Hullo there!" she called.

Domini looked up, put down her trug basket and came across the sun-baked red earth to the window. She was bewildered by the turn of events. Rowena looked transformed, her eyes bright, her cheeks flushed, her lips curving into a smile; and only half an hour or so ago, Francis had been to her with his strange request and a baffling lack of explanation.

"Heavens, what a sleep!" said Rowena, stretching and yawning.

"I'll get you some breakfast."

"Only the usual, Domini. I'm not hungry."

Would she ever be hungry again? Ever be anything but filled with this delight, this contentment, this certainty that all was now well with her world?

"Orange juice and toast?" asked Domini.

"Only orange juice, or I shan't be able to eat any lunch," said Rowena, and went back to bed and sat with her knees hunched up, a cigarette held lazily between her lips, her mind filled with the happy commotion of her thoughts.

Francis still cared for her. He must do, to have made love to her so enchantingly last night. He had not said much. He never did say much when he was making love to her. Speech spoilt his concentration on her, he used to tell her. But he had thrilled her in the old, remembered way, his arms as strong, his lips as compelling, all the little familiar tricks of his enjoyment of her the sweeter because for so long she had known them only in memory.

Now that she had broken down the barrier between them, now that he had yielded to her and had those hours of love with her, everything would be different, easier, happier. Never again, never, never, would she feel the lure of any other man. She had learnt her lesson. She knew now what Francis meant to her, all that he meant, he and he alone. He had forgiven her. The past was wiped out. The future was now hers, for happiness, for making up for all that they had lost.

Domini brought in the tray with her orange juice on it, waited whilst she drank it and then, rather doubtfully, gave her Francis's note.

"Your husband gave me this for you," she said.

Rowena looked at the envelope, startled. It had just her name on it, "Rowena," in his handwriting.

"Francis gave it to you? But—what for?" she asked, and then smiled and thought how unlike him, but how sweet of him, to write her a love-letter after last night!

She slid her finger under the flap of the envelope and Domini took the empty tumbler and the tray and left her.

The first words sent a chill to Rowena's heart, for he had written to her as "Dear Rowena."

"Dear Rowena, – This is a difficult letter to write and I think it is best just to say what I have to say and net try to put frills on it.

"Last night was a mistake, and a bad one. It was weak of me and I shall eternally regret it, for your sake even more than for my own. I have excused myself to Domini and Keith and gone away. I shall not go back home yet, but shall wander about a bit. Eventually, and by the time Domini tells me you are quite fit again, I shall come back for you. I will open an account for you meantime with the Standard Bank in Johannesburg, Commissioner Street, and if it is necessary for you to contact me before I come back, you may mite to me there.

"Francis."

Chapter Nineteen

Domini stood on the *stoep* watching, with narrowed eyes and a frown of perplexity, the two figures walking slowly over the *bundu* beyond the farm boundary. Soon they were lost amidst the trees and stubby bushes which distinguished the wild from the cultivated territory and she turned to go slowly into the house, where a dozen jobs awaited her. She knew that Rowena and Keith had counted on these pressing jobs to keep her from noticing that they had gone.

Mechanically she went about her work, into the house and to her little office to write cheques and letters so that they should be ready when Inkusi came to tell her he was starting for the town and the stores; into the bedrooms to see that clean linen had been put on the beds and the soiled linen made up into a bundle for the wash-girl; into the bathrooms to inspect the baths, the basins and the taps before the floors were scoured and polished; keeping at hand to make sure that the floors really were scoured and not merely smeared with thick polish and given a surface cleanliness only.

Keith should have done the letters, and the payment of accounts. She could not, however, leave this to him any more since the humiliating discovery that he had been systematically robbing the farm and herself by a clever 'cooking' of the books which enabled him to falsify the accounts for his own enrichment. There had been a bitter scene between them when Domini had made this discovery.

That had been on the very day when Francis Craye had left the farm, a day when her nerves had been frayed by other things, notably by Rowena's difficult reaction to her husband's abrupt departure, for which she gave Domini no more acceptable reason than Francis had done. She had stormed and wept, threatened to take her own life, so that Domini had felt it unwise to leave her alone at all, and finally had goaded herself into such a state that Keith had taken the car and gone into Pretoria for a doctor, who had given the angry, suffering girl a draught potent enough to put her into a profound sleep.

It was whilst Keith had gone for the doctor that Domini, obliged to go into the matter of an unsettled account which the books showed to have been paid, had discovered that all was far from well there. She had been in no mood for the discussion which had had to follow when Keith had returned and Rowena was asleep. Since then she had added to her already heavy burdens the farm accounts.

Keith should have been down on the half-acre devoted to the new piggeries, superintending the erection of the additional pens. Keith had told Domini only ten minutes or so ago that he was going down and Rowena at the same time had said she was taking a book and some needlework into the shade of the blue gums at the opposite end of the farm lands.

Yet there they were, unmistakably, going off into the *bundu* and there was nothing that Domini could do about it. Would it be any use even to confront one or both of them with it when they came back? They would probably lie to her so that she must either appear to accept their lies and let the matter drop, or else they would try to justify themselves, and there would be quarrels, scenes, all sorts of bitterness and disgust.

It was three weeks now since Francis had gone, and Rowena, who had at first been restless and talked of going back to Rhodesia, now appeared to have accepted the position and showed no sign of wanting to leave. Domini was able to let her alone to find her own occupation and amusement. It was not long before it became apparent that she was finding them with Keith, at first going with him, laughing and teasing him, when he went about his own work on the farm, but gradually either luring him from his work or being acquiescent when he abandoned it on his own initiative to take her riding, or out in the car on invented errands to town, or on some pretext or other to the outlying parts of the farm where they could not be observed from the house.

Domini was worried. She had felt that, though she did not understand the position and was not admitted to his confidence, Francis had left Rowena in her charge. During those first few days of anger, wild grief, resentment and extravagant submission, Rowena had spoken of her love for her husband, telling Domini that Francis was her life, that there would never be another man for her, that unless he came back to her and forgave her (she did not tell Domini for what), life would hold nothing for her any more and that she might as well be dead.

Yet so quickly she had consoled herself, or so it appeared, with Keith, and Domini knew her husband very well, his indolence, his weakness, his susceptibility where women were concerned, and there could be no denying Rowena's physical attraction, the greater as the days went by and gave her renewed health.

There were days when Domini lost patience altogether and demanded angrily of Fate how much of this she had to endure, and for how long. Had Rowena not been a guest in her house, and to some extent entrusted to her care, she would have been tempted to give up the fight, to tell Keith he could go whenever he liked and wherever and with whom, so long as he went out of her life. She would even have paid him to go, so that she might at last have some sort of peace.

But this morning she had been made aware sharply that there were other forces at work, and that this lonely peace was not all that might be achieved if she let Keith go, or made him go.

She had had a letter from Mark Teckler, the first letter. The typewritten envelope with a Johannesburg postmark had meant nothing to her, and she had put it with the other letters until she had time to read them, but when she had slit open this envelope and unfolded the sheet of typewritten paper, she had caught her breath with sharp surprise, for it had started 'My dearest love' and there was only one person in the world who might call her that.

"My Dearest Love, – It seems so long since I have seen you or heard from or of you that I must break the silence and ask you if you will not at least telephone to me so that I can hear your voice and know that all is well with you. I shall be here in my room, waiting for you to call me, every evening from 7.30 to 8, and if there is a more convenient time for you, please let me know. I must have word of you, Domini. I am staying here only because I cannot put more miles between us, and I always hope that you will come to me or let me come to you. My life is empty without you and could be filled to overflowing with you. Will you not yet make up your mind to come, my love? Even if you feel that Keith would not divorce you if you came to me, do not let that make any difference. You will be forever mine just as I am yours. Please telephone me, my darling. I shall live each day in expectation that you will.

"Yours only and forever,

"Mark T"

The jolt of her heart, the swift coursing of the blood through her veins, had told her all she needed to be told, that not only had she not been able to forget him, but that during these weeks the thought of him had been constantly with her, to uphold and encourage her even though at the same time it could fill her with the despairing sense of the finality of their parting and of the inadequacy of her life with Keith.

Her thoughts returned to the letter time after time during the morning, whilst behind it was the memory that Rowena and Keith had not returned, that his work was being neglected and almost certainly she and Francis being betrayed.

She found an opportunity of going across to the piggeries to find, as she had anticipated, two native boys lazily plastering mud on the flimsy foundation of dried thatching reeds. They looked startled and guilty at her appearance, and she rated them soundly, stood by whilst they destroyed all the work they had done, and told them she would return at a certain definite time to see that the proper skeleton framework had been made of wattle boughs before they started the interlacing of rushes preparatory to the mud plastering.

When she returned to the house from a final visit to the dairy and the kitchen, she found Rowena and Keith stretched in long chairs on the *stoep* with cool drinks beside them.

Rowena smiled up at her.

"Isn't it hot?" she asked. "Can I get you a drink?"

"Keith will get it," said Domini unsmilingly.

"Of course, darling," he said and got up with unusual alacrity to set a chair for her and fill a tumbler from the long jug standing in an ice pail. "I just happened to come along as Rowena arrived. I've been down with those lazy niggers at the piggeries."

She gave him a cold glance that made him uncomfortable.

"How are they getting on?" she asked.

"Oh, all right, you know."

"Have they made wattle foundations?"

"Oh, of course, of course. I'll go down again in a minute to have another look. You know how they scamp things if they get a chance."

"There's no need for you to go down," said Domini, taking the tumbler from him, her voice still very cool. "They have just demolished the reed and mud and started again and with wattle this time."

He stared at her, flushed and discomfited. Domini took her cold drink into the house with her, leaving him with Rowena.

Rowena turned to him at once.

"Keith, you're a complete idiot. She knows we've been together and that you haven't been near the piggeries."

He laughed.

"Oh, she'll get over it – and you were so damned enticing. What about going back this afternoon to that place we found?"

She shook her head.

"Not for me. For one thing, I was terrified of snakes all the time."

He grinned, looked quickly round and then bent and kissed her.

"You weren't. You didn't think of anything in the world except me, and you might as well admit it."

"All right. I'll admit it," she said. "But there's no sense in getting her mad – at least not if you want to keep in with her, as I suppose you do."

"I'm not sure that I do," said Keith airily, though he was watching her closely.

She did not reply, but lit a cigarette and sat with it between her lips, her hands linked about one bent-up knee as she lay in the long rattan chair, her dark head against a scarlet cushion, her whole attitude one of studied, conscious allure.

He hesitated, waiting for the reply that did not come, and, muttering something about the piggeries, he sauntered off across the garden, his hands in the pockets of his blue slacks.

Rowena watched him go, her eyes enigmatical.

What exactly did she want of Keith Ellman and mean to have? He amused and diverted her and kept her from thinking too often and too deeply of Francis, who during these three weeks had neither written to her nor sent her a message, though she had discovered that he was being generous to her in the amount of money at her disposal. She had not started consciously to play with Keith until she discovered that he was in love with her; that is to say, he was temporarily infatuated with her, wanted to kiss and fondle her and indeed to go as far as she would allow, but she felt that he also desired to keep in with his wife so as to be able to remain at the farm, where he had a comfortable home in return for as little work as possible.

She found him amusing and stimulating; also more than a little dangerous, since she had constantly to subdue and control his ardour. Her own emotions had been stirred into active life again by the one night she had spent with Francis before he had humiliated and enraged her by his immediate flight from her and his letter. Into those seething emotions, Keith Ellman had come as a dangerous new element, and it was only the thought of Domini, and her very real affection for her, that had kept her from allowing herself to become actually Keith's mistress, though she was honest enough with herself to admit that only the final act remained and that she had allowed him to believe that that was within his reach in the very near future. She had no illusions about him. She knew that he was idle, careless, selfish and untrustworthy, but she also felt that Domini had contributed to this by her attitude towards him, by doing too much for him and by allowing him to get away with his shiftless unreliability instead of making him take the consequences. She realised that, though she admitted herself to be Domini's inferior in most ways, she had reached something in Keith which his wife had not known how to reach. By laughing at him, deriding him, even showing contempt for him, she had roused in him a faint desire to stand well in her eyes, whilst it appeared he had not cared how he stood with Domini.

All through the afternoon, Domini too was quiet and remote, her thoughts ranging from her domestic problem to the aching longing which Mark's letter had produced in her. As the time grew nearer to half-past seven, she deliberately made a job for herself in the dairy, taking from Rose the weighing up and packing of the half-pound packets of her own special cream cheese, for which she had found a steadily growing market. The girl, delighted, scuttled off and Domini set herself resolutely to the task and forbore to look at the clock. She was weighing up the last pound when Keith put his head in at the door.

"Have you got to do that tonight?" he asked. "It's nearly half-past eight."

She drew a quivering sigh of relief and regret. It was too late now for this one night, anyway.

"Is it so late?" she asked. "No; I need not finish it," and she put the rest of the cheese, with the neat, silver-papered packets, back into the refrigerator.

"Tell Violet she can make the coffee, will you? I'll just go in and wash and then we'll have supper."

He hesitated, and, even whilst telling himself that fools rush in where wise men fear to tread, he burst out with a question.

"Is there anything wrong, Domini?"

She stopped for a moment and then closed the door of the refrigerator.

"What makes you think there might be?" she asked steadily.

His eyes fell before hers.

"Oh—nothing. Only—you've been very quiet all day. If it's the business of this morning—"

"What business, Keith?"

He flushed and fidgeted his feet on the floor of beaten earth.

"The—about the piggeries. Me not seeing that the boys did the work."

"Oh—that?" she asked, as if faintly surprised. "I've forgotten that."

He stood for a moment trying to find something to say, and then went out of the dairy. Domini watched him go, her hands hanging at her sides, a look almost of defeat in the slight drooping of her figure. What was the use of going on? Of trying to make something out of her marriage by herself, with no help from Keith? If it takes two to make a quarrel, it certainly takes two to make a marriage, yet she felt she was battling alone. Did he really want to go on with it? Was she forcing him into a position against his will? Had all that contrition and all his promises before she went to the Game Reserve been just hot air?

If he had gone back to Flora Pearce, or to any of the loose-living girls she had suspected him of having before her, she felt that now she would let him go; but it was Rowena Craye, the girl more or less entrusted to her, the wife of a man she sincerely liked and respected even if she did not altogether agree with his attitude towards Rowena.

She contemplated writing to him and asking him to come back, but there was ingrained in her a horror of interfering with the lives of others, and she let the days slip by without doing anything other than finding jobs for Rowena to do which would keep her for at any rate part of the day separated from Keith.

And each evening there came to her with increasing nostalgia the thought of Mark sitting in his hotel bedroom, waiting during that half-hour and probably much longer, since the long-distance telephone calls to and from Johannesburg sometimes take many hours.

And then one day she felt she could bear it no longer. She must speak to him, hear his voice, know that she was not as utterly alone as she felt herself to be. She put through a personal call to him for half-past seven that evening, and sat in her office and tried to concentrate on her accounts until, just before eight, the call came through.

"Domini? Is it you?"

"Yes, Mark."

Now that she heard his voice, the once-unfamiliar accent so dearly familiar, she did not know what to say but sat with the instrument to her ear, her love for him and her need of him surging through her brain and her body.

"Thank you for calling, love," he said. "I was almost afraid you wouldn't, but I was prepared to stay in Johannesburg until you did, even for the rest of my life."

She laughed, a quavering laugh that told him more poignantly than words that something was distressing her.

"Oh darling, to hear your voice again," she said brokenly.

"Then why haven't you telephoned before?"

"I don't know. Yes, I do! It's such madness. I know it's all wrong and that it will only make things harder afterwards, but I just had to hear your voice and feel—nearer to you."

"Domini, may I come out there? Just for an hour or so?"

"No, my beloved. No, it wouldn't do," she said quickly.

"Because of him?"

"Of course."

"Lass, you're unhappy. I can hear it. Why must you go on being unhappy when I am wanting you so much, waiting to give you happiness and everything else your heart could desire? Come to me, sweetheart. Please come. Or let me come to you and bring you away."

"You know I can't, Mark."

"Have we got to have this all over again? Surely if you ever had any responsibility for that waster, you've fulfilled it many times over. Haven't you any right to *any* happiness or life of your own?"

"I can't leave him, Mark. He would be completely lost without me. He'd just go to the bad, become one of these poor whites, a hobo living on sherry and sleeping out."

"I don't believe it. You've babied him, Domini, and you think of him as a helpless child instead of a man whose first instinct is self-preservation. I'm willing to bet that if you left him, he'd find his own feet and stand on them in no time. Domini, come to me. Please come."

She bent her head so that it rested on the pile of books on the desk, and when her voice came to him, it was faint and shaken. He could only just hear it.

"My heart's dearest, if only I could! Oh, if only I could!" and, groping blindly, scarcely aware of what she was doing, she replaced the receiver and let the line go dead, whilst at the other end he called frantically and in vain to her.

She stayed there a long time, her throat aching but her eyes tearless and gazing into space, into the future with Keith, not daring to see the future as it might have been with Mark.

In Domini's bedroom, Rowena noiselessly replaced the receiver of the other telephone. She had picked it up automatically when the bell rang, and at once had felt herself unable to put it down.

She felt no shame at having listened. The thing concerned her too deeply.

She sat on the edge of the bed and thought about it. She was not what is known as a woman's woman. She had never since her schooldays had a close woman friend. Until she had known Domini Ellman, she had never felt the need of one, and certainly had never admired and loved one as she loved Domini. It was queer, she thought ironically, that when she had found the one woman who could evoke her love, she had proceeded to take that woman's husband away from her.

Yet that conversation which she had just overheard brought her intense relief, for she knew now that she had not taken from Domini anything that she either valued or wanted.

Poor Keith!

Yes, and poor Domini. Mark Teckler was a rough diamond and not at all the sort of man Rowena herself could have fancied, but there was some quality about him which, in spite of his lack of culture, made him fit to be Domini's mate. His strength, his iron will, even his ruthlessness, must appeal to a woman who was herself strong and who, Rowena felt, could be ruthless.

And Mark Teckler stayed alone in Johannesburg waiting for her voice on the telephone, and Domini was here, tied to a man she did not want, a man who did not want her, but who was bound to her by her persistence in making him dependent on her. What was it Mark Teckler had said? That she 'babied' him. But how right! That was just what she did do, watching him, guiding him, guarding and protecting him even from himself, covering up his faults and failings from the eyes of others.

And gradually an idea was born in her mind, born with a strange assortment of food on which it must be nourished – a bitter sense of failure with regard to Francis, who only too obviously, cared nothing about her – a sincere love for Domini whose life was barren because of Keith – a sort of pitying tenderness for Keith, who, she felt, could become a man but for Domini.

Later that evening, she asked Domini whether it would be possible for her to have the car to go into Johannesburg the next day.

"I'm positively in rags," she said, "and I simply must get a few things. I'd like to start very early."

"I think that would be all right," said Domini. "We shan't need it for anything as far as I know."

"I'll drive you in, if you like," offered Keith. "I've got to see my own tailor sometime or other."

"I'd rather go alone," said Rowena coolly, and he flushed and did not pursue it.

She knew where Mark was staying in Johannesburg, having heard discussions about it before they left the Reserve, and when she reached the city, she parked the car as near as she could to his hotel and walked back to it along Kerk Street. She had telephoned him on reaching the city and he was waiting for her in the foyer of the hotel.

"Can we go somewhere to talk privately?" she asked him when he had greeted her.

"I've got a suite here," he said and took her up to it.

She looked about her. Obviously it was as she had surmised. Only a man very comfortably off could afford a suite like this at one of Johannesburg's best hotels for an indefinite period merely on the off-chance of hearing a woman's voice now and then.

"Mark, may I come straight to the point, even if it's rather a sharp one – sharp for me, that is?"

"I'd be glad if you would, Mrs. Craye."

"Rowena?"

He nodded, and she went on.

"I've got to admit that last night I did something most people would think rather low. I listened in to your conversation with Domini and I now know the whole set-up between you two. What *you* don't know is that there is another angle to it, the one between Keith Ellman and me."

She had rehearsed in her mind exactly what she was going to say, and Mark's calm silence helped her not to forget her lines.

"Yes?" he asked and waited.

"We happen to want each other. You know why Domini won't leave him, but, of course, she hasn't any idea what goes on with me."

"And just what does go on?"

She shrugged her shoulders.

"What do you imagine? Domini works all the hours of the day and some of the night too, whilst Keith more or less loafs about. In her heavenly kindness and generosity, she gave me her own bedroom, which is connected with Keith's by a mutual bathroom. You see what a convenient arrangement it has been."

"You mean that you have betrayed Domini with her husband?"

"If that's the right way to put it. My own has left me, and I'm very fond of Keith and he's nuts about me. Now that I know what you and Domini feel about each other—well!"

His eyes were very cold. He disliked her intensely, and yet realised that by this bold action she was helping to make things straight for him and Domini.

"Why do you come to me about it?" he asked curtly. "Isn't it between you and Ellman?"

"Not altogether. I said I would come straight to the point. Keith and I can't go away together because we've neither of us any money."

"And you want me to support the two of you?"

"You're able to come to the point too, I am glad to know. No, I'm not asking you to do that. I believe there is a lot more in Keith than Domini allows him to make use of, and if I take him away from her, I think I can make a man of him. He'll work for me because I shan't do it for him, and he's so crazy about me that I can twist him into any shape I like – just as Domini has twisted him into his present useless shape."

"Then what do you want me to do?" asked Mark bluntly.

"Give me enough money to pay our fares to England and to live on until I get Keith started. There's work there for everybody, and he can choose to a certain extent, but I shall see to it that he really does work and keep me."

He pulled his cheque-book from his pocket and crossed the room to the writing desk.

"I'll give you five hundred pounds now," he said. "That will get you both out of the country and allow you something to live on if you can't get a boat at once. When you prove to me that you have reached England, I'll cable an order to my English bank to put a further five hundred to your credit anywhere you like, but not in this country. Here's the first five hundred, drawn on my bank here. Have you an account?"

"Yes."

"Then pay this in. Don't carry all this in cash around with you."

"You're being very generous, Mark."

"I intend to be," he said grimly. "I want to make quite sure that you do go and that you take Ellman with you, though it beats me what you want him for. I can rely on you to take him with you, I suppose?" looking at her searchingly from under his strong eyebrows.

"Oh yes. You can certainly rely on that," she said.

"You're sure he'll go with you?"

"Absolutely. He loathes his life on the farm and is longing to get back to England."

"All right. Keep in touch with me, but of course, Domini must not know anything of this transaction."

"I agree," said Rowena, and folded the cheque and put it into her bag. "Goodbye Mark, and—thank you."

"I'm doing it for myself, and for Domini," he said grimly, opening the door for her, but not offering to shake hands.

"And I'm doing it for *myself* and Domini," thought Rowena wryly as she went.

Francis would, of course, have seen her to the lift if not to her car. Mark Teckler merely opened his door for her and did not even watch her to the lift.

Oh well, if that was the way Domini liked them!

There was no feeling of elation or triumph as she went to the bank and paid in Mark's cheque and then crossed the road to the Union

Castle offices to make enquiries about passages. All she could think of as yet was that she was finally breaking with Francis and that, whatever she felt for Keith Ellman, no man would ever again draw from her the love she had had for her husband. She felt bleak and empty. Perhaps some day there would be something for her out of this. In any case, she would have been the means of giving Domini her happiness, and since she was to have no more of her own, she must make that do.

Her lips curled and her eyes grew bitterly contemptuous.

This, then, was what she had made of her life in the end!

That night, for the first time, she unlocked the door that led from the bathroom into Keith's bedroom, and went in.

He had not started to undress, but had been standing staring moodily out into the darkness. He turned, astounded and delighted, to see Rowena there.

"Darling!" he said and hurried to her.

She let him take her in his arms and kiss her, and then drew herself firmly away.

"Sit down," she said. "I've come in here to talk to you, not to make love. I've got to ask you one thing, though. Keith, are you in love with me?"

He sat beside her on the edge of the bed, looking at her with that still incredulous wonder in his eyes.

"You jolly well know I am," he said.

"And you want me?"

"Heavens, just give me the chance!"

"I'm going to give you the chance – no, not here and now, so keep your distance!" pushing him away. "What I mean is, do you want me for keeps? Eventually to marry me if we can both get free?"

"Yes, definitely, though how the heck are we going to get free?"

"Domini would divorce you if you went off with me, and I'm pretty sure Francis would do the same for me."

Excitement was rising in him. He was not only madly desirous of possessing Rowena, but he was also actually in love with her – in love as he had never been before with any woman, not even Domini. Rowena never treated him as if he were a half-wit, never took away from him to do herself little jobs he undertook, always insisted on his finishing them. She gave him a feeling which was, or easily could be, pride and belief in himself.

"But—how could we possibly do it? Go off anywhere together?" he asked anxiously. "What should we use for money?"

"I've got enough to get us to England," she said.

He stared at her.

"But I always thought you said you hadn't anything but what Francis gives you? Surely he hasn't—"

"No," said Rowena sharply. "Of course he hasn't. I had this five hundred invested. I went into Jo'burg today to realise it, and it's now in my bank – enough to get us to England, and to keep us for three weeks in Cape Town whilst we wait for a boat. The Union Castle have given me a chit to their head office in Cape Town, and they think we can get a passage on the *Stirling Castle*. If not, we shall have to wait until we do get one."

He sat there looking at her, bewildered and half afraid to take in what she was saying.

"You're a fast worker," he said at last.

She nodded.

"Yes, when I want something; and I want this. Don't just stare at me like a goof. Isn't it what you want too?"

"Darling, of course—of course. Only—I can't quite take it in. You really mean we can go away? That you'll come with me? Back to England?"

"If you want to."

He took her in his arms then and she did not resist him. After all, this was all she was going to get out of it, and henceforth this was the man who had to make up to her for everything – for her life of ease, for her extravagances of dress and her expensive luxuries, and for Francis Craye, the man whom she still loved with all her heart and soul and for whom her body craved.

She clung to Keith.

"Make me love you," she cried a little wildly. "Make me love you!"

He held her away from him to look at her searchingly and with a frown.

"Don't you now?" he asked. "If you don't, why are you doing all this?"

"I do love you, and I want you and need you, but you've got to be much more to me than you are now. Can you be?"

He lifted his head up and looked over hers. There was a new light in his eyes, the birth of a new pride, a new hope and faith.

"Yes. I can be. I will be. You shan't regret it, Rowena—Rowena, my darling, darling."

She lay in his arms and let him love her. After all, what did it matter now?

But he was swearing that she should not regret it. How could he know that? How could she?

Chapter Twenty

Domini stood waiting for Mark to come to her. In the room behind her, Francis Craye was sitting, his long legs bent, his hands linked between his knees, his mind busy with the thoughts engendered by the conversation he had just had with her.

She had telegraphed him to come as soon as she had read Keith's note and realised that he and Rowena had gone.

When she told him, Francis was silent for a long moment, taking in all this meant. Then his face relaxed into his familiar, three-cornered smile.

"Well, there doesn't seem much to do about it, does there? You say Rowena left nothing for me? No letter or message or anything?"

"No. I think perhaps you'd better read Keith's note to me," and she handed it to him.

"Dear Domini [Keith had written], – Rowena and I are going away together. I can't soften that to you, though I am not very proud of myself after all you've done for me, but I'm in love with her and she with me. She says that that is what has been the real trouble between us, Domini, that you've done too much for me. Well, now I've got to look after her. We're going to England, and I shall get some job that appeals to me more than office work, but certainly not farm work. Will you divorce me, Domini? I want to be able to marry her as soon as possible, and we both hope that Francis will set her free. I can't thank you, Domini dear. There are not enough words.
                                    Keith."

"H'm."

Francis read the letter through twice and then folded it up and replaced it in its envelope and laid it on the table. "H'm," he said again. "That's rather that, isn't it? I suppose they've got a bit of money from somewhere, though I don't think Rowena's got much."

"Keith has something under two hundred pounds," said Domini with an edge to her voice.

She was thinking of one of her first reactions to his letter, which she had found when she came back to the house from her daily round of the farm, supposing Keith and Rowena to be still in their beds. She had gone from reading the letter to the small wall safe in her office. She kept the key on her own key-ring, but there was a spare one in case of emergency, and Keith knew where that was kept.

She opened the safe and pulled open the drawer in which she kept any substantial amount of cash. Yesterday she had received from the bank, sent out as usual by special messenger, the monthly amount needed to pay the wages and the outstanding bills, and in this particular month she had decided she could complete the payments for the small generator which supplied electricity, and she had had that amount in cash as well. She had told Keith what she intended to do, it having always been part of her policy towards him to tell him in detail what she spent on the farm.

He had chosen his time well, she thought angrily, finding the drawer empty. It was bitter food for reflection that Keith had not considered, or cared, how she was going to replace that sum. So far she had not herself considered how she was going to do it. It was an irresistible impulse which had made her send the telegram to Mark to ask him to come to her, rather than any thought that he would help her materially.

She was too proud to tell Francis how Keith had obtained the money with which, presumably, he would pay their fares to England. She discussed the other aspects of the situation with him, however, calmly and reasonably.

"Mark Teckler is still in Johannesburg," she told him. "I felt I could not be alone here, and as I did not know you were actually in

Johannesburg, and could get to me so quickly, I sent to ask him to come to me."

Francis nodded.

"He's a very sound individual," he said. "Now what are we going to do about these two? Do you want to apply for a divorce?"

"It's the only way," she said.

"Possibly. The thing is, do you want him back. Domini?"

"No."

She spoke the monosyllable with an instant closing of her lips, and looked away from him. She was bitterly hurt, defeated, all that she had tried to do flung back at her, and flung by the hand that had written that letter and at the same time had robbed her and left her with no thought of how she was to make good the loss.

No, definitely she did not want him back – and yet his going, even apart from the manner of it, had left her with a feeling of bewilderment, as if her life had stopped short.

"It's hurting you, isn't it?" asked Francis in a quiet voice.

"Only my pride," she said bitterly. "There's been nothing else between us for a long time. Only—I seem to have been a blind fool, don't I? And so pleased with myself. So sure of myself. You see what he says here? That, according to her, I've ruined him by what I've done for him, or tried to do. He won't look after her, you know, Francis. He isn't capable of looking after himself, let alone somebody else."

"I don't know," he said slowly. "I think perhaps you've rather under-estimated him, Domini, if you won't mind my saying so. You've been a little too much for him, too capable, too forthright. It's been too easy for him to leave things to you. Rowena will leave them to him. I know her. She won't carry any man as you have carried Keith."

"He'll let her down."

"Maybe. That won't be too bad for her, either. In a way, I've done the same as you have. I've made life too easy for her and never made her bear the consequences of her own actions or attitude – until now, when I had practically left her. And you see the result of that! She took Keith on instead, and it's my belief that she'll manage to make a man of him just because she'll force him to be responsible for her. I think we'd better do as they ask, Domini. We'd better set them free. What a pity we can't round it off nicely by falling in love with each other!" with one of his little chuckles. "I wonder why I never have fallen in love with you, Domini? I admire and like you tremendously."

She managed to smile at that, an uncertain effort.

"And I you, Francis," she said.

"In fact, I think we may say that our respective partners have shown shockingly bad taste, and a sad lack of the proper appreciation of values, in clearing off and leaving us," he said and again she smiled.

They could hear a car crunching over the rough roadway between the main road and the house.

"That'll be Mark," said Francis.

Domini nodded and went out to the *stoep* to wait for him.

Johannesburg. June to December, 1951.

ALSO BY NETTA MUSKETT

Give Back Yesterday

Helena Clurey has it all – a devoted husband, money and family. She is happy and secure, but her apparent contentment is about to be shattered by a voice from the past. Mistress she may have been, but that is not the way it is put to her: 'you were not my mistress - you were, and are, my wife.'

The Weir House

Philip wants to marry Eve. It is her way out - he is rich, not too old, and has been in love for years – but not a man she can accept. He has even secretly funded her lifestyle, such that it is. Eve feels trapped. Unlike her friend Marcia, who cheerfully accepts an 'ordinary' life without complaint, Eve has known better and wants better. A chance encounter then changesthings – Lewis Belamie pays her to act as his fiancée for a week. Adventure, ambition, and disappointment all follow after she journeys to Cornwall with him, where she eventually nearly dies after what appears to be a suicide attempt because of a marriage that has seemingly failed. However, the mysterious and mocking Felix really does love her. Just who is he; how does Eve end up with him; and what part does 'The Weir House' play in her life? Has Eve's restlessness and relentless search for stability ended?

ALSO BY NETTA MUSKETT

Through Many Waters

Jeff has got himself into a mess. It is, on the face of it, a classic scenario. He has a settled relationship with one woman, but loves another. What is he to do? It is now necessary to face reality, rather than continually making excuses to himself, but can he face the unpalatable truth? Then something beyond his influence intervenes and once again decisions have to be made. But in the end it is not Jeff that decides.

Misadventure

Olive Heriot and Hugh Manning had been in love for years, but marriage had been out of the question because of the intervention of Olive's mother. Now, at last, she was of age and due to gain her inheritance and be free to choose. A dinner party had been arranged at the Heriot's home, 'The Hermitage' and Hugh expects to be able to announce their engagement. Things start to change after a gruesomely realistic game entitled 'murder', which relies on someone drawing the Knave of Spades after cards are dealt. Tragedy strikes and other relationships are tested and consummated – but is this all real, or imagined?

18706041R00138

Printed in Great Britain
by Amazon